"*The Nature of Witches* is a timely, thoughtful tale of the responsibilities we have to our planet and to one another. Griffin's well-developed world building and complex main character make for a read that will resonate deeply."

—CHRISTINE LYNN HERMAN,
author of The Devouring Gray duology

"Seasonal magic abounds in this addictively thought-provoking tale of love, loss, and self-identity."

—DAWN KURTAGICH, award-
winning author of *The Dead House*

"I could have stayed lost in the pages and magic of *The Nature of Witches* forever. Griffin's lush prose and evocative imagery adorns and complements the thoughtfully designed world, and the well-drawn characters triumphantly carry the story from beginning to end. A stunning and timely debut."

—ISABEL IBAÑEZ, author of *Woven*
in Moonlight and *Written in Starlight*

"A bright, fresh read from a glowing new voice, *The Nature of Witches* is both timely and stirring. Griffin's emotional writing that cuts to the heart will make her a new YA favorite."

—ADRIENNE YOUNG, *New York*
Times bestselling author of *Fable*

"Vibrant and magical, *The Nature of Witches* is an achingly beautiful exploration of love and hope perfect for fans of Shea Ernshaw and Taylor Swift's *Folklore*. This book is a ray of sunshine."

—ROSIEE THOR, author of
Tarnished Are the Stars

"In her debut, Griffin ties the story of a witch learning her strength to the raw power of nature and places it in a world decimated by climate change. It's new, different, and well worth a read."

—*Booklist*

Also by Rachel Griffin

The Nature of Witches

WITHDRAWN

WILD is the WITCH

RACHEL GRIFFIN

sourcebooks
fire

Published by Sourcebooks Fire, an imprint of Sourcebooks
P.O. Box 4410, Naperville, Illinois 60567–4410
(630) 961-3900
sourcebooks.com

Cataloging-in-Publication Data is on file with the Library of Congress.

Printed and bound in the United States of America.
WOZ 10 9 8 7 6 5 4 3 2 1

For Mir,
who walks by my side down every path,
no matter how wild

prologue

The wind was starting to build. Iris knew she should focus on the words of the witch in front of her, but instead her attention was on the sound of the trees. She concentrated so intently that the sound replaced everything else, drowning out the blood rushing through her veins and her heart beating wildly in her chest, louder and louder until even the witch's voice faded to nothing.

Iris could feel the presence of the animals in the surrounding woods, the way their claws sunk into the forest floor and the way their ears perked up when a twig snapped in the distance. She didn't have woods like that back home, and it took all her strength not to break into a run and disappear into the trees. They were wild, those animals, and perhaps Iris belonged with them.

"Ms. Gray?"

Iris startled at the sound of her name, and she blinked several times, narrowing her focus to Ana and trying to ignore the call of the wilderness around her.

"Did you hear what I said?"

Iris reached into her memory for the words the witch had spoken, but she couldn't find them. Her mind was still stuck on that night one month prior, in a quaint blue house that overlooked the lake. The council had asked Iris to recount the events that had taken place that night, and she told them everything exactly as she remembered, every single detail down to the smell of putrid smoke and the sobs of her best friend.

Human flesh doesn't burn the same as wood. It doesn't crackle or spit sparks out in every direction. It isn't cozy on a frigid night or romantic on a rocky beach. It's horrifying the whole way through.

Iris wished she didn't know that.

She swallowed and shook her head. "I'm sorry."

Ana walked around the large oak table where the rest of the council members sat. Iris stood facing them, her jaw aching from the constant grinding of her teeth. Her fingers worked the fabric on either side of her stiff, gray dress, the color the same as the pebbles that lined the perfectly manicured path leading to the front door of her family's home.

When the witch reached her, she held out her hands to Iris. "With your permission, I'll begin the reading."

Iris looked to her right, trying to catch her father's eyes, but he kept his gaze on the soggy ground. Her mother, however, looked right at her, never one to shy away from her daughter. Not even in anger or sadness or fear. Not ever. She nodded once, and Iris turned to the witch in front of her.

"You have my permission."

Iris felt the magic working on her right away, the heat moving through her bloodstream and neural pathways, sliding through her mind in search of lies and deceit. She kept her eyes open, but the world around her disappeared until all she could see was a blanket of darkness with tiny pinpricks of light shining through, like the stars.

That was nature's give, ensuring that every human under the sun would know undoubtedly when magic was being used on them. They would know when all they could see was starlight.

Ana was one of the most powerful Stellars alive, a witch whose magic was strongest on humans, and she read Iris in seconds.

Iris blinked as the darkness faded and the world came back into view. Ana watched her carefully, then walked back to the table where the rest of the Witches' Council sat.

Iris tried not to think of how her best friend, Amy, had been rid of her ability to perceive magic in the very place Iris stood now, the cruelest of punishments handed down, even though Amy's oldest sister sat on the council.

Iris had been sleeping when Amy had done the unthinkable, when she'd pulled her boyfriend to the water's edge and turned him into a witch, just as he'd asked. Just as he'd wanted. Amy had been sure she'd be able to help him through the moments after, when he could suddenly see the magic of the universe and was desperate to pull it toward him, even though that magic could burn him alive. She'd believed she could stop him from commanding so much that it would incinerate him on the spot. She'd been wrong.

She'd been wrong, and Iris had been there.

Iris had woken to the sound of screams, and she'd run toward them. But she'd been too late, and the boy had turned from witch to ash before the moon had fully risen.

Iris closed her eyes, trying to rid herself of the memory. The council stood and took seven turns around the open field as they came to a verdict. Every trial was held outdoors, since a witch's intuition was strongest when surrounded by the natural world. The day was heavy with fog, and the witches slipped in and out of view as they circled the large expanse of wild grasses and blooming lavender.

Iris kept her eyes on the rain-soaked earth and the dozens of dandelions growing in the field. She looked to her parents once more but was again met only by her mother. As the council completed their seventh turn, Iris pushed her palm to her chest, trying to calm her racing heart.

The five witches reclaimed their seats at the long oak table and watched Iris, their facial expressions giving nothing away. Ana, the head of the council, stood as all the air fled Iris's lungs.

Ana folded her hands in front of her. The wind picked up, sending strands of her black hair over her face, but she did not tuck them back.

She looked Iris right in the eyes as she spoke. "You're free to go."

"I am?"

"Yes. You don't bear any responsibility for what happened that night. We will file our verdict with the state this afternoon.

Seeing as Mr. Newport's family declined to press charges against you, the court will accept our verdict as final."

Iris breathed out. The council was being too lenient. Iris had known something had been going on with her best friend, could feel in her bones she'd been planning something that Iris would never approve of. Iris should have stayed awake, should have been there to stop it.

But instead, she'd gone to sleep, and Alex Newport had burned.

"Thank you," Iris managed to say.

She wanted to move, to run to her parents and be taken home, but she stayed where she was, watching Ana and the rest of the council leave. Amy's older sister was last to stand, staring at the space Iris occupied but not truly seeing her. If only Amy's verdict had been as kind.

Free to go.

A light rain began to fall as Iris reached for her mother and clutched her as tight as she could. But her father held back. There was an inexplicable sadness in his eyes that didn't make sense given the verdict she'd received.

When they turned to leave, a gust of wind carried a single feather right past Iris, dropping it directly in front of her. She bent to pick it up and held onto the dark-brown feather dappled with white the whole way home.

one

two years later

The owl is watching me again. Most owls have vibrant eyes the color of fire, reds and yellows and oranges, but not the northern spotted owl. The northern spotted owl has eyes dark as pitch, and while he's supposedly nocturnal, he knows where I am day and night.

He took an interest in me as soon as we brought him into our wildlife refuge. Mom says it's a sign of good things to come—northern spotted owls are sacred to witches, after all.

But I can't help the way a chill runs down my spine when I feel his eyes on me, as if he's a harbinger instead.

He sits on the branch of an old fir tree, and we stare at each other for several moments. I finally turn away when my unease finds its way to my stomach. A wet nose collides with my fingertips, and I look down at Winter. She has been my loyal protector since Mom and I moved here two years ago, and she watches the owl with wary eyes.

"That wolf would die for you," Pike says from behind me. He says it as if it's an accusation, as if I charmed Winter into loving me, and I turn and fake a smile.

Pike Alder doesn't know what I am, and even if he did, I would never use magic to force affection.

Winter loves me because she can sense in her bones that I am worthy of her trust.

"I know." I pet Winter on the top of her head, and her eyes close. I would die for her, too, even though she would never allow it.

Pike frowns, the same frown that tightens his jaw and pulls at his lips whenever there's something he doesn't fully understand. I can feel him trying to figure me out, studying me through the lenses of his tortoise shell glasses, so I speak to halt his thoughts.

"Is there something you wanted?"

He cocks his head to the side, and I know I'm going to hate whatever it is he's about to say. "I just thought you'd like to know that I was once again rated higher than you on our feedback forms." He says it casually, but his chest inflates as he speaks.

I try to keep my expression neutral and hope Pike can't see the heat rising up my neck. I've worked hard to get comfortable speaking in front of the groups that tour our refuge, but it comes naturally to Pike. And as much as I hate to admit it, he's good at it. Great, even.

And he knows it.

"Congratulations," I say, keeping my voice free of the embarrassment I feel.

I give Winter a final scratch before stepping around Pike and heading back to the visitor's office. It's overcast out, a heavy blanket of gray covering the trees, the air dense with the promise of rain. I follow the trail through the forest of Sitka spruces, brown cones littering the path and crunching underneath me.

"I can sit in on your next tour and give you pointers," Pike says, falling in step beside me. "You know, take notes, speak up when you get something wrong, give you feedback after. Spring break is next week, so I have the time."

"How generous of you," I say, tucking a stray piece of hair behind my ear. "Is it really spring break already?"

"Yep. An entire week of eight-hour days together."

"Great."

"You know you love it when I'm here."

"Interesting word choice," I say, turning on the outdoor faucet and rinsing the mud from my boots. Pike does the same, then follows me into the small wooden building that serves as our office. It somehow still smells of the pine it was built from, and the wood floor groans when I enter.

"Come on, Iris, you'd be bored if it weren't for me. Besides, a little friendly competition is good for you—you'd hate for anyone to think you didn't actually earn your job here." He winks at me then and heads into the back office before I can respond.

Pike gives me a hard time because it's my mother's nonprofit, but he knows I'm better with the animals than anyone else. He's in school to become an ornithologist, dedicating his entire life to the study of birds. But his textbooks and binoculars are nothing compared to my magic.

Not that he can ever know that.

It's his arrogance that bothers me. Nature is all about balance, but Pike walks around as if the whole world is his. He doesn't understand humility or reverence, doesn't respect the chain beneath him because he's at the top.

Just once I'd like to show him all the things he doesn't know, all the facets of the universe he's missing by not having magic, but there's nothing that could make me foolish enough to share my secrets with another person. Not even an insurmountable dislike of Pike Alder.

I take a deep breath and begin cleaning up for the day, gathering all the visitor forms from the last tour group and putting away the unclaimed brochures. I wipe down the glass display case where our Foggy Mountain Wildlife Refuge merchandise is kept and ignore Pike when he walks out and turns on the television hanging on the wall.

We typically only use it to show our tours a quick video explaining the mission of the refuge, but Pike prefers background noise to silence. I usually tune it out, but the word *witch* comes through the speakers loud and clear, followed by a name—a name that sits heavy on my chest as if it's a physical thing, cumbersome and painful.

Images from that night on the lake invade my mind, and I squeeze my eyes shut, trying to banish them. But they continue to play, over and over as if they're the only movie in a twenty-four-hour theater. I force myself to go about my chores, making sure Pike can't see the way I'm hanging on every word from the news anchor's mouth.

But it's no use. My hands slow as I listen carefully to the report, and I turn my gaze to the screen. *"...early release has been granted. Amy Meadows was convicted of involuntary manslaughter by the courts and rid of her ability to use magic by the Witches' Council..."*

I exhale, a piece of that night breaking off my insides, not quite as heavy now. Early release has been granted. Amy's going home.

"Bad call," Pike says under his breath, shaking his head at the screen.

The glass cleaner slips from my fingers and drops to the floor, and I quickly pick it back up, trying to fight the knot forming in my chest. I spray more liquid on the case and wipe it up in fast circles, then do it again.

"They can't be trusted," Pike says. Then after a moment, his voice comes again, right behind me. "I think you got that spot."

I jump at his nearness and almost drop the bottle again. I want to tell him he's wrong, that there was a time I trusted Amy with everything. But it's dangerous, letting him see me worked up over a witch, so instead I stand and say, "I once again find myself doing more chores because you can't manage to do yours well."

"I think I know how to clean glass," Pike says.

I point to the upper corner of the case, where Pike likes to steady himself while cleaning. "Your handprint is so well defined I could cut it out and give it to your mother as a Christmas ornament."

Pike laughs, but my focus is back on the television. The broadcast continues, and Pike's words echo in my mind as if they were spoken in a canyon.

Bad call.

They can't be trusted.

The door swings open and Mom walks inside, ensuring I don't say anything I'll regret later.

"Honestly, Pike, you know how much I hate finishing my day with the news." Mom swats his arm before turning off the television, but she gives me a meaningful look as she does.

"Sorry, Isobel," he says. "I was just leaving."

"See you tomorrow," Mom says before heading into the back room.

Pike is almost out the door when he stops and turns. "Shoot, I forgot to clean the sloth enclosure," he says, giving me an overly apologetic look that's anything but sincere. He checks the time and shakes his head. "I have plans tonight, and I'm already running late. You don't mind doing it, do you, Gray?" His expression slips, and the right side of his mouth pulls up into a smirk.

"I'd believe you just a little more if it weren't the third time this month you'd 'forgotten,'" I say. "And yes, I do mind."

"Why, do you have someplace you need to be?"

I grind my teeth and don't say anything. He knows I don't, that I never do, and his smirk gets bigger. "Didn't think so," he says. With that, he hops out of the office and lets the door shut behind him, sending a burst of cold spring air into the small space.

"Not even a thank-you," I say, turning around and grabbing my things, grateful he can't see the way my skin burns with frustration. I don't want him to know that he gets to me, that his words actually mean something.

Mom comes out of the back room and turns off the lights,

holding the insulated mug she uses every morning for coffee. She slips into her jacket and untucks her straight blond hair, a stark difference from the brown, curly mess I got from my dad.

I used to love it, but now I'd trade it in for my mom's if I could.

Mom locks up the office, and we walk outside, the cloud cover from earlier getting darker as the day recedes.

"Pike left me to clean the sloth enclosure, so I need to do that before we head home," I say, failing to keep the annoyance from my tone.

"That sounds like him," she says with a casual laugh. "I'll get the walk-throughs done while you're cleaning." She starts off toward the aviary and looks over her shoulder. "Meet you back here in twenty minutes," she calls.

We walk in opposite directions, and I take a deep breath, letting the cool coastal air calm me. The sloth habitat comes into view with a bright-yellow sticky note attached to the door, standing out against the dusk. I recognize Pike's handwriting and squint to read the words: Thanks slow much!

I roll my eyes and pull the note off the door, crinkling it in my hand and tossing it into the trash. I get started cleaning, doing my best not to disturb the sloths, most of whom are sleeping. All of the money we get from the tour groups goes directly toward caring for our animals, and while the wolves are the biggest draw of the tours, the sloths never disappoint.

Once their habitat is clean, I check the temperature before slipping back outside. Mom is already waiting for me, and she wraps her arm around my shoulder.

"How are you?" she asks, leaning her head against mine, and I know she's asking about Amy.

"I'm glad she's going home," I say. "She deserves to."

"She does," Mom says, giving me a tight squeeze before pulling away.

What happened that night was so much worse for Amy. All she wanted was to share the magic she adored with the person she loved, and instead she watched him die. But there was so much collateral damage, so much pain, and I'm still working my way through the wreckage.

I want Amy to go home. I want her to find happiness and love and a way to move forward. I want to reach out and ask how she is, but we haven't spoken since her trial, and I don't know how to start up again. At first, she didn't want to speak to anyone, and I was okay with it because I didn't know what to say. I was so mad at her, and so devastated for her. It was complicated, and it still is.

Eventually, weeks passed, then months, then years. And after all this time, I still don't know what to say.

"Maybe it can help give you some closure." Mom drops her work gloves onto the office railing and looks at me.

"Maybe," I say, even though I don't know how a person gets closure from something like that. If closure is even something I want. The pain of it keeps me sharp, a constant reminder that some things are best left hidden.

I don't say anything more, and Mom doesn't push it. She knows there was a fundamental shift inside me after my trial, that I began to close off the parts of myself I'd previously held open to the world. I think it makes her sad sometimes, the way I built so many walls around myself for protection from something she can't see. The way time and distance didn't bring as much peace as she thought they would.

"You take him way too seriously, you know," Mom says after several minutes, interrupting my thoughts.

"Who?"

She raises her eyebrows and tilts her head expectantly.

"Oh, Pike. Honestly, Mom, I'm a little surprised you don't."

"He's hardly the first person to make a joke about witches."

"I don't think he was joking. But even if he was, he works with us. And after everything I've already put us through—"

Mom cuts me off. "How many times do I have to tell you that what happened that night wasn't your fault?" I'm about to argue, but Mom continues. "Besides, look around you," she says, motioning to the acres of land surrounding us. To the animals we're lucky enough to take in. "Tell me that having to move isn't one of the best things that ever happened to us."

I suppose she's right. Mom and I fell for the Pacific Northwest the moment we arrived, and being forced from our old home in the plains of Nebraska led us here, to a place neither of us could ever imagine leaving. Mom was able to start her own nonprofit, and now we operate one of the most diverse animal sanctuaries on the West Coast.

Sometimes it feels like a dream.

We love it here, but we don't talk about how the Pacific Northwest can't fully fill the hole my dad created when the fallout from that night on the lake required us to move and he refused. How his desire to stay outweighed his desire for us.

How who we are became too much for him.

And yet, I believe my mom when she says she's happier now. I can see it in the way she moves, with a lightness she didn't have before.

"Maybe it is," I say, and she leans into me. She takes a breath as if she wants to say something more, but no words follow.

"What is it?" I ask.

"Pike's a good kid, and he's the best intern we've had."

"He's also infuriating."

She frowns at my words, and I stop and look at her. "Just say what you want to say, Mom."

"Our life here is pretty great," she starts, her voice hesitant. "Don't create a problem where there isn't one."

I sigh. I know she's right. Our life here *is* great, but that's why I cling to it so tightly, why I want to protect it with everything I have. Maybe Pike really is just making stupid jokes that mean nothing, but I'm unwilling to let my guard down enough to find out.

"It really is great," I say, softening my tone.

"It is." She squeezes my hand and pushes through the gate that leads toward the house, but I pause.

"I'll catch up with you in a few minutes," I say.

"Give Winter a scratch for me."

I smile at her words, at the way she knows my routine so well. It's almost dark now, and I take my time walking to the woods where the wolves roam. Pacific tree frogs croak in the distance, and a crescent moon illuminates the clouds, casting the forest in a soft glow. I let myself in through the metal gate, then whistle for Winter. She comes running, the way she does every night.

I sit on the cold ground and stroke her silver fur, resting my head against hers. She leans into me, and I think that maybe Mom is right, that maybe the universe meant for us to be here all along.

There is magic in my blood, but this place has its own kind of magic. I feel it every time the evergreens sway in the wind and whenever the treetops are swallowed by fog. I can feel it in the salty air and the fern-covered ground.

This is my home, and I know it as sure as I know how Winter is feeling just by looking at her.

This is where I'm meant to be.

I sit with Winter for several minutes before giving her one final pet good night. I stand and let myself out through the gate, beginning the walk home, but a chill rushes down my spine and I stop.

Slowly, I turn. I have to squint to see him, his shape nothing more than a shadow in the dusty twilight, but sitting in an old spruce tree is the northern spotted owl.

Silent, still, and watching.

Always watching.

t w o

Most people think magic is created, that it goes from nonexistent to existent in the span of a moment.

That isn't true.

Magic is always present, always close. It exists along with all the atoms and particles of the universe, and when enough of it is brought together, it produces a reaction most would call extraordinary. But the reaction itself isn't the magic; it's the existence of it in the first place that is.

Witches are able to recognize the energy around us and reorder it in ways to produce certain outcomes. It's a sixth sense that most people don't have. We can harness all the chaotic particles and bring them together into something brilliant.

And because magic is born of the universe, of the same stars that created everything on Earth, it can be used in three ways: on plants, on animals, and on humans. For every witch, one of the three forms comes most easily to them. Mom and I are both Lunars—our magic is strongest on animals.

It's that sixth sense, that innate connection to the world around us, that gives us our power. It's why I'm able to soothe animals and feel their needs, why I know their history just by touching them.

It's also why I have to work so hard to hide who I am, because being a witch isn't just casting an occasional spell. It's seeing the world differently than the way others see it. It's living in the same space but experiencing it in a totally singular way.

It isn't that witches have to hide. We don't. Once it became common knowledge that it's impossible for magic to be used on a person without their knowing about it, witches have been welcomed into society. And magic is highly regulated, especially for Stellars, whose power gravitates toward people.

The combination of those two things led to less fear and more trust, to witches being open about their magic and respected in their fields. It's been that way for generations now, and magic has become wholly intertwined with society, from Stellars who specialize in pain management to Solars who work with farmers around the globe.

But I've seen firsthand what a fragile acceptance it is, and I don't trust it. After the trial, I wasn't Iris anymore. I was a witch, and when the word was sprayed in black paint across the home my father had worked so hard to build, he no longer felt up to the task of raising a girl with magic in her blood.

And I had it easy compared to Amy. The way she was treated made me certain that what is best for me is to hide the magic I love. So I do.

Mom and I are lucky, though. Our home borders the wildlife refuge, and since so much of the work we do is with animals, we're able to use our magic regularly. It's a quiet, invisible kind of magic that will never get us shunned. It will never require us to start over, to move to a different town where whispers and sidelong glances and spray-painted words don't follow us.

Foggy Mountain Wildlife Refuge gave me my life back, just as we try to do for the animals that come here, and I'm thankful every single day that this is where we ended up.

I check my watch. I only have fifteen minutes before I need to be at work, but fifteen minutes is enough. The news of Amy's release has me feeling exposed and vulnerable, and the memories I've tried so hard to forget are all I see when I close my eyes. I still haven't forgiven her for begging me to go to the lake house with her, for not telling me what she and Alex had planned. I thought we trusted each other with everything, but it turns out I was wrong.

Give it to the earth.

That's what my grandmother used to say, when my feelings felt bigger than the whole world, when I was sure I'd collapse from the weight of them all. She taught me to cast spells I would never use, as if I was writing a letter I would never send. I've been doing it since I was young, and at times, it's the only thing that calms me, that anchors me to this place.

I gather dried herbs from the cottage behind our house—mugwort, lavender, and lemon balm—and put them in a small pile on the ground. They're surrounded by a circle of stones and rest on top of ashes from all the other spells I've written but never used, all that's left of my worries and frustrations and fears.

I sit down on the dirt, facing the circle, and begin. I'm not a Stellar, but I know how to write a spell that would sear into Amy's mind and expose all the messy feelings I have about that night. I know how to rearrange the magic around me to let Amy understand I want the best for her, even though I don't know how to show it. Even though I'm still upset.

So that's what I do. All at once, the particles of magic in the area make themselves known, and I pull them closer. They hover in the space between me and the stone circle, and I silently speak the words, magic morphing in front of me as I do.

A sharp, metallic scent tinges the air, too faint for anyone but a witch to sense. But it's there, the undeniable scent of magic, the spell I've crafted for Amy overcoming my senses.

In one quick motion, I release it to the herbs, binding them together as one. The spell clings to them, a living thing I could send to Amy if I wanted. But magic is regulated, and casting a spell to make myself feel better isn't an acceptable use.

This is just for me, a spell that won't do anything other than be absorbed into the earth. A letter left unsent. But the ritual of it is enough, and my shoulders relax as I go through the motions my grandmother taught me.

I take the remaining magic and send it directly over the herbs, the particles heating up as they collide into each other. I send them around and around until so much heat is produced that a small spark jumps to the ground and the herbs go up in flames, taking the spell with them.

Smoke rises into the cool morning air, the remnants of magic caught on the wind and burned into ash. It, and all my feelings surrounding Amy, belongs to the earth now, and even though my spell will never reach her, I feel better.

I stand and wipe the dirt from my jeans, then walk to the office. The wind is strong this morning, and the tops of the trees sway back and forth against the overcast sky. My hair blows out behind me, and the cool air feels good against my warm skin. The calm of this place moves through me, and by the time I reach the office, some of the knots that had formed in my stomach have loosened.

Pike is already there when I walk inside, hanging his coat in the back room. I run my fingers over the engraved logo in the wooden desk, the way I do every morning. I trace the wolf howling at the full moon and the outline of mountains behind it, the letters that spell out the dream that Mom turned into reality.

"Feel better?" Mom asks, raising an eyebrow at me.

She never took to my grandmother's ritual the way I did, and she doesn't approve of me writing spells that aren't technically legal, even though they're never put to use. She believes all magic should have a purpose, that crafting spells that aren't used for anything is wasteful.

I've tried to explain the way it calms me, the way it helps me work through my feelings and release the things I can't change, but she doesn't get it. Still, she's never told me not to do it—even though she doesn't understand, she knows it matters to me.

"I do," I say, kissing her on the cheek. "I'm sorry I'm late."

Mom looks at the clock. "Three minutes is hardly late. Pike doesn't apologize until he's at least ten minutes late," she says, loud enough for him to hear.

"Hey, that's unfair," Pike says, walking out from the back room. "That's only happened a few times, when I've been enthralled by my coursework. Some would say you're lucky to have such a studious intern."

"A studious intern who stops for coffee regardless of how late he's running," I say, and Mom laughs, shaking her head. Her cell rings, and she steps into the back to answer it.

"Wow, way to throw me under the bus," Pike says. "You're not still worked up over the sloths, are you?"

"You mean am I still worked up over you purposefully leaving your chores for me because you decided your time is more valuable than mine?" I ask, moving behind the desk and pulling a jar of vitamin D drops from the drawer. "No, I'd forgotten all about it."

I make sure Mom isn't looking, then I take off the lid to her mug and put a drop in her coffee. Her doctor told her to start taking it, but she never remembers, so I remember for her. I don't think she'd care if she knew I put vitamin D in her coffee, but she already thinks I worry about her too much, so I try to be subtle.

"Well, it sounds kind of rude when you put it like that," Pike says.

"It was rude." I push the lid back on Mom's mug and put the vitamin D away just as she walks out, interrupting Pike's reply.

"That was Dan. Animal rescue is going to be here in a few minutes with a wolf they found on the ridge. It's pretty bad, from what it sounds like, and I'll need your help bringing it in. Pike, can you handle the ten o'clock tour?"

"Sure thing," he says. He gets the office ready for the first group, and Mom takes a quick sip of coffee before grabbing her coat. I follow her out of the office without giving Pike another glance.

"How bad is it?" I ask. It's a cold spring day, the kind that feels as if it's still touching winter, and I wrap my arms around my chest. Mom and I are both wearing Foggy Mountain baseball caps, and our boots trudge through the mud as we make our way through the trees.

"I don't have many details," she says.

The treetops sway in the breeze, and several pine cones drop to the ground when a larger gust blows through the branches. Raindrops from the night before glisten on the ferns and moss, and amber sap clings to the bark of the nearby pines. I hear tires over gravel in the distance, and Dan's truck comes into view just as we leave the cover of the trees.

"Hi, Isobel," Dan calls from the driver's side. He turns off the engine and steps out, pulling on his jacket as he does. "Iris," he says, nodding.

"Hi, Dan," I say, walking to the bed of the truck.

"What have you got for us?" Mom asks.

"Male. Four or five years old. Struck by a vehicle in eastern Washington."

I release the back of the truck, and pale yellow eyes lock on mine. The gray wolf is lying on his side, his head tilted toward me, and he takes a shuddering breath. Mom keeps Dan busy so I can focus on the wolf. I feel the connection form between us, an invisible string tying us together, and I let the wolf see my intentions.

He knows he isn't in danger.

He knows I want to help him.

He knows I'll do everything I can to save him.

His eyes close, and I quickly survey the damage. His right side is covered in blood, caked in his fur, making it impossible to see the wound. I close my eyes and listen to his breathing, feel the way the air doesn't fill up his lungs. The rhythm of his heart echoes in my mind, and it's too fast.

Whatever internal bleeding he's sustained has slowed, and if Mom and I work fast, we can save him.

"We need to get him inside," I say. "I'll grab the cart."

I rush to the side of the shop, where a small cart with a cargo bed waits. The forest-green paint is faded and dirty, and the Foggy Mountain logo is covered in mud, making the words difficult to read. I start the engine and drive back to where Mom and Dan are waiting.

We carefully transfer the wolf to the cart and drive him into the shed, where a long metal table is prepped and waiting. Mom interned for a veterinarian years ago, long enough for her to learn the basics of surgery. Everyone in town assumes Mom is a vet, and she's never done anything to correct the assumption.

Her connection with the animals tells her what needs fixing, and she does it.

We get the wolf situated on the table, and after making sure he isn't a risk to us, Dan leaves.

Mom closes her eyes and strengthens her connection to the wolf, sounding off his injuries as her magic scours his body.

"Three broken ribs." Pause. "Moderate internal bleeding." Pause. "Major organs are okay." Pause. "No sign of infection."

She opens her eyes and looks at me. "Let's get started."

I pull up a chair and sit at the end of the table where the wolf's head is. He whines, and I slowly move my hand to his snout. He sniffs a few times and lets me pet his fur. Mom turns on the electric razor to shave the wolf's side, and he tenses when he hears the noise. I send more magic into his system, and he relaxes into my hand.

Contrary to popular belief, we can't create more magic than what's already in the world. Nothing is created or destroyed. It all simply exists, and we direct it in the best way we can. Much of what we do is a combination of magic and science, magic and medicine, magic and research. It all works together in perfect harmony, keeping things in balance. That's why Mom can't simply look at the wolf and heal him; magic is a tool, but it's only one of many.

Most importantly, we can't exert control over animals or plants or people. Magic works *with* the natural world, never against it. I can't make an animal do something it isn't willing to do, but I can show it my intentions, let it know it's safe, and let my magic flow through it in a way that's reassuring. I can try to direct it, use magic to coax it in one way or another, but what to do is ultimately always up to the animal.

They're wild, after all, just as they should be.

Once Mom is done shaving, she starts cleaning up the gash in the wolf's side, and I keep him as calm as I can. It's a two-person job: Mom can't use her magic to calm him and address his injuries at the same time, and having a scared wolf trying to escape is a disaster waiting to happen. So I sit with him and pet his fur, letting my magic wrap around his instincts until every part of him tells him he's safe.

Mom works quickly, and once she has stopped the internal bleeding, she stitches up his side. When she's done, I hear the wolf's heartbeat slow, feel the relief in his lungs when they're able to take a full breath.

He's going to be okay.

We take him to a private enclosure at the edge of the refuge, where he'll be able to heal without interference from the other animals. Winter runs over and shoves her snout through the metal fence, trying to get as close to the new wolf as possible.

"He's not a threat," I tell her. "He's hurt and needs to heal. Keep an eye on him."

I could live a thousand lives and never be loved by anyone as much as I'm loved by Winter. I scratch her head, then turn toward the office for a clean set of clothes.

Pike is in the office when I get there, eating a sandwich and reading a book.

"You look like you're working hard," I say. I walk around him and into the back room, where I keep an extra sweatshirt. The one I'm wearing has dried blood smeared on it, and I pull it up and over my head, and my T-shirt goes up with it, revealing my stomach.

Pike is watching me, and I catch his glance before he quickly looks away. I pull down my shirt and put on the clean sweatshirt, and when I look back at Pike, a blush has spread across his fair skin. He clears his throat before taking another bite of his sandwich.

"It's my lunch break," he says, returning to whatever book he was reading. It's large, with a detailed drawing of an owl on the left page and a close-up of a wing on the right.

"Are you not quite ready for books with words yet?" I ask him, looking over his shoulder.

He rolls his eyes and doesn't look at me. "It's a textbook," he says. "You know, for studying. Not all of us are lucky enough to have a job we didn't earn waiting for us after high school."

I graduated last year, and Mom and I talked briefly about college, but it didn't make sense. I already have all the skills I need to work at the refuge, and spending four years in a classroom, when I can gain more experience under the cover of evergreens, wasn't something I wanted.

I look at the drawing of the owl. It's lifelike and detailed, with all the anatomy precisely labeled. The owl's dark eyes stare at me from the page, reminding me of the spotted owl outside. I walk around the desk and put on my raincoat.

"I may be lucky, but I earned my place here. That book can't teach you intuition or warmth. It can't teach you the things you'd need to learn to be even half as good with the animals as I am."

"Maybe not, but at least I'm working at it. What are you working on? Because it certainly isn't your people skills."

"I'm more comfortable with animals," I say, ashamed when my voice gets quiet.

Pike doesn't seem to notice, though. "It's too bad you aren't a witch, then you could just force people into liking you. Did you hear that the girl on the news was released after only two years?" He shakes his head. "Ridiculous."

"What's your deal with witches?" I do my best to keep my voice steady, even, not letting him know how hard it is to ask the question. If he's going to be interning with us, I want to know.

His hazel eyes get glassy, and he looks down at his book for several moments, staring off into a place I can't see. "I don't trust magic," he finally says.

The words make me sad for some reason. I trust magic more than anything else in the world, more than I trust most people. I shake my head and turn to leave the office.

"That was a rather big sigh," Pike says, any hint of seriousness gone from his voice.

"Did I sigh?"

"A big one," he says. "An 'I'm so exasperated with Pike I can't even be here anymore' sigh."

"Well, you do have that effect on me." I try to match his joking tone, but I don't quite succeed, and the words sound mean and aggravated. I walk back to the desk and lean my arms on it. "Seriously, why do you hate witches so much?"

I'm surprised when my voice breaks, threatening to expose all the things I keep hidden. I want him to say that he doesn't, that he's just joking around. My palms sweat, and I suddenly feel like I'm that girl back in Nebraska, staring at the word *witch* graffitied across the front of her home, not understanding how anyone could use the word as an insult. Not understanding how anyone could see it as anything other than wonderful.

Pike stands and walks around the desk, just inches away from my face. "You really want to know?" His voice is soft and low.

All I can do is nod. My heart races, and I swallow hard. I wait for him to laugh and say it's nothing, to wave it off as one big joke. But he doesn't.

He leans in close to me, so close I could snatch the glasses off his face or smooth down his wavy brown hair. So close I can smell the spice of tea on his breath. "I'm not going to tell you," he says. "But I will say one thing. The girl on the news? She should have been the one to burn."

He turns and walks out the door before I can respond.

three

When Mom and I get home that night, Sarah is already in the kitchen. The house smells of herbs and spices, and I take off my coat and breathe deeply, trying to forget the words Pike spoke to me earlier. Trying to forget the way his voice held a darkness that scares me.

She should have been the one to burn.

Mom goes upstairs to shower, and I walk into the kitchen and sit down at the counter. I always love seeing Sarah in our home—she brightens everything. She lives a couple miles down the road, but she's here all the time, and I suspect that one day I'll realize she came for dinner and never left.

She's a big reason I believe my mom when she says moving is one of the best things that happened to us. Mom and Sarah have been friends for years, and when we moved out here, their friendship deepened.

Now, when I see the looks that pass between them, when I hear my mom hum to herself around the house, it eases the sting of guilt that lingers in my chest. A few months ago, Mom told me that their love changed to *in* love, and the words healed something in me I thought was forever broken. After everything she went through with my dad, she found her person in the heart of the Olympic Peninsula, and all I want is for her to keep smiling and humming and laughing.

It's all I want for Sarah, too.

"How was your day, hun?" She hands me a few slices of bell pepper, the ones she didn't chop because she knows I like them raw.

"It was fine," I say between bites. "We got a new wolf today. He was hit by a truck on the other side of the mountains, but he'll be okay."

"Such majestic creatures," she says, and I smile because it's what she always says when we talk about the wolves. Sarah was my mom's first close friend who is also a witch, and the awe she has for the world around her is unbridled.

She stirs her sauce and tastes it before adding more salt, then hands me a spoon to test it as well.

"Delicious," I say.

She winks at me. "It'll do."

Her long black hair is pulled back in a ponytail that can barely hold the volume of her waves, and her warm, beige skin is dotted with sweat at her hairline. Mom's footsteps echo through the house as she walks down the stairs, and Sarah pours her a glass of wine and hands it to her as soon as she enters the kitchen.

"Thank you," my mom says, giving her a grateful look.

I set the table while Sarah plates the food, and Mom turns on some classical music to play in the background. There were many things that Mom changed when we moved here, many habits she broke and traditions she severed, but playing classical music over dinner is one of the things that stayed.

I wonder if it makes her think of Dad.

Sarah and Mom exchange stories about their days, Mom talking about the wolf, Sarah talking about the breakfast café she owns, and I run over the past ten hours in my mind, my thoughts snagging on what Pike said in the office.

She should have been the one to burn.

It's the only time he has ever sounded mean, truly mean. And it scares me because after everything Mom and I have been through, the last thing we need is a witch-hating intern working for us.

But it's more than that. I hate the way I held my breath when he spoke, the way I hoped it was nothing, something I'd built up in my mind that didn't match reality. I hate the way his words stunned me and how, for one awful moment, I thought I might cry.

"Iris?" Mom asks.

I look up from my food. "Sorry, did you say something?"

She sets down her glass and looks at me. "What's on your mind?"

"Nothing; it's not a big deal," I say, but Mom and Sarah watch me, waiting for me to tell them what I'm thinking. They don't need magic to know when something's bothering me, unfortunately. Hiding how I feel has never been a strong suit of mine.

"It's just something Pike said. About witches. He said they can't be trusted, but there's something in the way he said it that worries me. Like it's really important to him or something." I leave out the part about Amy because I can't bring myself to repeat it, to say the words out loud.

Mom pours herself another glass of wine and tops off Sarah's as well. "A lot of people don't trust witches." She says it as if it doesn't faze her, as if it doesn't make her angry or upset. "After the way you reacted to the news the other day, he's probably just saying it to rattle you."

"Pike says a lot of things to rattle me," I say. "This was different. He sounded...cold, I guess. Mean. I just don't know if we should keep an intern around who clearly doesn't like witches."

"He's harmless," Mom says. "And he'll never find out anyway. Unless you keep getting worked up over the news broadcasts, that is." She gives me a pointed look, and her mouth pulls up on one side. "You just don't like that he gives you a run for your money at work."

"He does not," I say, sounding more defensive than I mean.

Sarah bursts out laughing and leans onto her elbows conspiratorially. "Is he the kid in glasses who looks like he belongs in an ad for fair-trade coffee?"

"I don't know what that means," I say, but Mom is leaned back in her chair, nodding excitedly at Sarah. "Ew, both of you," I say. "I've never even noticed his looks."

That's not entirely true. The first day of his internship, I most certainly *did* notice the way his thick brown hair looked perfectly mussed up and the way his glasses seemed to bring out the hazel in his eyes. I noticed the smattering of faint freckles across the bridge of his nose and the way the rim of his glasses stood out against his pale skin.

Then he opened his mouth, and it's been hard for me to remember seeing him as anything other than what he is now: a person I thoroughly dislike.

"Of course you haven't."

I set down my glass, and it hits the table harder than I intend. "You guys aren't taking this seriously enough," I say. "He could be a real problem for us."

"Iris, honey, I love how protective you are. I love how you only want what's best for us. But please believe me when I say you need to relax a little. What happened two years ago, it was tragic and awful, but it wasn't the norm. Witches aren't shunned and run out of their homes—we're as much a part of society as anyone else. I understand why you want to keep that part of us hidden, I really do, but I hate the idea of you living in fear." Her voice is gentle, and she tucks a piece of hair behind my ear. "If it makes you feel better, Pike's internship is up at the end of the semester, and the only way he'll ever know you're a witch is if you want him to."

"I would never want that."

"Then you have nothing to worry about," she says. She pauses and takes a sip of water before speaking again. "You know, honey, someday there will be someone worthy of keeping your secrets." She stands up from the table and grabs her plate.

I help Mom with the dishes before making myself a cup of

tea and heading to my room, but I feel unsettled. I hate having secrets, and for a while I didn't think I needed any. In our last town, I didn't hide who I was. We were friends with our neighbors and had my dad's boss over for dinners. We went to church pot-lucks and participated in the high school's bake sale.

But that night with Amy changed everything. No one believed that Alex truly wanted to be turned into a witch. No one believed that it was a misguided plan borne of first love. And no one believed that I wasn't involved.

The narrative quickly became that of dark intention, of two witches having fun with the unsuspecting high school boy, and it spread like wildfire, burning through the whole town. We couldn't escape it. Even after my trial, after the Witches' Council let me go and the town knew the verdict, nothing changed. It only got worse.

We tried to weather it, to ignore it all and get on with our lives, but we couldn't. That night by the lake followed me every-where I went. It followed my parents everywhere they went.

So we decided to leave.

I knew as soon as we started talking about it that Dad's heart wasn't in it. Even prior to that night, Dad had been suggesting I stop spending time with Amy and make new friends—friends who weren't witches. He asked my mom to stop her work with the exotic animal rescue and try to get involved in other things. *Normal* things to go along with the normal life he worked so hard for.

And when it came down to it, he didn't want to leave. We'd had to move once before, when my grandmother accidentally set the house on fire with a spell gone wrong. Insurance wouldn't cover the damage, so we packed up and moved to a small town in Nebraska where the cost of living was lower and we could start over.

I think that's when he stopped thinking magic was wondrous and started to resent it instead.

Dad loved that town. He loved his job and the white picket fence and the Toyota Camry that sat in the driveway. He loved the stability and routine, and when it came down to it, he loved those things more than he loved us.

So we left, and he stayed.

And the thing that kills me is that now what I want more than anything else in the world is to stay here. And I don't know how to be angry at him when I want the exact same thing he did.

To stay.

Mom and Sarah are still downstairs talking, and I finish my tea and get ready for bed. But I can't sleep. I'm frustrated that, after everything, Mom can be so casual about Pike Alder, that she can be so sure he'll never find out who we are. He's a danger to us, and she isn't fazed by it at all.

I never used to have secrets, and now I cling to them as if they're my lifeline. Ever since we got here, I try to make up for everything we lost. I try to protect us. I try to ensure that we can stay here for the rest of our lives. But Mom isn't a worrier, she's relaxed and easygoing, and I feel like I'm constantly having to compensate for that. Even after everything that happened in our last town, she wouldn't be hiding the fact that we're witches if it weren't for me. She does it because she knows it's what I want, knows it makes me feel more secure. But she'd never choose this on her own.

I don't think we have the luxury of being easygoing, though, and every time my mom tells me to relax, it makes me want to tighten my control even more.

I hear the front door close, followed by an engine starting and tires rolling down the gravel driveway. Moments later, Mom's footsteps echo up the stairs and pause in front of my door. She quietly turns the knob, and I shut my eyes and pretend to sleep, not wanting her to know that the worries she wishes I didn't have are keeping me awake.

She softly shuts my door and walks down the hall to her room. The house is quiet except for the sounds in the walls as the temperature cools and the house settles.

I close my eyes once more, but all I see is Pike leaning into me, his voice cold and mean, his eyes too intense for comfort.

I know I should let it go, breathe it out and try to get some sleep, but my heart is racing and my mind is awake, filling with worry and nerves and unease.

After another half hour of unsuccessfully falling asleep, I get out of bed and get dressed. I quietly slip out of my room and walk down the stairs, pausing at the front door to make sure my mom didn't wake. Her room remains quiet, and I pull on my jacket and boots before grabbing a flashlight and heading out into the night.

If Mom is going to insist that Pike continues his internship, I have to find a way not to care as much. I have to stop my dislike of him from growing stronger than it already is. I have to find a way to ease my worries, and as I walk toward the cottage out back, my body thrums with excitement, the magic inside me anticipating what's to come.

It doesn't matter that I just wrote a spell for Amy. Pike's words settled under my skin, and I haven't been able to focus since he said them. So tonight, under the cover of darkness, I'll give Pike Alder to the earth.

I'll write a spell I'll never use and let the ritual of it ground me, release my fear so I can move on.

And since the spell will vanish before it's ever used, it can match the tone of Pike Alder's voice.

It can be mean.

four

The night is cold and clear. Thousands of stars shine overhead, and I turn off my flashlight and tilt my head back. I can see the Milky Way, the echoes of white in a pitch-dark sky, and I take a breath as if the entire universe can fill my lungs.

Winds from the Pacific collide with the tops of the spruce trees, sending them back and forth, swaying in an otherwise silent night. I pull my jacket tighter around my torso and walk to the workbench outside the cottage.

A small, dirty lamp hangs from the gutter, and I tug on the pull chain. It flickers several times before clicking on, and fluorescent light spills into the night. The lamp buzzes above me, and two moths flit around in circles.

There's no spell book or cauldron, no repeated phrases or rings of fire. There's just the draw inside me that calls magic from its scattered position and pulls it into something potent.

I push open the old cottage door and collect wormwood and

safflower, then head back outside and gather enough twigs and branches to create a satisfying fire. Then I begin.

Witches have a kind of internal switch that allows us to regulate when we're receiving magic. We believe in leaving things as undisturbed as possible, in letting the earth exist on its own without our constant interference. We only flip the switch when needed, a call to the magic around us, inviting it to assemble into something new.

I exhale and concentrate on the energy around me, the protons and neutrons and photons and muons, and I dismiss them all until the only thing remaining is raw, untouched magic.

I flip the switch, and it rushes toward me in an incredible surge, thousands of particles of magic snapping into me as if I'm a magnet. My skin heats up and prickles with the weight of it, a physical reaction I will never tire of. I am the cosmos and energy and the matter of the universe held perfectly together with skin and bone.

Winter howls in the distance, a long cry that gets the other wolves going as well. I listen as they take their turns until one final howl echoes through the night and fades to nothing. I suspect it's Winter's way of checking on the new wolf, saying hello in the middle of the night when the humans aren't around to keep him company.

I smile at the thought.

My skin burns hot with the mass of magic blanketing me, and I turn my attention to Pike Alder and his arrogant demeanor and hatred of witches and constant rotation of flannel shirts. I think about the way he laughed at the newscaster and rolled his eyes and dismissed Amy as untrustworthy without a single thought.

I think of the way his tone turned to ice, permeating my skin and turning my whole body cold.

She should have been the one to burn.

What is the one thing Pike Alder would hate more than anything else in the world?

The answer slams into my mind instantly, a spell so cruel it can only be called a curse.

A curse to turn him into a witch, to make him become the very thing he hates.

But the memory of that night on the lake makes me hesitate. There's a reason it's illegal to turn a person into a witch, a law that's upheld in both regular courts and witches' courts. It's dangerous and unpredictable, and Amy was willing to risk everything because the person she loved wanted so badly to experience magic.

By the time I reached the lake that night, Alex was already engulfed in flames. I couldn't see his face behind the red-and-orange light, couldn't meet his eyes. Amy was crying, still trying to pull the magic from him even though it was too late. She was a Stellar, and if she couldn't help Alex when her magic was most effective on him, I knew my Lunar magic wouldn't be enough.

And I was right. It wasn't.

I squeeze my eyes shut and focus on the sounds of the night around me. I'm not on a quiet lake in Nebraska. I'm at my home on the Olympic Peninsula, surrounded by hundred-year-old spruce trees and briny sea air from the Pacific. It's just me and a tradition I learned from my grandmother—there is no one here for me to hurt.

The spell will burn away with the pile of herbs, and that will be it. Hopefully, it will take my fear and frustration with it, make it easier for me to work with someone who hates what I am. Pike will never know, and I'll feel better.

A lot better. I get to work.

The magic around me vibrates in anticipation, turning my skin to pins and needles, morphing into the shape of a curse that can turn a boy into a witch. I prepare to bind the spell to my pile of herbs when a series of four loud hoots punctuates the air.

I stumble back and squint into the night sky, even though trying to find the owl in darkness is a fool's errand. But I'm certain it's the spotted owl. I know because I can feel him watching me, feel his big eyes boring into me as if I'm prey.

I watch the sky for several moments, and when he doesn't make another sound, I get back to my magic. Then it happens again, this time closer.

Louder.

Four short hoots with the middle notes closest together.

My heart races, and my skin crawls, not with the vibrant feel of magic but the awful creep of dread. The owl continues his call, again and again, louder and louder until I'm terrified the sound will wake up Mom, will wake up this entire peninsula.

I can't concentrate on what I'm doing, and I release the magic from my control, letting it scatter and flee into the night. The curse will have to wait.

"Stop!" I shout in the direction of the owl, my voice unsteady and rough.

He listens. The hoots stop in an instant, replaced with the

gentle sway of towering trees, a silence that is somehow worse than the owl's incessant screams.

I rush to the workbench and turn off the light, then grab my flashlight and head back to the house. I walk fast and keep my head down, wrapping my arms around my ribs, but I feel his eyes on me the whole way there.

It isn't until I get inside that I realize how fast and shallow my breaths are coming, and I quietly shut the door and lean back into it. I let my eyes close and my lungs fill, inhaling deeply in the safety of this house that so quickly became my home.

I hang my coat on the rack and take off my boots, then silently slip up the stairs and into my bedroom. I change into my pajamas and crawl into bed, trying to release the tension in my body so I can sleep.

I tell myself I was overreacting, that I let a lonely owl frighten me so much I ran back home. But even as my muscles relax and I sink farther into my mattress, I can't make myself believe it.

A gust of wind kicks up, howling through my old bedroom window, and I get out of bed to pull down the shades. Large shadows move in the distance, and even though I know it's impossible, I'm sure I see the sacred owl in the branch of a tree, watching me through the glass.

When I wake up the next morning, I'm still feeling uneasy. A restless night of sleep did nothing to calm my worries, and as I walk down the stairs and into the kitchen, I know I need a release before work. I leave Mom a note telling her I'm heading out early, and when my tea is ready, I pour it in a travel mug and walk into the chilly morning air.

It rained overnight, a fresh spring rain that covers the forest in an earthy smell that fills my lungs, the scent calming me from the inside out. I learned a long time ago that nature has a way of easing the wound-up gears in my chest, of loosening the knots I've tied tighter and tighter over the years.

The smell of rain is one of my salves. The sound of rushing water is another.

And when those things don't work, when the worry becomes too much, I give it to the earth, just like my grandma taught me.

The world is starting to brighten, dawn giving way to the light. The soil is damp beneath me, and the trees rustle in the early-morning breeze. A layer of fog hangs heavy in the sky, shrouding the treetops in a veil of mist, and house finches sing in the distance.

The herbs and sticks I gathered last night were scattered by the wind, and I pick them up and set them back in the same circle I used for Amy's spell, and for all the spells that came before it. I take a long sip of tea, the warmth sliding down my throat and fighting off the morning chill.

I've never left a spell unfinished before, and that combined with a night of playing Pike's words over and over has left me even more tense. I want to let it go like Mom says, release the fear and worry, and this is the only way I know how.

I get started.

Everything around me is peaceful, and when I call the magic toward me, it slides into place as if it has been waiting for me to return since last night. It surrounds me in a layer of warmth, and an energetic buzz dances over my skin.

When I picture Pike Alder, the magic shifts in response, heavy with the intent to turn him into a witch. Or, more precisely, turn him into a mage.

Witches are born of the earth, entering the world blood-slick and silent, halting their cries to marvel at the feel of magic on their skin for the very first time. Anyone who acquires the ability to direct magic later in life is a mage, and there aren't many of them.

Witches are forbidden from turning other people, and the mages who exist today almost entirely consist of people who were turned illegally or who were drenched in magic by accident when a witches' power spun out of control.

Either way, intentional or not, the overwhelming presence of magic makes them aware of that sixth sense, that switch inside us that recognizes the fragments of the universe. But mages are dangerous—they gain access to the magic around them in a single instant, and if there isn't a witch present to teach them how to control it, the consequences can be dire.

That's what happened to Alex Newport—he grabbed all the magic he could, engulfing himself in it, and Amy wasn't strong enough to help. She couldn't stop him from pulling more and more until the reaction was fatal.

But I needn't worry about that. The beauty of what my grandmother taught me is that I can write a spell that will never be put to use. I can let it hold all of the feelings that are building inside me like a brewing storm, acknowledge the fears and hurts that would otherwise be all-consuming, and do it in a way that respects the world around me.

I may not like Pike, but I appreciate the order of the universe. I have no wish to change it, and while turning Pike into a mage might make him see that magic isn't bad, that witches aren't deserving of the animosity he has toward us, I would never actually do it. Still, it's comforting to go through the motions, to let myself imagine doing something to Pike that he would view as truly awful—even though it isn't awful at all.

Magic is a gift, one that Pike Alder is wholly undeserving of.

But the point of a curse is to deliver a consequence that is unimaginable to the victim, and being turned to a witch would be unimaginable to Pike.

It's the perfect curse for him.

I speak my intentions as the particles of magic shift in the air, following my voice and transforming into a curse. Once it's formed, I focus on the herbs in the stone circle. A spell of this nature has to bind to something powerful in order to stay intact, which is why the herbs are the perfect vessel—they're strong enough to hold it, but once I burn them, the curse will disperse on the wind as if it never even existed, taking my fears along with it.

A ritual almost as perfect as the woman who taught it.

The curse gets clearer, and when a dense mass of magic radiates in the space in front of me, I know it's ready. I inhale, filling my lungs with all my worries, with all my too-big feelings and painful vulnerability, and on my exhale, I release them along with the curse.

The curse rushes toward the herbs, but before it can bind to them, a solid stream of air blows into my face as a brown object enters my peripheral vision and flies past me in a blur.

I watch in horror as the northern spotted owl comes into focus, directly between me and the stone circle, the curse slamming into his chest. He lets out a rough bark before flying upward and stopping in a nearby tree, watching me from above.

I drop to the ground and scramble toward the wormwood and safflower, searching them for any sign of magic, any sign of the curse I created.

But there is none.

I slowly stand and turn toward the expanse of trees. The fog has lifted enough for me to see the owl with perfect clarity. I close my eyes and concentrate, finding a connection to the bird right away. And there, sitting heavy in his chest, is the curse.

I have to undo this. Magic is a living, breathing thing, which means it will stay with the owl as long as he's alive. But if he dies, the curse will be released into the wild, where it will seek out and find Pike Alder.

My heart slams into my ribs, too fast, and an awful chill rolls down my spine. I break out in a cold sweat and tell myself to breathe.

All I have to do is get the owl and remove the curse from him. Then I can bind it to the herbs like I originally intended, burning it all together until it vanishes into smoke and scatters on the wind.

The owl continues to watch me from his perch in an old evergreen, and I slowly walk toward him, keeping my eyes on his the whole time.

He cocks his head to one side and spreads his wings.

Please, I beg. *Don't*.

Then he flies away.

five

I search everywhere. I run to the refuge and look in all the areas the owl likes, the old-growth trees surrounding the property and the hollows in the massive firs, but I don't see him. I walk to the aviary, a foolish hope that maybe he's finally flown back to the cage he escaped from over a week ago. The woodrat we left out for him is still there, untouched, and his cage remains empty.

He prefers to be in the trees and the hollows, and I don't blame him. We were treating him for a wing fracture when he escaped, and it's the first time he has been able to fly in weeks. But he's still healing, and it's too soon for him to be out on his own.

Mom hasn't been worried about his escape because he's been keeping to the property, and she says he'll return to the aviary when he's ready. But I can't risk him leaving the refuge.

When my initial search doesn't yield anything, I run back to the cottage where all our books of magic are kept. I push through the door and breathe in the musky air, the jars of dried herbs rattling on the old wooden table.

The books are on shelves in the very back of the room, covered in a layer of dust. We rarely use them—magic is all about intuition and reacting to what's already present. Even the spells I craft, they aren't prescriptive; they're written from feeling and instinct.

I pull the large leather Lunars book from the top shelf, a rain of dust floating down with it. I sit on the cement floor and carefully open the front cover. The pages are yellowed and worn, and I run my fingers over the long-dried ink. We may not use the books as much as our ancestors did, but seeing their writing, reading about how they used their own magic, grounds me.

I flip through the book until I find the section on birds of prey, and my heart races when the northern spotted owl is the first bird written about. Goose bumps rise along my skin as a horrible realization slides down my spine and claws at my chest. I force myself to take steady, even breaths, but the weight of it is too much.

My eyes scour the words on the page, searching for anything to contradict what I know in my gut to be true. But instead, the word stands out like the full moon on a cloudless night.

Amplifier.

The northern spotted owl is sacred to witches. And it's sacred because it's a powerful amplifier of magic.

I can't believe it took me this long to put the pieces together, but now that I have, I'd give anything to undo it. As soon as I see the word, a memory of a childhood story flashes in my mind, and nausea roils my stomach.

My mother's voice was calm as she told me the story of a

witch who lived hundreds of years ago, who used one of the sacred owls to bring death upon the home of the man who killed her husband. But she didn't understand how powerful the owl was, and the curse destroyed not only her village but all the villages surrounding hers. It stretched on for miles and miles, destroying everything in its path, and it took over one hundred years for any signs of life to return to the desolate land.

The story says that the ghost of the owl still haunts the location of the old house, circling high above, bound to the land it was originally cursed to.

I keep reading, and, sure enough, the book recounts the same tale.

I press my back against the wall and pull my knees to my chest, forcing my head between my legs. The book slips off my lap as I try to outrun the panic that's threatening my body, try to remember the breathing techniques I learned, but I can't think.

If the owl is an amplifier and the curse is unleashed, Pike isn't the only one who will be affected by it. The story goes that the curse far outreached the intended target—if this curse is unleashed, anyone in the general area could be impacted. Would they all be at risk of turning to mages? Visions of Alex by the lake run rampant in my mind, the memory of putrid smoke so strong I can smell it now. I have no idea what would happen, no idea how the curse I wrote would echo throughout the region, but it would be bad.

Unthinkably bad.

Tears burn my eyes and slip down my cheeks, and it aches each time I swallow, as if I'm forcing a rock down my throat. We don't have the kind of resources we'd need to aid an entire region impacted by an amplified curse; that kind of disaster hasn't happened in years, maybe not since the witch my mom told me about. And that was a curse on the land, not on people.

Is that what will become of my life, a story mothers tell their children at bedtime?

I press my palms into the cold stone and try to ground myself, try to slow my heart and even my breaths.

The only good thing to come from all my reading is that the curse can be unbound from the owl just as easily as it was bound to him in the first place. It just needs what the book calls a "kindred home."

I stand and gently put the book back on the shelf, then I run to the refuge. When I get to the oldest part of the forest, I slow to a walk and slip behind a tree, just in case anyone is walking the property. I've seen the owl enough to draw a perfect mental image of him, his dark eyes and curved beak, the white feathers that form half-moons around his eyes. His brown feathers and white spots. And even now, though I haven't found him, I'm sure he's close.

There is magic in him as sure as there is magic in me, and I close my eyes and search for him, seeking out his energy amid everything else. He carries a curse that I wrote—I'll be able to locate him, and when I do, I will track him.

But maybe that won't be necessary. I feel him almost instantly, close by, and I slowly turn in the direction of the pull and open my eyes. There, not four trees away, is the northern spotted owl, watching me from the hollow of an old fir tree. If he only knew the magic he held inside him, the curse that could change my whole world.

I tentatively take one step closer, then another. He watches me but doesn't move, and if I can just get close enough, I can remove the curse from him and bind it to something new. A kindred home.

I take two more steps, then pull the herbs from my pocket as the owl's gaze follows my movements.

"There you are," a voice says behind me. "How's my second best?"

My magic scatters, and the owl snaps his neck in the direction of the voice. I watch helplessly as he takes off from the tree and flies up up up, past the aviary and visitor's office, over the fence, and well into the land beyond the refuge.

Gone.

"What is wrong with you?" I yell at Pike, not caring that my voice is loud and frantic. "Now he's gone!" I shout, my hands shaking and my vision blurring.

Come on, Iris, I tell myself. *Stay in control. You're okay.*

"Whoa, whoa, whoa," Pike says, holding his hands up. "Relax. I didn't even see the owl."

"Now I'll never find him." I watch the sky for another moment before turning to Pike. "Please tell me you have something important to say. I can't bear the thought of you scaring off

the owl for literally no other reason than that's just how obnoxious you are."

"Ouch," Pike says, and even though his tone is casual, I wince
as I replay the words in my head.

"I'm sorry," I start, but Pike waves it off as if it's nothing.

"Your mom is looking for you. She wants you to meet her at
your house for something," he says, shoving a hand through his
thick hair. His glasses have slipped down the bridge of his nose,
and he pushes them up with one finger and looks at me.

I tilt my head toward the sky, hoping to see that the owl has
come back, knowing all the while he hasn't. Still, I slowly scan the
treetops, searching for him.

"It's gone," Pike says. "Did you know the northern spotted owl
was practically famous around here during the logging debates in
the nineties? Its population has been declining for years as our
old-growth forests are cut down. It's too bad you lost ours."

"I didn't lose ours," I say frantically, shaking my head and starting to pace. But he's right: the northern spotted owl is getting close
to vanishing from Washington altogether, and I went and lost the
only one we had at the refuge. I stop moving when I feel Pike's eyes
on me, when I realize he's watching me as I come undone.

"It looks that way to me," he says, his voice teetering on the
edge of mocking. I turn away so he can't see my eyes glisten or my
skin redden, and I slip my hands in my pockets to hide their shaking. If Pike weren't so thoughtless, weren't so arrogant, weren't
so casual in his cruelty toward witches, none of this would have
happened.

I know he didn't force me to cast the spell, but all I want in this moment is to be away from him. I needed relief from Pike, needed to vent my frustrations so my dislike of him could ease, and instead it's worse now than it has ever been before.

"Would it kill you to be nice for once in your life, or are you actually set on making my day worse?" He looks surprised, like he doesn't realize how upset I am, but he doesn't say anything. I shake my head. "I'm going to find my mom."

I know I should walk home, tell my mom what happened, and get her help in fixing this, but I'm terrified. The magnitude of it is unthinkable, and the thought of putting that weight on her makes me sick to my stomach. So instead, I walk to the acres of forested land where our wolves roam.

I let myself in through the metal gate, walk to my favorite tree, and lie down beneath it. It isn't long until Winter finds me and licks my face, then sits down next to me and watches the fence line. My faithful protector.

I stare up at the trees above me, trying to make my thoughts slow down so I can form some kind of plan. I once again picture the owl in my mind, and I'm able to form a connection, feel his presence even though he's miles away by now.

I could track him. Unbind the curse before it hurts anyone.

That's my only hope.

I push myself to sitting and lean into Winter, petting her fur and taking comfort in her steadiness, in the way she would follow me to the ends of the earth. Farther than my own father was willing to go.

I give her a quick hug, then stand up and walk home. I've wasted too much time already, and I need to tell Mom exactly what happened so I can begin my trek to the owl. I don't know what all the consequences would be if the curse was released, but I know with absolute certainty that I don't want to find out.

six

As I walk home, I begin working out everything I'm going to say to my mom. How I'm going to tell her about the owl and the curse and the enormity of the situation, but I stop when I reach the driveway. Sarah's car is parked out front, and I suddenly wonder why I was called home in the first place.

I rush through the door and call for my mom, but I'm instantly greeted with laughter coming from the kitchen.

"Mom? Is everything okay?" I ask.

Half-drunk glasses of champagne are sitting on the kitchen table, surrounded by massive piles of food, and I suddenly feel as if I'm interrupting something.

"Aren't you guys supposed to be working?" I ask because I can't think of anything better to say.

"Always the responsible one," Mom says, wrapping her arm around my shoulder and kissing me on top of my head.

"I'll wait outside." Sarah grabs her glass of champagne and walks out the back door.

"I want to ask you something, honey. Sit." Mom motions to the table, and I sit down, my heart racing.

"You're making me nervous," I say. "What is it?"

Mom pulls out the chair next to me and grabs my hand. "I know Sarah and I haven't been dating for very long, but we've been friends for over half my life," she begins, and I take in the scene around me once more and it clicks into place.

"Oh my God," I say, shoving back to look at my mom. "Are you engaged?"

A huge smile spreads across her face, and she nods excitedly. She holds up her hand, and a gold band that looks like ivy sits on her finger.

"Oh, Mom," I say, pulling her into me. "I'm so happy for you."

And I mean it. I mean it with every part of me. She pulls away and wipes a tear from her cheek, and I'm so overcome with happiness for her that it erases everything else just for a moment.

My mom is happy again. After everything we've been through, after everything my dad put her through, she's happy.

"You're okay with it?" Mom asks, looking at me intently.

"Okay with it?" I ask, laughing. "I'm thrilled. I love Sarah, and I love how happy she makes you."

Mom nods and pulls me into another hug, and then the back door opens and Sarah is wrapping her arms around both of us. There was a time I believed we wouldn't get through the pain of leaving our old life behind, and my chest aches, knowing that this was waiting for us on the other side.

But then the owl pops into my mind and my insides turn cold.

Mom and Sarah pull away, and Sarah holds up her matching band to show me, but I can hardly respond. I watch my mom, the way she smiles and laughs and wipes at her cheeks, and I can't do it. I can't tell her about the curse and rob her of this moment she's fought so hard for. I can't.

"Iris?" Mom asks. I look up, meeting her gaze. "Honey, are you okay?"

"I'm sorry," I say, forcing myself to smile. I will not ruin this moment for them. "I'm wonderful. I'm so, so happy for you both."

Mom leans back in her chair and takes a sip of water. "Iris, what is it?"

They look concerned, and I realize if I don't say anything, they might worry I'm not happy about their engagement. So I settle on a half-truth.

"It's just something with the refuge. I can tell you about it later," I say, grabbing both of their hands. "I want to celebrate with you."

"We've been celebrating all morning, darling," Sarah says. "Tell us what Pike Alder did this time."

"It's shockingly not about him," I say, even though deep down, it's entirely about him. "It's the owl."

"What about it?" Mom sits up in her chair, the smile slipping from her face.

"He's gone," I say. "I watched him fly out of the sanctuary. I can still feel him, but he's far away. Miles into the mountains."

"He's not ready to be back in the wild," she says.

"I know."

Mom sets her glass down and looks at me. "That owl is sacred, and with so few of them left…" She trails off, and I sigh in relief.

I was counting on her reverence for the animal to get her to agree to my plan. The northern spotted owl is a threatened species, and she couldn't bear to lose one that was in our care.

"I want to go after him," I say. "He won't get very far with that wing."

Mom is quiet for a few moments, thinking it over. "It would be good experience for you, tracking him. Do you think you could be back here in a few days?"

"If he stays relatively close, yes. I just need to figure out how to get him to come to me once I actually find him."

Mom is quiet, and I can tell she's running through something in her head. "I can give you some supplies to help with that. But I don't know…I don't like the idea of you out in the woods by yourself."

"I'll be fine," I say, trying to keep the desperation out of my voice. "He isn't too far away—I'll be gone two days, tops."

But Mom is shaking her head, and my heart drops as I feel my options slipping away. "I don't want you out there by yourself."

"It really doesn't bother me," I say.

"But it bothers me." She pauses, then a big smile spreads across her face and I know just by looking at her that I'm going to hate whatever it is she's about to say.

"If only there were an ornithologist around who could help you."

"No," I say. "Absolutely not."

Mom stands up and finishes her champagne. "It's a great idea."

"It's a horrible idea." I stand and follow her to the kitchen. "Seriously, Mom, no. What's he going to do? I'm the one who can track the owl and bring him back here. I don't need Pike."

She leans against the kitchen counter and watches me. "There's no way you can expect to carry all your gear, as well as an owl, down a mountain on your own. If he's up for it, Pike's going with you."

She walks back to the dining table and sits next to Sarah, and I helplessly follow, trying to get her to see my side of this. "He hates witches, Mom. If anything, having him with me is a liability. I can do this on my own."

"He's just kidding around, Iris. He's not out to get you, I promise."

"You don't know that," I say, panic stirring inside me.

Mom gives me a sad look and pats the chair in front of her, but I don't sit down. I pace around the room, trying not to think about how much time I'm losing to this conversation.

"Oh, honey, is that what you really think? That he's out to get you?"

"No," I say, coming to a stop. "Yes. I don't know." I sink down into the chair and look at my mom. "I just don't like him," I finally say.

"I'm sorry, honey, but I'm not comfortable with you going on your own."

I look at Sarah, my eyes pleading. "Can you come with me?"

"I wish I could, darling, but I have to be at the café."

I rub my temples, trying to think of any other solution than trekking through the woods with Pike Alder.

"If you don't want to go with Pike, then I'll have to call the council, and they can handle it. With the work they do to conserve the amplifiers in the wild, they can help," she says. "Come to think of it, I believe Cassandra was stationed here recently."

The mention of Amy's older sister makes goose bumps rise along my skin. The last time I saw her was at my trial, watching me with a neutral expression from behind the long oak table. Bile rises up my throat, and I swallow it down.

"No," I say, too quickly. "Let me do this."

If Mom gets the council involved, they'll detect the curse. I would be put on trial for cursing a boy to turn into a mage, the punishment of which is a merciless spell that would destroy my ability to perceive the magic around me.

It would vanish, as if it was never there in the first place.

Just like what happened to Amy.

My body shakes as I imagine the consequences, and I take several deep breaths, trying to stay present. I can't go through another trial. I can't lose my sense. I can't. I'd be losing the part of me that makes me *me*. I have to at least try to get the owl back.

I get up and move around the room again, running my hands through my hair.

I only have one option, then.

"Fine," I finally say. "I'll ask Pike to go with me. But don't call the council—I want to do this myself."

"Deal," Mom says, satisfied with herself. "It'll be great practice for you."

"If he'll even agree to do it."

"I can help with that," Mom says.

"What do you mean?"

"Pike's been bugging me to submit the paperwork to his university so he can work here through the summer and get credit."

"You can't be serious. The entire summer?"

Mom gives me an apologetic look. "I haven't gotten around to it yet and obviously wanted to talk to you before making a decision either way."

"That's just...so many days with him around."

Sarah laughs, a light, breezy sound that would put a smile on my face under different circumstances. She stands and starts clearing the table, but Mom watches me intently.

"I won't do it if you don't want me to. This refuge is ours, and we make all the decisions together."

"Thanks, Mom," I say. "I'll see if he'll agree to go with me first without having to offer him something."

"A last resort," she says, barely hiding the smile creeping onto her face. "Smart."

I shake my head and walk into the kitchen. Pike's a good intern, I'll give him that, but I wish Mom would take him more seriously. Instead, I get the impression she's enjoying this. If she only knew what was at stake.

I give Mom and Sarah another round of hugs and congratulations, then I set off to find Pike. Anything is worth keeping that smile on my mom's face, hearing that lightness in her voice.

Anything.

Even spending several days with Pike Alder in the woods.

seven

Pike is standing outside the office thanking the tour group, and I watch as he smiles and waves. A girl who looks to be around my age gives him a shy smile and tips her head down when he thanks her for coming, a slight blush spreading across her cheeks. She hands him a small piece of paper, then rushes to catch up with her parents.

On a normal day, I'd want to warn the poor girl, but now all I see is a future that might not happen because of this curse. Because of me.

My body aches to turn around and handle this alone, without Pike, but I think about the way Mom and Sarah looked back at the house. I'm doing this for them. Then I call his name.

Pike looks up from the piece of paper and slips it into his pocket.

"You're back," he says. "Everything okay?"

"Everything's great," I reply, too quickly. "I mean, with my mom. Everything's good."

"Okay."

I pause, kicking my boot into the mud, not able to make the words leave my throat. A strong wind picks up, blowing my curly hair in every direction, and I slide my hands over my head to tame it. Pike is watching me as if he's amused, and it makes me angry.

"Why are you being weird?" he asks, raising an eyebrow and tilting his head.

"I'm not being weird," I say, even though I'm acutely aware of how weird I'm being.

He raises his hands in the air as if in surrender, then walks back into the office.

"Wait," I say, and he turns to face me. "Do you want to go for a walk?"

"A walk? Not really."

I sigh, hoping he can hear it from where he's standing. "Humor me."

"Okay," he says, grabbing his jacket and shrugging it on. "Let's walk."

I shove my hands into my pockets, and we make our way to the trail that winds through the forest bordering the refuge. "That owl is really important to me," I finally say. "There aren't many northern spotted owls left, and he's not ready to be back in the wild with his wing. He was under our protection, and we failed him." I'm embarrassed when I realize my voice is shaking, and I swallow hard and take a steadying breath.

"*You* failed him," Pike says. "I was busy with the tour groups.

Had I been working in the aviary, he wouldn't have escaped in the first place."

"Seriously? You're going to point fingers when I'm trying to fix this?"

"I'm just setting the record straight."

"You're being an ass," I say, the words flying out before I can think better of them. Pike stops walking and raises an eyebrow at me.

"At least I'm an ass who's right."

"I'm honestly shocked that you have any friends," I say, giving him an exasperated look.

"And I'm not shocked at all that you don't have any."

His words sting, and I'm embarrassed when my gaze drops to the ground. I used to have friends; back in Nebraska, I had lots of friends. At least, I thought I did. Then Alex died and Amy went to jail, and my phone went silent and my lunch table emptied. People whose voices used to greet me in class faded to whispers behind my back, and the fact that I was a witch mattered in a way it never had before.

Mom encouraged me to make new friends when we moved here, to get involved in school activities, but we were starting the refuge, and every day I wanted to rush home and see our animals. I missed them during the day, and I knew they missed me, too. They became my best friends, and somewhere along the way, I forgot about making human ones.

"Are you going to let me get to the point or not?" I ask, keeping my voice even.

"Go ahead." He starts walking, but his words are still heavy in my chest, and I take several seconds before catching up with him.

"I want to go after the owl," I say. "Try to find him and bring him back."

"I didn't realize he was tagged," Pike says, and I suddenly feel sick. Of course Pike would think the only way to go after the owl would be if we had tagged him with a location transmitter. Which we hadn't. I'll be able to track him using magic, and when we reach the bird and Pike sees there's no transmitter on him, he'll likely have a lot of questions.

Questions I can deal with, though. An amplified curse I can't, so I lie. "Yeah, the day after he got here."

"That would make it easier," Pike says, more to himself than to me. The wind gets stronger and it starts to rain. I pull my hood up over my head, and Pike does the same. "You don't need my permission, you know."

"Obviously," I say, turning back toward the office.

"Then what are you asking?"

"I just...thought it might be easier with two people." I force the words out and keep my gaze on the forest floor.

Pike stops and stares at me. "Are you asking me to go with you?"

"Unfortunately," I say, unable to reply with something kinder.

Pike lets out a loud laugh. "You know it could take days, right? And that's if we're lucky. Where is he now?"

"Near Cedar Creek, in the Olympics."

"So you want to backpack with me through the mountains? Just the two of us?"

"*Want* definitely isn't the word I'd use."

The rain is falling hard now, but I need an answer. I put my hands on my hips and look at him, watch the raindrops as they splatter on the lenses of his glasses. He shakes his head.

"I'd love to help you, Gray, I really would, but traipsing through the woods with you on my spring break isn't my idea of a good time."

"I don't love the idea, either, but I thought it might be good experience, given your chosen field of study. Besides, you were going to spend all your days at the refuge anyway."

"Did it occur to you that I might have evening plans?"

"Not really, no," I admit. "Do you?"

Pike smiles. "*National Geographic* is airing a four-part special on birds of prey," he says excitedly.

"Those are your plans? To watch *National Geographic*?"

"Yes," he says, not a hint of embarrassment in his voice.

I sigh. "Come on, Pike, help me out."

"Why?"

"Because you claim to care about the animals here."

"I do care about the animals here. I care so much, in fact, that not one of mine has managed to escape," he says, and I'm so fed up that I almost walk away. Then Pike's mouth quirks to one side. "I'll do it."

I pause. "You will?"

"If Isobel files the paperwork for a summer internship with my university." He smiles triumphantly, and I groan. So much for using it as a last resort.

"We already talked about it. She'll do it," I say.

"Then I believe you have yourself a deal." He holds out his hand to shake on it. I don't take it, but that doesn't seem to faze him. "I still haven't landed on a project for my final yet, and I'll be able to use this trip. My professor will love it."

"Well, as long as your professor loves it," I say.

Pike rolls his eyes. "You know, Iris, as long as we're going to be stuck together, I could help you work on your people skills. I wouldn't mind."

"Has it ever occurred to you that my people skills are fine and it's you that's the problem?"

"No," he says. "Not once."

I sigh loudly and shake my head. "I'm already regretting asking you."

"I'm already regretting saying yes."

Pike's eyes catch on mine, and something passes in them that I can't read. He almost looks sad. Then it's gone. "Just so you know," he says, leaning in closer, "I would have gone for the owl. But getting the chance to annoy you all summer is a definite bonus."

I want to be frustrated, to turn around and leave him out here, but instead I'm relieved, and I'm horrified when my eyes start stinging. I blink several times and look away.

"Thank you," I say. "For coming."

Maybe this will be one of those wild stories I tell when I'm older, how I almost single-handedly destroyed the Pacific Northwest because of a boy who hurt my feelings. Maybe I'll even laugh about it.

What's more likely is that I'll carry this mistake in my chest for the rest of my life, a physical ache that reminds me of how fleeting happiness is, that it can be taken away with a single choice. And that's assuming I can fix this, undo the mess I made.

"You know we might not get him, right?" Pike says, interrupting my thoughts. "Even if we know where he is, he'll be difficult to spot in the trees, and he'll be most active at night. It's not like we can just ask him to fly down and step into a cage."

"I know that," I say, walking back toward the office.

"You just look so relieved, and I want to make sure you know that we might not be able to bring him back here."

"I said I know." The words come out fast and tense, and I push my hand to my chest, trying to ease the tightness that's beginning to form there. Even if Pike is right and we can't bring him back, I can try to unbind the curse in the woods if I can get close enough to him. That would entail using magic in front of Pike, though, so it's an absolute last resort.

Pike doesn't say anything else, and we walk back into the office and take off our coats and boots in silence. He turns toward the back room when I grab his arm. He looks down at where my fingers are wrapped around his forearm, then slowly brings his eyes to mine.

"Look, I don't expect you to understand, but I need to have hope. I know it's unlikely, I know we have a lot working against us and that he's a wild animal with a mind of his own. I know all that. But I need to have hope." I pause before speaking again. "Please let me."

"Okay," he says, and it's the first time I've ever heard him sound gentle. It doesn't quite fit him, the contrast so stark against his arrogance and sarcasm.

I nod and let go of his arm, but he doesn't move right away. He keeps his eyes on mine for a moment longer than expected, then he walks into the back room. I slowly let my breath out and bring my fingertips to my temples, trying to rub my headache away.

I've already shown him too much, made him aware of how much this matters to me. And now it's time to get back to normal, to try as best I can to hide my fear. Because the way I cope with it, the way I anchor myself to this world is through magic, and if I'm going to be alone with Pike, I have to ensure that every second of every day is spent with that switch turned off.

He can never see it, not even for a moment, not even one so fleeting that he questions if he saw anything at all. Because once someone suspects, they never really forget. That's the thing about magic: people want to see it and feel it almost as much as they want to dismiss it entirely.

It's an echo of something just out of reach, a whisper that says there's more to this life than what meets the eye.

Everything about this trip will pull at the edges of Pike's mind, hinting at magic. He'll be in a forest that's been growing wild for hundreds of years, trees so giant and old they're covered in it. He'll be following a bird bound by a curse that was written for him. And he'll be doing it all alongside a witch who will be tracking the bird on instinct.

He will be surrounded by magic in a way he's never been before, and I will have to protect myself every single second, keep my guard up as high as it will go, hiding my secret as if my entire life depends on it. Because it does.

"Hey," Pike says, emerging from the back room. He pulls on his coat and looks at me. "You look terrified."

"Oh," I say, waving a hand through the air as if it's nothing. "I was just thinking about the sheer terror of spending several days in the woods with you." I'm thankful when my voice is even again, easy and light.

Pike smirks and grabs his coat. "There's nothing more terrifying than backpacking with an experienced hiker who is always prepared and has a vast array of bird knowledge."

"I was factoring your personality into the equation as well," I point out.

He laughs at that, a genuine laugh that surprises me. "You're no picnic yourself," he says.

"Yeah, but the difference is I don't think I am."

He shakes his head, but he's still smiling. "I'm going home to pack, and you should do the same. Let's plan for two nights to start and hope it doesn't take any longer than that. Meet me back here in two hours."

We haven't even left yet and he's already telling me what to do. Two nights sounds unbearable, but I know it's small compared to the crisis we're trying to avert. I know it will be worth it if we can get the owl back here safely.

"Two hours," I say, heading for the door. "Don't be late."

e i g h t

Mom and Sarah help me get ready. Mom fills my backpack with the necessities, and Sarah makes sure I have enough homemade granola to last me a week. Neither of them seems worried, and if anything, they almost seem excited.

What I really want is to grab my mother's hands and tell her what an awful situation this is, how badly I messed things up. I want to tell her this isn't a game, that it isn't funny. That I'm scared Pike will somehow see through me, and I'll give our secret away.

But what I want more than anything is to not be terrified of showing who I am, to not care if Pike finds out in the first place. There would be so much freedom in not caring, so much comfort. Amy used to tell me that I care too much about people who care too little. I can only imagine what she'd have to say about Pike.

Once I double-check that I have everything I need, I secure my tent to the bottom of my pack and check the time. I have twenty more minutes until I meet up with Pike.

"All set?" Mom asks.

"I think so," I say, grabbing a fleece from my closet and throwing it on over my T-shirt. "Are you sure you're going to be okay managing the refuge for the next few days?"

"I'll be fine. Sarah's going to help me in the afternoons, and we don't have another tour scheduled until the weekend."

Mom is sitting on my bed, and I sit down next to her. "I'll be as quick as I can."

"We'll be fine," she says again. "Just be careful and do your best with the owl."

"I will," I promise.

We're quiet for a few moments, then Mom shifts and pulls out something from her pocket, keeping her hand around the object so I can't see what it is. Then she looks at me apologetically, and an embarrassed smile tugs at her mouth. "I know you hate him, but be safe," she finally says.

I look down at her closed hand and back to her face in horror.

"That better not be what I think it is," I say, mortified, sure my skin has turned a bright shade of red.

"Just in case," she says defensively.

I stand up and grab my backpack from the floor, sliding it onto my shoulders. "I can guarantee you that won't be necessary."

Mom stands too and adjusts my straps, then moves behind me and opens one of my pockets. "Just take it. You won't even notice it's there," she says, tucking it inside. Then she laughs. "Ha! Isn't that one of their marketing slogans?"

At this point, I might actually die before getting a chance

to find the owl. "Okay, great, thanks so much," I say, leaving my room and hurrying down the stairs.

Sarah is waiting for me at the bottom, and she almost laughs when she sees me. "What happened to you? Your face is the shade of my favorite marinara."

"Mom happened."

"Ah," she says. "Here, take this. It'll have you feeling better in no time." She hands me a blackberry scone that's still warm from the oven, then gives me a hug.

"Those smell amazing," Mom says, reaching the bottom of the stairs and smoothing a hand over my hair.

"I saved you one."

"Make it two?" Mom asks, then pulls me into a hug. "I'll miss you, baby girl."

"I'll miss you, too. I'll check in when I can, but I'm not sure how reliable cell reception will be. I'll call you on Wednesday if I can't before then."

"Sounds good," Mom says, handing me my jacket. "You've always been more at home in the trees than you ever were in the confines of a house. If anyone can bring back our owl, it's you."

"Thanks, Mom."

"No magic and no talk of witches. That's all you have to remember."

"I know," I say, shifting the pack on my shoulders. "Anything else?"

"Yeah," Mom says, taking my hand in hers. She gives it a quick squeeze and smiles. "Have a little fun."

I know she means it innocently enough, but after our conversation upstairs, I can't help the incredulous look I give her. She seems to put the two together, and her expression morphs into one of alarm. "I didn't mean it like that!"

"Like what?" Sarah asks.

"I'm going now." I walk out the door before Mom has a chance to answer.

It's starting to rain again. I pull my hood over my head and make sure my rain protector is covering my whole pack. I turn around to see if Mom or Sarah have come outside, but the yard is empty. A rabbit dashes out from the shrubs and into the woods, and I quickly slip into the cottage where all our herbs are kept.

The bundle of wormwood and safflower that was meant for Pike's curse is waiting for me untouched, and I take it along with some sticks for kindling. I pull some calamus root from a jar to help strengthen the binding spell, then I put it all safely in my pack.

I don't anticipate needing it, since my goal is to bring the owl back to the refuge and deal with the curse here. But I'm not comfortable unless I have a backup plan, and I'll be ready to unbind the curse in the mountains if that's what it comes to.

I turn off the light and shut the door to the cottage, then take the trail to the refuge. The fenced woods where the wolves spend most of their time comes into view, and I let myself in and call for

Winter. Seconds later, she's bounding toward me, circling my legs when she reaches me.

"I'm going away for a few days," I tell her, running my fingers through her fur. "Take care of Mom while I'm gone, and I'll try to take care of everything else."

I'm giving myself three days to try to handle this on my own, and if I can't, I'll get help. The Witches' Council stations Solars in parks wherever there are amplifiers to maintain and preserve their habitats, and my greatest hope is that I find the owl before they do. But if the worst happens and the owl is injured, at least there will be someone within a few hours who can offer assistance.

Winter pushes her head into the outside of my thigh, and I give her several more pets before letting myself out through the gate. She runs to the fence and shoves her snout through it, watching me as I walk away, and the image of her makes my heart ache.

How easily this could all be taken away.

I don't know how I feel about Cassandra being stationed nearby, knowing she might get involved if I can't handle this on my own. She was on the council for Amy's trial, and when the verdict was read, she insisted she be the one to rid Amy of her ability to perceive magic.

Maybe she couldn't bear what she'd done and asked to be reassigned. Or maybe it was simply procedural. Either way, something about her presence in the Olympics makes this feel more dire, more urgent, as if she could show up at any moment and take away my magic, too.

I know it's selfish, worrying so much about my magic when

there are other things at stake. But losing the thing I love more than anything else in the world would be devastating.

I take a deep breath and push the thoughts aside for now. That's an absolute worst-case scenario, and I'm not there yet. Not even close.

Pike and I arrive at the office at the same time, and I can't help it when a laugh tumbles out of my mouth. He's not particularly tall, he's thin, and his backpack looks as if a family of five could live comfortably inside it.

"Your backpack is bigger than you are. How are you even standing upright?" I ask, shaking my head at how ridiculous he looks.

"It's called being prepared, Gray."

Before I can stop him, Pike snatches my pack from my shoulders, pulls off the rain protector, and opens it up, inspecting the contents inside. I have no idea where Mom stashed the condom, and I desperately claw at my pack in his hands.

"If we run into trouble, what will you save us with? Your pound of KIND bars?" he asks, holding the pack above his head as I grab for it.

I shove him aside and pull it from his grasp, closing the top and securing it over my shoulders once more. "Staying nourished is a critical part of survival," I say, thanking everything that is good that Pike didn't see the condom. "And KIND bars last a long time."

"If we end up in a situation where we're relying on your KIND bars for our sustained nutritional needs, things have gone very wrong."

"Look, you're prepared in your ways, and I'm prepared in mine. And I never said I'd share them with you."

"Already arguing and you haven't even left yet? You guys are off to a great start," Mom says from the door of the office.

"Hey, Isobel," Pike says, shoving a hand through his hair. "Just sticking with what we know."

"Why don't you branch out a little? You never know, it might be fun."

Fun. There's that word again.

I sigh and give my mom a hug. "Thanks for seeing us off."

"Of course. Good luck out there."

Pike leaves the office first, and I give my mom an exasperated look and roll my eyes. He really is so obnoxious. She laughs, and I wave before following Pike to his car.

He throws open the hatch of the old Subaru, and it's filled with more gear. Coolers and expanding chairs, hiking poles and gallon jugs of water.

"How long did you say you were packing for again?" I ask, sliding my backpack into the trunk.

"Two nights," Pike says, missing the sarcasm in my voice. He watches me pile my things into his car and sighs. "You're doing it wrong."

He pulls out my pack from the trunk, then rearranges things before putting it back in. "I didn't realize there was a wrong way to load a car," I say.

"There's a wrong way to do most things."

He spends a few more minutes arranging everything in the

trunk, then we get into the car and Pike starts the engine. I watch out the window as we make our way down the gravel road, putting my fingers to the glass when we pass the woods where Winter is, her snout still through the fence, watching the car as we drive away.

If this entire thing fails and the Witches' Council comes after me, if they turn off my ability to perceive magic, will Winter still feel our connection? Will she still know me at the deepest level, even if my magic is gone?

The thought is too much to bear. Pike turns on some music, and I almost ask him to turn it off, sure that whatever he's chosen will be as awful as he is, but it isn't awful at all. It's nice.

"What is this?" I ask, the first words I've spoken since we left the refuge.

"The Album Leaf," he says, looking at me from the corner of his eye. "Do you like it?" He asks it as if it's a test and if I say the wrong thing he'll kick me out of his car.

I don't answer right away, and instead, I listen. It's gentle and calming, the way a rushing river might sound if it were music. It fills the car with slow notes, taking its time, and for just a moment, it transports me to a place where there is no curse and no Witches' Council and no fear. It makes me feel as if I'm safe.

"I love it," I say, and the hint of a smile pulls at Pike's mouth. He doesn't respond, but he reaches out and turns up the volume. I rest my head against the cold glass window and close my eyes, picturing the owl and the way it will feel when we bring him home.

I replay the events of the morning over and over in my mind, trying to figure out where I went wrong, how something that was supposed to make things better made them so much worse. And the thing that makes goose bumps rise along my arms is the way the owl seemed to do it with intention, swooping down from the trees at the exact right second to steal the curse.

Like he knew what I was doing.

The owl has been inaccessible to me. I can track the curse inside him, know when he's watching me, but I can't get to his center, can't feel what he wants or needs the way I can with Winter and most of the other animals at the refuge. He's a mystery to me, and yet I have this gnawing suspicion that I'm totally exposed to him.

"Would you check and see if the owl is still in the same place?" Pike asks, interrupting my thoughts.

"Why?" I ask, too quickly, and instantly reprimand myself. If I don't want Pike to pick up on anything suspicious, I have to stop acting this way. "I'm just trying to save my battery," I add, hoping the explanation makes sense.

He raises an eyebrow and gives me a quick glance before looking back at the road. "Our exit is coming up, and I want to make sure we're still headed to the right place," he says. "And I brought power banks for charging."

Of course he did. "Because you're very prepared."

"Exactly."

I pull out my phone and go to the tracking app, silently thanking the gods that I have the app at all. We've tagged animals in the past and had some come to us with one already in place, and I open the app and pretend to search for the northern spotted owl.

As I'm doing that, I find my connection to the bird and feel the particles of magic align between us, a steady stream that extends from the curse in his chest all the way back to me. I'm amazed by how strong it is, by the power of the magic within him. Many animals live in old-growth forests, but the spotted owl is the only true amplifier.

It's an extraordinary creature, one I'm both in awe of and terrified of.

"He's still there," I say.

"Good. Hopefully he found an old nest or hollow he likes. I was looking at the maps earlier, and there's a logging road that winds up in that direction. We can probably keep the car fairly close to where we camp, depending on the owl's exact location."

"Sounds good to me," I say.

The song hits its final note, and the car fills with silence. Before I can ask to hear it again, Pike reaches out, presses Play, and the album starts over.

nine

We pull off the main road and turn onto a narrow dirt path wide enough for a single car. The road is covered in potholes, and we bounce around as we make our way farther up the mountain. The gear in the back rattles, and I grip the handle on the door to steady myself.

"Almost there," Pike says.

We drive for a few more minutes, then come to a small gravel parking strip. We are the only people here.

It's been raining the whole drive but miraculously stops once we park. Pike takes out a map that shows all the trails in the area, and he studies it, looking for the best way up. He pushes his glasses up his nose and taps a pencil on the dashboard while I start unloading the gear from the back.

It's overcast, thick gray clouds covering us, and it won't be long before the rain starts again. Spring is when the weather in the Pacific Northwest gets confused, bouncing between hail and sun and rain all in the same day. Sometimes all in the same hour.

There's something playful about it, as if the weather is enjoying every facet of its personality, appreciating all the ways in which it covers the earth.

I pull my backpack from the trunk and slip into it, securing the straps around my chest and waist. Pike seems to have found whatever he was looking for on the map, and he rolls it back up before grabbing his pack as well. He shrugs into it, and I have to try not to laugh when he stumbles back a step.

He adjusts the straps, then pulls a small cooler from the car.

"What's in the cooler?" I ask, surprised that he wants to carry it all the way up with us.

"Food," he says, grabbing a second container from the back before slamming the hatch closed. "I mean, it's nothing compared to your stash of KIND bars, but it will have to do."

"Okay, I get it, you don't like KIND bars. If we're stranded and they're our only option for survival, I promise I won't make you eat one."

"That's all I ask," he says.

He hands me the second container, which looks like a pet carrier on further inspection, then locks his car and stuffs his keys into his pocket. "That one has food for the owl."

He starts toward the trail, and I follow close behind. It's late afternoon, but with all the cloud cover, it's dark and cold. We're silent for a while, and I listen to the sounds of our breaths as we climb higher and they come faster. It's peaceful, though, and something about the protection of the trees makes the task at hand feel less daunting.

Maybe we'll find the owl and bring him back.

Maybe my curse won't be unleashed on the entire region.

Maybe Mom will be able to enjoy her happiness, to get so used to it that she forgets there was ever a time she was unhappy.

I take cautious, patient steps, not wanting to slip on the roots and rocks that are slick with rain. Drops of water fall from tree branches and land in my hair, and wet ferns catch my ankles, making my socks damp.

But I don't mind the rain. I never have.

"Can I ask you something?" Pike says after not speaking for most of the hike. He doesn't turn around or slow his steps.

"Sure," I say.

"Why don't you like me?" The question catches me off guard, and I hesitate before answering. We're only a couple hours into this trip and he's already asking hard questions.

We walk in silence for a few more steps while I figure out what to say. I decide to go with honesty. Having to hide so much of myself makes me ache to be honest with the rest of my life. "Because you're arrogant. You think your way is the best way and anyone else who does it differently is wrong. You like to compete just for competition's sake. And while you spend hours studying birds, you often fail to recognize the sheer wonder of their existence. You watch them with facts bouncing around in your head instead of awe. It often feels like you think you have something to teach them instead of the other way around. I think maybe that's the biggest reason: you act as if you have nothing left to learn."

Pike doesn't say anything for several seconds, and I start to think he won't respond at all. But then he does. "That's a long list," he says. He doesn't sound hurt or upset. More indifferent, as if I was talking about someone other than him.

"Is it an unfair one?"

He stops at that, slowly turns and looks at me. Sweat is glistening along his forehead and his glasses have slipped down the bridge of his nose. His eyes scan my face as if he's searching for something. "No," he finally says.

When his eyes land on mine, I refuse to look away. I owe him that after what I said, and we watch each other for several breaths. His facial expression reveals nothing, and after another moment, he turns and starts walking. We're quiet the rest of the way up, and I follow when Pike cuts off the trail toward a clearing. It's obviously meant for backpackers, with a pile of ash surrounded by rocks in the center of the site and level ground where we can set up our tents.

The river isn't far, rushing in the distance, close enough for me to hear. Everything is wet, the earth and the trees and the rocks, and even though it isn't raining yet, I can feel the water in the air. Pike takes off his pack and unclips his tent from the bottom, and I close my eyes and search for the owl. My heart beats faster and hope blooms in my chest when I realize how close he is, probably a twenty-minute walk deeper into the forest.

I instinctively follow the trail of magic, stepping out of the clearing and into the dense woods.

"Where are you going?" Pike asks.

"To look for the owl."

"It's almost dark," he says, unrolling his tent. "We need to set up camp."

"But he's close," I say.

"It doesn't matter how close he is. There's no way we can get that owl down the mountain in the dark, and we need a place to sleep. Owls are creatures of habit—if he found a place he likes, that's where he'll stay."

I stand at the edge of the clearing, every part of my body wanting to race toward the owl. Pike is right, though. The responsible thing to do is get set up and make sure we're ready for the owl when the time comes.

I walk back into the clearing and slip out of my pack, taking a quick sip of water before I get started. I set up my tent a few feet from Pike's, and dozens of memories run through my mind as the smell of nylon fills the air. My dad used to love camping, and it was something we did every summer for as long as I can remember.

I'm not sure if I even liked camping at first or if it was the way being in nature seemed to turn back the clock on my dad. The way it made his eyes brighten and the tension in his shoulders loosen. He taught me how to fish and cast a line, how to filter water and start a fire. He taught me how satisfying it could be to use my hands instead of magic.

Now I wonder if he taught me that because he resented magic. That's one of the worst casualties of being hurt by someone who was never supposed to hurt you: you start to question all the beautiful things that led up to the ugliness, start to wonder if some of the moments you thought were perfect were actually painted with a dirty brush.

The wind picks up, blowing the scent of nylon far away, clearing my head of the memories. By the time my tent is set up, Pike has already started a fire.

There's a large lighter by the circle of rocks, and I raise an eyebrow. "That's cheating," I say.

"That's being efficient," he counters.

He grabs a tarp from his pack and spreads it out over the ground, then he motions for me to sit down. He opens the cooler and starts on dinner, and I'm amazed at how prepared he is. I will never tell him that I was ready to spend the next several days eating only Sarah's granola and KIND bars.

"Can I ask you something?"

Pike looks up from what he's doing, his eyes meeting mine from over his glasses. He nods.

"Why don't you like me?"

His hands slow over the sandwiches he's preparing, and when he speaks, he keeps his eyes on the food. "Because you act as if the whole world is your enemy. You're slow to trust and quick to spurn. You don't give anyone the benefit of the doubt, and you're so preoccupied with what might go wrong in the future that you never stop to enjoy what's happening in the present." He grabs a bag of chips and carefully places several on top of each sandwich.

The words have a weird effect on me, the opposite of what

I would have thought. Instead of feeling insulted or upset, I feel exposed. It's uncomfortable and my skin prickles, every part of me wanting to turn in on itself and hide.

If he can see those things so clearly, what else can he see?

"That's a long list," I finally say.

"Is it an unfair one?" He looks up at me then, holding my gaze for several seconds. The firelight dances off his glasses, and a wave of hair falls in his face.

"No."

He nods and gets back to work on our dinner. I need to clear the air of his words, so I ask the only thing I can think of while watching him prepare our food. "Are you putting chips in our sandwiches?"

"I am," he says, pushing the top piece of bread over the layer of chips. "Please don't tell me you've never had chips in your sandwich before."

I watch him, and I must look unconvinced because he hands me the sandwich and says, "This is about to change your life."

"Doubtful," I say.

"Just try it."

I take a bite while Pike watches, and I'm delighted by what a difference they make. "Okay, that's actually pretty good."

Pike looks pleased with himself, and he settles onto the tarp next to me. "I'm glad you like it."

"Most people don't recognize the near-perfection of a cold cheese sandwich," I say.

"I think this is the first time I've had one. I've never seen you eat meat, so I tried to come up with something that was vegetarian and easy. And chips work on everything." He takes a bite and leans back, so casual, and for a moment I can't respond.

Pike noticed that I'm a vegetarian, and not only did he notice, but he brought me food to accommodate it. This new piece of him doesn't fit with all the other pieces I have, and I study him in the fading twilight.

"Thank you," I say. His eyes meet mine, and I blink, bringing my focus back to the food in front of me.

The fire crackles as we eat, and the wind is blowing in the perfect direction, sending the smoke away from us. I look up into the trees and check on my connection to the owl, and sure enough, he's in the same place.

I breathe out in relief and eat my dinner as quickly as possible. Once I'm finished, I stand and clean up, then stop in front of Pike. "Okay, time to go," I say.

He looks up at me from where he's sitting but doesn't make any move to stand. "We're not looking for the owl tonight."

"Yes, we are," I say.

"Iris, he's going to start hunting soon. It will be dark by the time we even get to him. There's no way we'll find him, let alone capture him. We have to wait until morning."

"I'm sick of waiting," I say. "Why did we come up here today if we were just going to waste it?"

"To get prepared," Pike says. "You can't just go up to the owl and ask him politely to join us for dinner. It doesn't work that way."

"Oh, because you're so knowledgeable about tracking owls through the forest?"

"It's just common sense," he says, exasperated. "He'll hunt tonight. He'll be calm tomorrow. We'll go after him as soon as we get up. There's nothing we can do when it's this dark, so just relax a little."

"God, I'm so sick of people telling me to relax all the time." I say the words under my breath, more to myself than Pike, but he responds anyway.

"Maybe you should listen."

"It's that easy, huh? Just decide to relax." I look away. "You don't get it." I'm too tired to argue, too tired to get into a sparring match where the person with the quickest wit wins. Pike is all sarcasm all the time, but I just want to think before I speak and say what I mean. I don't want to have to be clever when I feel anything but.

"Am I supposed to?" he asks.

"Are you supposed to what?"

"'Get it.' Because I have the distinct impression that you're not interested in me getting you." The way he says it hints at something deeper, but I can't pinpoint what it is.

"I don't make a habit of explaining myself to people who seem set on misunderstanding me."

He doesn't respond to that, and after watching me for another breath, he shifts his attention to the fire.

"I won't go tonight," I finally say. The owl is safe and seems happy where he is. We'll have a better shot of getting him in the morning.

"That's a good choice." I catch the satisfaction in Pike's tone, but I don't say anything. "Why don't you let me make you a s'more instead?"

"You brought ingredients for s'mores?"

"Obviously."

I sit down on the tarp and watch as he sticks a marshmallow on the end of a stick and roasts it over the fire. Tendrils of gray smoke blow into the trees and the dusty blue of twilight gives way to the darkness. I lean back on my hands and try to appreciate the majesty of this place, even though I'm here with a boy I tried to curse.

Pike concentrates on the marshmallow in the fire, and for a single moment, I feel guilty for what I did, guilty that Pike has no idea what's at stake for him on this trip. But then I replay so many of the conversations we've had and I feel justified in it.

Of course, the owl stealing the curse wasn't part of the plan, but I know why I wrote that curse in the first place. I wanted to give him to the earth, and I *still* want that.

Pike pulls the marshmallow out of the fire, and a tiny flame blazes from it. He blows it out, then sticks it between two graham crackers with some chocolate in the center.

"Dessert," he says, handing it to me.

I take it from him and watch as he makes his own, and I can't figure out why he's doing this. Why he brought me food, why he intersperses his arrogance and patronizing comments with moments of kindness. It would be so much easier if he was awful all the time. But as it is, my stomach drops and a sick feeling rises in my throat when I think about him finding out what we're really doing here. I try to stay calm, stay present in the moment I'm in, but it's so hard.

That's what people like Pike don't understand. I don't enjoy what's happening in the present because I *can't*. It feels impossible to enjoy these small moments when I know all the possibilities that await me on the horizon, and to be disliked for it feels particularly cruel. Suddenly, I don't want to be sitting next to him anymore.

"I think I'm going to go to bed," I say, standing.

Pike looks up at me. "You don't want another s'more?" The question catches me off guard, as if he's disappointed that I'm leaving. He says it so simply, and it does something weird to my stomach, this genuineness that's so rarely there. I almost sit back down, but I stop myself. The last thing I need is to start ascribing meaning to things that have none.

"No, thanks." I walk to my tent without another word, and I feel his eyes following me. An ache has lodged in my throat, making it difficult to swallow.

I turn on a flashlight and change into my sweats, then I slide into my sleeping bag and pull it all the way up to my chin. I can hear Pike in the campsite, cleaning up and getting rid of any traces of food or garbage. Then he douses the fire, zips up his tent, and the world goes still.

I keep my eyes open and stare at the ceiling of my tent, even though it's so dark I can barely see anything. I wonder if Pike has fallen asleep or if he's staring at the ceiling of his tent, too.

Tree branches whisper in the wind and a light rain starts, tapping on the nylon fabric. It sounds nice, calming, and I burrow into my sleeping bag.

Just as my eyelids get heavy, I hear four loud hoots in the distance.

t e n

I wake to the sounds of scratching outside. I blink several times and let my eyes adjust to the light, then sit up and listen. A shadow crosses the front of my tent, and a low, guttural noise follows. I quietly slip out of my sleeping bag and put on my shoes, then I unzip my door and look outside.

Pike is quiet. He's still sleeping, with the front of his tent fully zipped. I scan the campsite, and a large female cougar is pacing by the firepit. I step out and slowly stand to my full height. The early morning air is cold, and I shiver in place.

The animal snaps her head toward me. Her ears are lying back, and she snarls loudly, agitated.

"Hi," I whisper, looking directly at her. "I'm not going to hurt you."

She watches me, and I carefully locate the magic inside her, assembling it in a way I can connect to. The particles snap into place and form a strong invisible string from the cougar to me. She looks surprised and snarls again, but I'm not afraid. She has likely never encountered a witch before, never felt the way magic can come alive inside her and all around her.

Even the fiercest creatures know to fear vulnerability.

I pull on her magic and let it search me from the inside out, let it see every part so that she knows she's safe. She keeps her eyes on me, but her ears relax a little. Slowly, her stance becomes less aggressive.

"That's it," I say. "Time to go."

I can't force her, but I put the instinct to leave in my magic as it wraps around the animal. Still, it's her choice. The cougar watches me for another moment, then gives in. She turns and begins to walk away when the zipper on Pike's tent breaks the silence.

"Pike," I say, keeping my eyes on the cougar, "stay in your tent."

But he doesn't listen and trips on the lip of his tent on the way out, falling face-first into the dirt. This would normally be the high point of my day, but there's a cougar in the area and Pike just made himself look like prey.

"You really can't listen, can you?" I say, my voice tense and annoyed.

Pike scrambles for his glasses and puts them back on, and I see the exact moment he notices the cougar. His eyes go wide, and he sticks his hand out toward me, as if to stop me from going anywhere.

"Iris, don't move! There's a cougar."

"I know that," I hiss. "That's why I told you to stay in your tent."

The cougar snarls and stalks toward Pike.

"Okay, don't move. Make loud noises. Don't look it in the eye.

Shit, my bear spray's in the tent." Pike rattles off facts as if they're his salvation, but he's still frozen in place.

"For the love of God, stand up! She thinks you're prey!"

But it's too late. The cougar lunges, and Pike covers his head with his arms. Frantic, I find the string of magic once more and pull, bringing the cougar's attention back to me.

"Stop!" I yell.

She's surprised and on edge, confused by the magic coursing through her. But she veers and comes to a stop, just barely missing Pike. She stays frozen where she is, and I try to calm her down as much as possible. Slowly, the cougar adjusts to the connection we have and relaxes again. Pike manages to get to his hands and knees, the cougar not two inches from his face.

Pike looks from the animal to me and back again.

"Stand. Up," I say.

Pike does as he's told, and I swallow hard and straighten my stance. I direct the cougar's magic back to my own, tell her over and over again that we aren't prey.

"Go," I say to her, quietly enough so Pike doesn't hear.

She snaps her head back to Pike one final time and snarls. Then she looks at me, turns around, and runs away.

I let out a huge exhale and run my hands through my hair. Sweat is beaded all along my hairline and down my neck, and I pace around the campsite, trying to expel the nerves building in my system.

"What the hell was that?" Pike asks, tense and bewildered.

"A cougar."

"You know that's not what I'm asking," he says, taking off his glasses and wiping the lenses with a cloth he pulls from his pocket. That's when I notice that Pike is in pajamas, matching navy pinstripe pajamas with a collar, buttons, and pocket that he seemingly keeps a cleaning cloth in. I don't think I've ever seen anyone in a legitimate matching pajama set, and I force myself to swallow the laugh that's building in my chest.

"Nice pajamas," I say, trying to diffuse the tension he's carrying. But the longer I watch him, the better he looks, and I force my eyes away, embarrassed.

They're nice on him.

"Be serious. That cougar was ready to attack me, and it stopped, as if by your command."

"You mean serious like those pajamas?"

He doesn't say anything, though, and I realize how bothered he is. How he's replaying what just happened and can't get it all to add up.

"They don't like loud noises," I finally say, keeping my voice as calm as possible. "Yelling was the only thing I could think of, other than throwing a rock."

There was no rock, but I need Pike to believe this was nothing. To believe we got lucky.

"I didn't see you throw anything," Pike says.

"You were a little preoccupied."

"I would have noticed if you'd thrown a rock," he insists. I see him working through it in his mind, over and over, but it never quite makes sense. He frowns.

"You were facedown in the dirt when I did it," I say, keeping my voice light. "Cut yourself a little slack."

He doesn't reply, and a knot forms in my stomach, seeing how disoriented he is. I want to tell him he's right, that he can trust what he saw, but I don't dare. "You know, a 'thank you for saving my life' might be nice," I say.

He raises an eyebrow at me. "I could have held my own."

"You tripped getting out of your tent, Pike. You were starting at a pretty significant disadvantage."

The faintest shade of pink colors his cheeks, and if it were anyone else, I would find it adorable.

"For the record, that's never happened before."

"Well, I'm glad I got to see it."

He laughs and shakes his head, then runs a hand through his hair. He starts to relax, and as he does, my heart begins to slow. Maybe he doesn't suspect anything. Maybe whatever questions he had have already left his mind and I didn't give anything away.

"At least let me redeem myself by making breakfast?"

I don't want to have breakfast. I want to get on the trail and find the owl, capture it, and bring it back to the refuge. But Pike just face-planted in front of me before almost being attacked by a cougar, so I feel like I owe it to him.

"Sure, breakfast would be great."

He looks relieved, and he heads back to his tent and grabs the cooler. I watch him, embarrassment pushing his shoulders in and tipping his head down slightly. The blush is receding from his cheeks, but he looks vulnerable in a way I've never seen him.

"What?" he asks, and I realize I've been staring.

I clear my throat and quickly look away. "Nothing. I'm going to take a quick walk while you're making breakfast." I head into the trees without waiting for a reply, trying to ignore the way my eyes wanted to stay on him, trying to ignore the way embarrassment turned him into a softer version of himself.

I start to feel sick, a wave of nausea rolling through me as I walk. We haven't even been here for twenty-four hours, and I've already had to use magic in front of him.

I tell myself that his embarrassment will overshadow anything else, that he won't be able to remember his questions through the fog of his bruised ego. And even if that isn't true, he didn't see anything because there wasn't anything to see.

I inhale and let the crisp morning air fill my lungs. This was just a bump along the way, and it will be smooth from here on out. It has to be.

Pike calls my name, and I give myself one more long breath before meeting him back at the campsite. He presents me with a plate of biscuits and gravy, and now that it's in front of me, I realize how hungry I am.

I sit down on the tarp, and he gives me a fork, his hands dirty and scratched from his fall. I set my breakfast aside and scoot closer to him.

"Are you hurt?" I ask.

He follows my eyes and turns his hands over, so they're palm up. The way he's showing me instead of hiding eases something in my chest.

"My pride hurts more than anything else," he says.

"I suspect that will take some time to heal. But at least let me help with your hands."

"They're fine," he says, but I'm already up, searching in my pack for the first aid kit. Once I find it, I grab my water bottle and a clean T-shirt.

I bring it all back to the tarp and sit down in front of him with my legs crossed. Without saying anything, he holds out his hands to me. I pour some water over both of his palms to clean off the dirt, pat them dry with the shirt, then tear open an antiseptic wipe.

"This is going to sting," I say. I take his hand in mine and go over the cuts with the towelette. He takes a sharp breath, and I lift his hand close to my mouth, gently blowing on his palm to ease the pain. I feel him watching me, but I don't meet his eyes. Then we switch hands and do it again.

His skin is warm and rough, and when I finish cleaning his cuts, he doesn't move right away. He looks at me with an odd expression, almost as if he's studying me, and for some reason, I find it hard to breathe. I sit as still as possible, even when the wind blows my hair in front of my face and my napkin jumps across the tarp. Then he seems to realize that his hand is still in mine because he slowly pulls it away and clears his throat.

"Thanks," he says.

I blink a few times, bringing myself back to the present, erasing whatever it was that passed between us. Nothing. It was nothing. "No problem."

I put the first aid kit away in my tent, and after giving myself a few minutes to regain my composure, I rejoin Pike on the tarp. We eat our breakfast in relative silence, listening to the sounds of the morning birds and the rushing river as it winds beneath the trees. It's peaceful and calm, and I wish I could enjoy it more, wish I could breathe it in and know that the only thing required of me in this moment is to be.

Just be.

But instead, my mind is restless, anxious to find the owl and get this whole thing over with.

"What are you thinking about?" Pike asks, looking at me over his glasses.

"The owl."

He sets his plate on the tarp and leans back, looking up toward the trees. "Why do you care so much? About the owl, I mean. I know it's a threatened species, but it seems personal to you."

My palms begin to sweat, and I remind myself that Pike doesn't know anything. I set my breakfast aside and rest my elbows on my knees, trying to look as casual as possible.

"I guess it's a few things. It is threatened, like you said, and there aren't many left in Washington. And losing one that we could have otherwise saved breaks my heart to think about. But it isn't just that." I pause, deciding a half-truth is the best answer to give. "I know it sounds ridiculous, but ever since he got out of his enclosure, he's been watching me. He follows me around the refuge and seems to always know where I am. And I guess I just feel like after a week of him coming after me, watching to see that I'm safe, I owe it to him to do the same."

I shrug and tilt my head back, letting the wind wash over me. I don't tell Pike that the owl felt like an omen, that every time I saw him watching me, a thick dread would coat my stomach. The truth is that the owl makes me uneasy, a feeling I rarely have with animals, but answering Pike's question in a way he'll understand is crucial.

"That doesn't sound ridiculous." He's quiet for several moments, and I start to think he won't say anything else. Then he looks at me again, and his eyes are oddly serious. "I have another list," he finally says.

That's not what I was expecting, and I wonder if he misheard me. "What?"

"Besides the one with all the reasons I dislike you."

"Ah," I say, unsure of where he's going with this.

"It's a list of things I like about you. And your devotion to animals is on it."

I stare at him, stunned by the words. Pike is never serious, which is one of things I dislike about him, but right now, there's no joking in his tone. There's no sarcasm or punchline. We watch each other, and I realize he means it. And not only does he mean it, but he managed to pick out one of the things I like most about myself.

I flinch and look away.

"Thank you," I say quietly, not meeting his eyes.

"Yeah, well, don't get all weird on me. It's a short list." He stands and stretches, reaching his arms toward the sky. His pajama shirt climbs up his body with the motion, revealing a strip of pale skin with a trail of hair leading south.

South.

Heat rises up my neck, and I quickly look away, hoping with everything that Pike doesn't notice. I don't like him—I shouldn't care if he has a nice list about me or if I'm senselessly intrigued by a trail of hair.

I stand and look everywhere except at him, distracting myself with the trees and the sky, and I'm relieved when he speaks again.

"Let's go get your owl," he says.

The words are so perfect, so lovely, they almost make me forget what I just saw.

Almost.

eleven

I grab my hydration pack and slide a KIND bar into my pocket, then meet Pike out by the firepit. He has unfortunately decided against pursuing the owl in his pajamas and is now in muted green hiking pants and a white T-shirt. It's a clear morning, the clouds from last night moving out to reveal a crystal-blue sky, and the air is cool with the perfect amount of bite. The trees are still, the only sounds are those of nature, and I think if I were the owl, I would have come here, too.

Sunlight reaches through branches and dots the forest floor in patches of gold, and I silently talk to the owl, asking him to stay where he is.

We're almost there, I tell him. *Just stay.*

"All set?" Pike asks, and I nod. He grabs the carrier with food for the owl, then pulls out a compass from his pocket and begins walking.

"I'll lead," I say, quickly moving in front of him.

"I have the compass." He picks up his pace to catch up with me, matching my strides so I can't get ahead.

"I have the coordinates."

He exhales loudly and looks at me for a few seconds, then shakes his head and gestures for me to go first. "It's never easy with you."

I want to tell him that it's *much* easier with me, since I feel where the bird is. We won't have to stop and look at maps or compasses or tracking devices. But instead, I say nothing and move ahead of him.

"I studied the map extensively against the coordinates," I tell him. "I know exactly where he is."

"Whatever you say."

We leave the campsite behind and begin our trek through the forest. There's no trail or path this far in, and we go slowly as we step over fallen trees and exposed roots, around ferns and moss-covered boulders. The ground is damp with the recent rain, and the woods smell earthy and clean.

After a few minutes, the gradient gets steeper, and soon we're walking at a noticeable incline. Pike breathes behind me, even and deep, and the sound is comforting in a way. Maybe it makes me feel like I'm not in this alone, like I have another person to weather it with.

But that's not true, and hoping for it is foolish. If my dad taught me anything, it's that a person who doesn't have magic will never choose to weather the storms with a person who does. It will always become too much for them, sooner or later.

Still, I listen to Pike's breaths against the sounds of the forest, and for just a moment, pretend I'm on a hike with a boy that I like instead of a boy that I cursed.

"We should name him," Pike says, interrupting my thoughts.

"Name him?" I ask.

"The owl. We didn't name him when he came to the refuge, but now that we're traipsing through the forest trying to find him, it feels like a good time."

A low branch is blocking our path, and I push it aside and wait for Pike to pass before letting it snap back into place.

"I like that idea," I say. "Have any suggestions?" I get in front of Pike once more and keep climbing, the air getting colder as I do.

"I've always been partial to the name Alfred," he says.

"He doesn't look like an Alfred." I press my palm into a nearby Douglas fir, taking a quick breather. The thick gray bark is ragged and feels rough against my skin, with deep furrows that run the length of the tree. Pike stops next to me and takes a sip of his water.

"Got anything better?"

Omen. Harbinger. Carrier of the Curse. But I can't say those, so instead I suggest Twilight.

"Like the book?" he asks.

"I was more thinking the time of night, but I'm delighted you thought of the book first." I unclip the hydration tube from my pack and take a long sip of water.

"It wasn't bad," he says, and I almost choke.

"You've read *Twilight*?"

"I have. I grew up not far from Forks, so I figured I'd see what all the hype was about."

"And?"

"I thought it was earned." He shrugs and takes another sip of water. My mind runs away with images of Pike reading, pushing his glasses up his nose, enthralled in a love story between a human and vampire. I wonder if he reads in his matching pajamas, the thought smoothing out the rough edges I so often see with him.

I clear my throat and look away. This is Pike. Witch-hating, arrogant, sarcastic Pike. But for the first time, it isn't totally clear to me why I cursed him, as if this trip is covering our past interactions in a softer light.

"You're full of surprises," I finally say. Once I've had a chance to catch my breath, I start hiking again.

"Will you check the compass? Are we still going northeast?"

"Remarkably, yes," Pike says. "You weren't kidding when you said you studied the map."

"You aren't the only one who's prepared."

The sound of the river is getting more distant, and I walk faster, realizing how close we are to the owl.

"Okay, back to the name," Pike says. "How about MacGuffin?"

"MacGuffin? As in the plot device?"

"Exactly. The owl flying away is what prompted us to go on this trip. He's a quintessential MacGuffin."

"Wow," I say, exaggerating the word. "That's exceptionally nerdy, even for you."

"It's an amazing name and you're just angry you didn't come up with it yourself."

"I don't think he'll like it," I say, forcing out the words between rapid breaths. My chest is getting tighter the higher we climb, and I slow my pace. "He has a serious look to him."

I hear Pike trip behind me, but by the time I look back, he's righted himself.

"Nothing to see here," he says. "He can be a serious MacGuffin. It totally works."

I sigh, shaking my head. "Fine. MacGuffin it is."

Sticker bushes scratch at my ankles, and my chest burns with the effort of breathing. Finally, I stop and swing my pack to my front, digging in the pocket for my inhaler.

"You have asthma?" Pike asks.

"Yes," I say, taking two slow puffs from my inhaler before putting it back.

"I didn't know that."

"Why would you?" I ask, realizing how little we know of the other. Trivial work competitions and bickering don't add up to any kind of real connection, and sometimes it feels as if all his joking and all my silence are really just shields meant to keep the other out. But I know there's a real person there, with fears and hopes and aches and wants, and I think it might be nice to see those things.

But he has no reason to show them, and I can't blame him. I cursed him, after all.

"Yeah, I don't know," he says, his voice quiet and unsure.

Before I start walking again, I check on my connection to the owl, and the magic reaches me instantly, strong and bold and vibrating with excitement. I pull out my phone and bring up the maps I downloaded on the way here, zooming in to show Pike the coordinates.

"We're here," I say.

"Damn, Gray, I'm impressed. You didn't take a wrong turn once."

I take a small bow, then turn my eyes to the trees. "Now all we have to do is find him."

"Okay, look for cavities or old nests. Platforms, too. Those are the likeliest areas for him to be."

"Got it."

We spread out, and I watch as Pike pulls out his binoculars and slowly walks through the trees, looking for the owl. I want to tell him he's getting warmer when he walks in the right direction, but I keep my mouth shut and give him time to find the owl on his own.

I know where to go, but I walk the opposite way so I don't seem suspicious. I pretend to look in cavities and squint to see faraway nests, weaving slowly through the old trees. These woods hold so much magic, upwards of two hundred years' worth, absorbing particles and holding them in their trunks for safekeeping. It fills me with rage and heartache in equal measure, knowing these forests are getting smaller and smaller, fewer and fewer. Knowing the habitats that are being destroyed along the way.

We don't know for sure why the northern spotted owl is an amplifier, but we suspect it has something to do with its preference for old-growth forests, spending its days and nights in a place drenched in magic. But if these forests cease to exist, the northern spotted owl will, too.

After a suitable amount of time has passed, I make my way toward the owl, keeping my pace slow so Pike still has a chance to find him. When he turns and goes the wrong direction, I follow my connection to the bird, and there in a low hollow of a towering Douglas fir is the northern spotted owl.

His big eyes stare at me, unblinking. He doesn't look surprised or startled or afraid. If anything, he looks...satisfied. As if he has been waiting for me to find him.

"Hi," I say, quiet enough so Pike won't hear. MacGuffin is in the lowest cavity of the tree, and one sweep of magic through his system tells me his wing is in worse shape than it was when he left the refuge.

Hope begins to bloom in my chest, an aching pulse that moves through my entire body. I found him. Now all I need to do is get him back to the refuge and unbind the curse. Then I can focus entirely on healing his wing.

"Pike," I say, keeping my eyes on the bird. "I found him."

Pike comes over and stands next to me, binoculars hanging from a strap around his neck. He looks into the hollow, and a smile spreads across his face.

"Hi, MacGuffin. Aren't you a sight for sore eyes?"

MacGuffin stares at us and cocks his head, and it isn't the first time I feel as if he's orchestrating this in some way I don't understand.

We keep our distance, several yards away so he doesn't feel threatened, but that doesn't seem like much of a concern. He recognizes me.

"He's a beautiful bird," Pike says, looking through his binoculars.

"He's a pain in the ass," I mutter, then immediately mouth an apology.

Pike laughs and brings his binoculars down. "He wouldn't be a very good MacGuffin if he weren't."

"Wow, you're *so* proud of that name."

"I really am," Pike says, setting his pack on the ground. "It was a total stroke of genius."

I take a few steps to the side and survey the hollow, getting the best possible view of the owl. He looks calm and comfortable, happy in the massive old tree. He watches us with interest but doesn't make any move to fly toward us. With his wing the way it is, I suspect he hasn't done much hunting, but he doesn't seem agitated or weak.

Back at the refuge, we have tools for capturing animals when needed, but they're still wild with minds of their own. I could use magic to try to entice him, but he's already shown that my magic doesn't have much of an effect on him. He's used to the feel of it and isn't as compelled to follow its pull as an animal first encountering it.

And even though his wing is injured, it still works. If he starts to feel threatened, he'll fly away.

The frustrating truth is that Pike and I can try all the tricks we want, but the only way we'll get him over here is if he wants to come. If he doesn't, we're out of luck.

"So, what's the plan?" I ask, setting my pack next to Pike's and leaning against a nearby tree. "He looks awfully comfortable in that hollow."

"Yeah, he does," Pike agrees. "I think we dive right in with the modified trap. It's pretty basic since we don't want to hurt him, but it's our best shot, especially if he didn't have a successful night of hunting. Most animals, wild and domestic, are extremely food driven," he says. "MacGuffin isn't any different."

"Sounds good to me."

Pike pulls out two flat boxes from his pack and assembles them, then hands me several towels. He fills the bottom box with one towel, then props up the lid of the box with a stick, readying the trap for the owl. The longer I watch him, the more my fears surface.

The curse is so strong in the owl, so powerful, I can feel it from here. And Pike is only yards away from it, from this curse that could turn him into a mage, that could ignite him like a tree in a California drought, engulfing him in flames instantly.

I swallow hard and try to keep my focus, blinking away memories of Alex and visions of Pike, forcing myself to stay present. There is no fire, no flames. No immediate danger.

We're okay. Pike is okay.

"Iris?" Pike asks, and I look at him. "I lost you for a minute."

"Oh, sorry," I say, realizing the trap is almost ready. "I got distracted."

"Well, pay attention because this next part is tricky." He picks up the carrier and opens the lid just enough to grab one of the woodrats. The animal scurries in his hand, and after a few tries, Pike successfully sets the trap.

The owl watches us the entire time.

"Okay, let's give him some space and see if he's hungry," I say.

Pike and I walk away and sit behind a large tree, close enough to see what's going on but far enough away for the owl to feel safe. Of course he knows we're here—he can still hear us, and he always seems to know where I am anyway—but the likelihood of him coming out for food is much greater if he doesn't feel threatened by us.

We settle into the dirt, and Pike raises his binoculars to his face, watching MacGuffin. We don't speak, and I silently beg the owl over and over to come out of his hollow and eat. But even from here, I can tell that the owl isn't eyeing the woodrat; he's eyeing us.

Several hours pass, and when it's clear the owl has no intention of moving, I shift my focus to Pike. "He's not interested in eating," I say, frustration creeping into my tone.

"Just give it time."

"He's an animal. If he wanted it, he would have taken it already. Wild animals don't typically subscribe to the delayed-gratification approach to things."

Pike raises his binoculars again, even though the owl hasn't moved.

"What are you looking for?" I ask.

"I don't know," Pike says, his voice tense. "You're frustrating me."

"And looking through your binoculars is helping with that?" I try to keep my voice down, not wanting to scare the owl, but we need a different plan.

"No, but it makes me feel like I'm doing something," he says. "Just let me do this my way, okay?"

"Your way isn't working."

Pike doesn't respond, and instead, keeps looking through his binoculars. I reach my hand up to snatch them away, but he jerks back, glaring at me. "These are the Swarovski Optik 8.5 by 42 EL Binoculars with the FieldPro package. Don't touch them."

He rattles off the exact model without hesitation, as if this is something he brags about quite a bit, and I give him an exasperated look.

"Seriously, Pike, it's time for a new plan."

"This plan is working just fine." He doesn't shift where he's sitting, nor does he turn his head to look at me. He stays stubbornly still, watching the owl in the hollow as if he'll fly down to join us at any moment.

"I'll do it myself," I say, standing and wiping the dirt from my pants. My herbs are in my daypack, and I'm not going to risk letting the owl get away again. I'm not.

I grab the towel from the ground, but I'm not quick enough, and Pike grabs the other side. He stands and faces me.

"Are you being serious right now? You're going to tug-of-war this towel?" I try to pull it away from him, but he grips it even tighter.

"If that's what it takes. Why did you bring me all the way out here if you weren't going to listen to me?"

"I'm sorry, at what point did you hear me say that I'd submit to your every command if you came along?"

Pike yanks on the towel, and it slips through my fingers. "I know more about this stuff than you do."

"Yeah, all your time in the classroom is really paying off."

Pike opens his mouth to respond when the owl lets out one shrill scream.

No.

I rush toward the hollow, desperate to see the owl, to calm him down and reassure him that he's safe. That everything's okay.

But I'm too late.

He swoops from his place in the tree then flaps his wings, flying up and up and up. His wing is too fragile, and I shudder at the thought of how much this is taking out of him.

"No!" I call, begging the owl to come back.

I run, chasing after him, but I can't catch up. I reach for the magic inside him, wrapping it with my own, doing everything I can to coax him back to the ground. I let him feel my utter terror, pleading with him to come back.

But it doesn't work.

He's used to magic, and he's used to me.

He finds a clearing and flies out of the canopy of the trees, then he's gone. Taking all my hope with him.

twelve

We hike back to the campsite in silence. Pike is several paces in front of me, making a show of storming off, which is fine. My eyes are stinging, and I don't want him to see me cry. It's not that I think crying is a sign of weakness—I don't. It's that crying feels vulnerable, and I'm careful about choosing who I'm vulnerable with.

It's getting harder to see, twilight enveloping the trees and shrouding everything in a dusty gray. A whole day wasted with nothing to show for it. I stop walking, lean my back against a weathered spruce, and cry.

My mom always says that there's not much an epic cry-fest can't fix, and while I don't think leaning against a tree with tears streaming down my face will help me find the owl, I can't deny that it helps me feel better.

I'm not sure how long I stand here, but by the time I wipe my cheeks and start walking again, the night forest is waking. Bats flit overhead and crickets chirp, but Pike's footsteps are long gone by now. I don't dare use magic to find him—it would have to touch him to work, and he'd see the unmistakable starlight that accompanies it.

Then he'd know.

But there's nothing else in our campsite for me to draw magic from, and Pike has our only compass.

I'm lost, just like my hope. Just like the owl.

I look around and exhale slowly. There's no point in trying to make my way back to the campsite now; I'll never find it in the dark. It's better to stay here—on the same path Pike and I traveled together—than risk going too far off course.

I sink to the ground and pull my knees to my chest, then lean my head against the trunk of the spruce and close my eyes. Its roots snake through the dirt, cradling me in its arms, telling me I'm safe. My eyes are tired after crying, and I hug my arms to my chest, exhaling into the tree, sinking in deeper.

When I start to get cold, I wrap myself in magic, thousands of tiny fragments rushing to my skin and colliding, creating enough heat to keep me warm. Once I stop shivering, I reach for the owl, giving all my attention to finding him.

I breathe out in relief when I feel him right away, so thankful he's still out there.

Our connection is strong, with the owl giving me access to his magic, wanting me to come after him. He may not let my magic influence him, but he wants to be found. I concentrate on the pull, the direction of the stream, and locate him about eight miles northwest of here. We'll have to pack up tomorrow and drive to a new trailhead, but at least he's still close.

Still living and breathing and carrying my ill-fated curse.

Now that I know he's safe, I can rest. I burrow back into the spruce, wrapped in magic and cradled in roots, and slowly drift toward sleep. For just a moment, I feel at peace.

Then: "Iris!"

I jolt forward and open my eyes, squinting into the darkness.

"Iris!" he calls again, his voice getting closer.

"Pike?" I'm still half asleep, and I rub my eyes.

"Stay where you are," he calls. "I'm coming!" His voice sounds urgent. Worried, even. A faint smile tugs at my lips.

"Over here!" I call back, realizing that Pike probably thinks I'm scared, lost and alone in the woods.

He's close enough for me to hear his footsteps, then his headlamp comes into view, bobbing up and down in the darkness. His light crosses my face, and he rushes toward me.

He kneels on the ground in front of me, his eyes scanning the length of my body. "Are you hurt?"

"No, why would I be hurt?"

"Because you're not with me," he says. "What the hell happened?"

"Nothing. I was upset about the owl and stopped to gather my emotions for a bit. I didn't realize how late it'd gotten."

"Jesus, Iris, I was worried sick." He stands and shoves a hand through his hair. "You can't do stuff like that, okay? If you need a minute, fine, but at least tell me first."

"I'm sorry," I say, standing up and wiping the dirt from my pants. They're soaked through, and I shiver. "I'm sorry. I won't do it again."

Pike stops moving, his headlamp crossing over my face,

illuminating the trees behind me. I wish I could see him better, see the way anger and worry pull at his features. His tone, his urgency, his tense stance all tug at something inside me, shifting my pieces ever so slightly.

"Thank you for coming back," I say.

He doesn't respond for a minute, but I can feel him looking at me, feel the way his eyes settle on my face.

"I'm glad you're okay," he finally says, and even though it's dark, I look down, unsure of how to respond.

I pick up my pack, resting it on my shoulders once more, and follow Pike back to the campsite. He doesn't say anything the rest of the way and busies himself with the fire once we're there.

"Thank you again," I say, breaking the silence.

Pike pauses what he's doing and looks up at me, his expression unreadable. Then something in him shifts, and he looks down. "You're welcome."

"I really didn't mean to worry you."

"I know," he says, his voice softening, letting go of some of the heaviness from earlier. "It doesn't seem like I had anything to worry about, anyway. You looked pretty comfortable when I found you."

"I was almost asleep," I admit.

He laughs at that, big and loud, the sound filling me up in a way I don't expect. "Of course you were."

"I've always liked the trees," I say. "I used to beg my parents to let me sleep outside. Something about being surrounded by nature has always calmed me down."

"Did you need that a lot as a kid? To be calmed down?" He

pauses what he's doing and looks at me, his face dim in the evening light.

"Yeah," I say, my fingers working the hem of my jacket. "I guess I did. I've always been really aware of the things I could lose. Too aware, probably."

"What kind of things?"

"Everything," I say. "My family, my friends, my home, my health. Everything."

Pike keeps working on the fire, and suddenly the flames spring to life, casting a warm orange glow on his face. He dusts off his hands and sits on the tarp, then his eyes meet mine.

"Have you lost things?"

I swallow hard. "Yes," I say, embarrassed when the word comes out hoarse.

"And life goes on. And somehow, you find a way to go on with it." I watch him, no longer sure we're talking about me. Then he clears his throat and leans back, taking a deep breath. "The trees really do help," he says.

I don't respond right away, caught between the present moment and the ghosts of my losses, reminding me of how much more I stand to lose. I wonder what kind of conversations Amy and Alex had leading up to that night, if they talked about loss or if all their words spoke of magic.

"Water helps, too. Rivers and lakes and rain. Even listening to water rush out of a faucet can help in a pinch," I say. I'm suddenly self-conscious, and I look down, not wanting to see Pike's face. I'm scared he'll make a joke of it, of this thing I've never told anyone I do.

I feel him studying me, and heat blooms in my neck, fighting against the cool spring night. He takes a breath. Then: "You're a remarkable person."

My reaction is so visceral that I feel the words more than hear them. That's not an ordinary thing to say to someone, not a *you're cool* or even an *I like you*. And the way he says it, as if it's a fact, something entirely undeserving of the weight I'm giving it, makes it hit me even harder.

"That almost sounds like a compliment," I tell him, keeping my voice light, trying to restore some balance.

"You know *unusual* is a synonym for *remarkable*, right?" he says, cocking his head to the side.

That gets a laugh out of me, and I'm suddenly thankful for Pike's easy demeanor, for the way he followed me from heavy to light in the span of a breath.

"Are you up for some s'mores?" he asks. "We've got ingredients left for a few more."

"Sure," I say. "Just let me change first."

I stand and head toward my tent, but Pike stops me. "Iris."

He steps closer, so close I can feel his breath on my skin. Goose bumps rise along my arms, and I stay where I am, stuck in place by the nearness of him.

"I meant it as a compliment," he says, his voice quiet. We're far enough from the fire that I can only see the shadow of him, the whisper of his body in front of mine. And maybe it's better that way, better that I can't see if the words touched his eyes or if his gaze fell to my lips as he said it.

Better that he couldn't see the way I searched for his face, aching to see what he looked like in that moment.

Better.

I keep walking, unsure of what to say or if I trust my voice to remain steady. When I'm in the safety of my tent, I replay his words in my mind, trying to figure out when Pike went from someone who delighted in giving me a hard time to someone who searches for me in the woods.

The familiar pang of guilt enters my chest, thinking about the curse that set this whole thing in motion. Pike makes me food and comes after me in the woods and thinks I'm remarkable. And I cursed him.

Dread stirs in my stomach, and I reach for the owl once more, making sure my curse is tucked safely beneath his wings. His magic rushes toward me, and I breathe out, telling myself to enjoy a s'more, get a good night's sleep, and start again tomorrow.

I change into my sweats and put my hair up in a topknot, then I grab my blanket and meet Pike on the tarp. Heat pours from the fire, and Pike roasts a marshmallow on the end of a stick.

"Perfect timing," he says, pulling the marshmallow from the fire and placing it between two graham crackers and a piece of chocolate. "This one looks good."

He hands it to me, and I devour it immediately, not realizing how hungry I was.

Pike makes one for himself, giving me an apologetic look once he's finished. "I wish I had more for us."

"We can get the ingredients when we stop for supplies tomorrow," I say, pulling the blanket up so it's covering my lap, wrapping my hands in the fabric to keep warm.

"You still want me to go with you?" he asks, sounding genuinely surprised.

It strikes me that I assumed he would, that I didn't even consider going alone. "Sure," I say, keeping my tone casual. "If you want to."

"I do," he says.

"Then it's settled."

I lie down on my back and look up at the stars, thousands of white lights in a sea of darkness. Sometimes I'm overwhelmed by it all, the vastness of this life, the absolute miracle it is that I exist in this moment in time. How much magic is out in the universe, stretching beyond what the eye can see, reaching distances the mind can't even comprehend?

The tarp crinkles as Pike lies down, too, mere inches from me. Without a word, I pull the corner of my blanket over to him, and he takes it, covering his legs. The fire crackles beside us, but the night is otherwise quiet. Still.

"Did you know that it's completely silent in space?" he asks, staring up at the sky. "There's no atmosphere, so sound has no way to travel." He pauses before speaking again. "Sometimes I wonder what it would be like, to be surrounded by that kind of silence."

I'm surprised that Pike would ever want to be surrounded by silence, and it feels as if I'm seeing a totally different side of him.

"Perfect," we say at the same time.

I slowly turn my head to look at him, and he does the same. Firelight dances off his glasses, casting shadows over his features.

His eyes find mine. "I'm sorry about earlier," he says.

"I'm sorry, too. I shouldn't have gone off the way I did."

"I didn't really give you much of a choice," he says, looking down as if he's trying to decide if he wants to say something more. He chooses not to, and silence fills the space between us.

We're quiet for several minutes, then I reach into my backpack and grab what's inside, holding it out for Pike to see.

"Iris Gray, are you offering me one of your precious KIND bars?"

"I am," I say solemnly, handing it to him with care. "An olive branch, of sorts."

"I'm touched, truly." He reaches out to take it, and his fingertips brush my hand as he does. My breath catches in my throat, and I don't move, suddenly more aware of my hand than I've ever been before.

This was supposed to be a silly gesture, a joke, but he looks at me with a seriousness that makes the space deep in my core churn with something I don't recognize. My hand is still, frozen in the air, Pike's fingertips resting gently on my skin. There's enough firelight to see the way his gaze changes and finds my mouth, the way he looks at me with a question instead of an answer.

He swallows, and I watch his throat move with the effort. Slowly, he takes the KIND bar and pulls his fingers from my hand, the cold night air invading the space.

"It's getting late," he says, standing.

I blink a few times, coming back to myself. Pike offers me his hand, but after the moment we just had, I don't trust myself to take it. I stand on my own and grab my blanket from the tarp.

Pike cleans up our garbage, then douses the fire. He turns on a flashlight and walks me to my tent, illuminating the way for us.

"Thank you again," I say, not quite meeting his eyes. "For coming back for me."

"You're welcome."

"Good night," I say, unzipping my tent and ducking inside.

I slip into my sleeping bag and pull my blanket up and over my body, remembering how just moments ago Pike and I were underneath it, staring up at the stars. I listen as he unzips his tent and shuffles around, getting ready for bed. Then the night gets quiet, the only sounds those of the animals who live here.

Still, I strain to hear him, wondering if he falls asleep quickly or if he lies in bed thinking, the way I do. I've never been able to quiet my mind on the best of days, let alone the days that leave me replaying every little detail until I want to scream.

Pike says there's complete silence in space, that sound can't travel, and I wonder if that could extend to my thoughts. I wonder if I could float up and up and up, and at some great height my mind would just...still.

I close my eyes and try to sink into the vision, imagining myself rising toward the heavens, the world getting quieter and quieter until suddenly there is nothing.

A rustling noise comes from Pike's tent, and I wonder if he's

still awake or just turning as he dreams, fast asleep. Then I hear
the unmistakable sound of a package opening, and my hand flies
to my mouth to stop the laugh rising up my throat.

Pike Alder is eating the KIND bar I gave him.

And for some reason, it makes me inexplicably happy.

thirteen

I wake to the sound of Pike walking around the campsite, humming to himself. I rub my eyes and yawn, then remember the owl flying off and immediately send myself into a panic. I reach for the bird, an urgent assembly of magic, needing to know that he's still close.

The image in my mind gets more and more defined as the magic tracks him down, and finally it's clear as crystal, confirming his location. I breathe out, long and heavy.

He's in the same place he was yesterday when I first sought him out after he flew away, and something tells me he'll stay there. Waiting for me.

I slip out of my sleeping bag and pull my hair into a bun. I'm sure I'm a mess, my curly hair wild and my eyes showing how tired I am. But I've never cared to impress Pike Alder, and I won't start now.

When I step out of my tent, Pike is already taking his down. Most of his stuff is piled up neatly to the side as he pulls out his tent poles and tosses them onto the ground.

"Morning," he says, turning to look at me.

It takes all of my self-control not to ask him how his midnight snack was, but I resist. "Morning," I say, grabbing the bag of Sarah's granola and shoving a handful into my mouth.

"What's that you're eating?" Pike asks, throwing me a glance over his shoulder. His eyes linger on the bag, and I almost laugh.

"Homemade granola," I say, handing it to him. "You're welcome to have some. Sarah gave me enough to last a year."

Pike eagerly grabs the bag and dumps a pile into his hand before giving it back to me. He's well-acquainted with Sarah's baking, since she often sends Mom and me to work with the recipes she tests at home.

"God bless her," Pike says after he finishes his handful. I give the bag back to him, and he takes more.

"She really is wonderful," I say, and I'm instantly hit with the memory of her engagement to my mom, and a joy so strong fills me up that I can physically feel it. "My mom and Sarah got engaged," I blurt out, wanting to share it with someone.

"Whoa," Pike says, finishing more granola. "That's awesome. They're great together."

"I think so, too," I say.

Their relationship has always seemed so natural, and I wonder how long Mom and Sarah were together before they knew they were together. Maybe they just one day realized they never wanted to say good night to the other person again, the way the darkness makes you see the stars—they've always been there, but it takes a cloudless sky away from the lights of the city to notice.

Pike looks at me then. "How do you feel about it?" His tone is kind, like he really wants to know, and I can't help the smile that spreads across my face.

"I'm thrilled. I adore Sarah, and she makes my mom happier than I've seen her in a very long time."

"I don't know how she couldn't, given all her amazing food."

"I know, and that's just a bonus. She's wonderful, and I can't wait until she moves in. She's a light to have around."

"She seems that way, from the few times I've met her."

The comment makes me happy, knowing Pike has noticed that in her as well. He notices more than he lets on, he's more thoughtful than he lets on, and I wonder why he tries to hide those things, why hiding so often feels like the only option.

Pike gets back to organizing his stuff, and I realize that I just shared something personal with him, something that makes me exceedingly happy, and he could have ruined the moment with one of his sarcastic comments or deflecting jokes, but he didn't. He celebrated it with me, and that feels big for us. Important, somehow.

"I'll get packed up," I say, turning back toward my tent.

"Want some help?"

"Oh, sure," I say.

"Don't sound so surprised."

"I don't think you've ever once offered to help me at the refuge," I point out.

"That's different. At the refuge, we're adversaries. It wouldn't make sense to help you. But here, we're allies working toward the same goal."

"I can't believe you just used the words *adversaries* and *allies* to describe us," I say, pulling my pack out of my tent.

"Really? I feel like those are both words I'd readily use."

"I mean, they are. I guess I'm still just shocked that you're like this."

He laughs at that, and an odd sensation comes to life in my stomach, like I'm proud to have made him laugh. I dismiss the thought and continue clearing out the rest of my things.

Pike gets started taking down my tent while I pack up, and once we check the site to make sure we haven't left anything behind, we begin our hike back down to the car. When we're almost to the trailhead, I stop for some water. Pike fishes his phone out of his pack and turns it on, and it dings several times in a row.

"Back in service," Pike says, looking at the screen. Then his facial expression changes, and he looks worried.

"Is everything okay?"

"Yeah, it's just... Oh man, I feel terrible. I had a date last night and totally forgot. She texted me a bunch and called twice."

I've always assumed that Pike dates, but hearing it unsettles me. I take a sip of water and try to look natural. Disinterested.

"Your girlfriend?" I ask. I have no idea if Pike has a girlfriend or not, and the question is out of my mouth before I think better of it.

He pauses his typing and looks up at me, his mouth quirking to one side. "Are you asking if I'm taken, Iris?"

"No. Why would I care?"

"I don't know, you tell me," Pike says, enjoying himself too much. His thumbs hover over his keyboard, but he doesn't resume typing.

"I'm just making friendly conversation," I say. I take one more drink of water, then begin descending again, annoyed at Pike for not answering and annoyed at myself for caring.

"Well, as a friend, why don't *you* date?"

"What makes you think I don't?" I ask, bothered by his assumption even though he's right.

"Do you?"

I pause. "No."

"Why not?"

"I don't know. I just...don't think I'd be good at it." My voice gets quiet, and I hope he doesn't notice. I'm glad that he's behind me, that he can't see my face. "I'm not like you. I can't just sit down with a random person and find something to talk about. It takes me a while to get comfortable with someone."

"You're doing just fine with me," he says.

"I'm not trying to impress you," I counter.

Pike stops walking, and I turn around. "That's your problem right there."

"What is?" I ask, exasperated, ready to move on from the subject.

"You shouldn't be trying to impress anyone. It should be the other way around."

"Coming from the person who says I don't have people skills," I remind him.

"I'm being serious. You're smart and talented and one of the most interesting people I've ever met. And you're best friends with a wolf, which is pretty badass." He pauses. "You don't need to try."

I laugh and roll my eyes, but he watches me in a way that makes me stop and listen.

"You're the one to impress, Iris." He says the words slowly, clearly, as if he wants me to repeat them back to him, as if it's imperative that I understand.

I look down, unsure of how to respond. "Well, if I decide to grace the dating pool with my presence, I'll keep that in mind." I say it like a joke, but I mean it. I'll remember what he said.

When we get back to the car, Pike lifts the hatch and starts loading our gear while I pull up the maps. I sit on the hood, looking at my screen, and he comes and sits next to me.

"She's not my girlfriend," he says, leaning into me as he speaks, like he's telling me a secret. It makes me oddly happy, knowing he's been waiting this whole time to say it, hoping I'd ask again. "It was going to be a first date."

"Probably not your best work, for a first date."

"No, definitely not," he says, laughing. He peers over my shoulder, looking at the maps.

"How do you think our owl's doing this morning?"

"I think he's fine," I say. "Pleased with himself that he's being so difficult to catch."

"You're being too hard on him. He's a wild animal, you know."

I want to tell him that if he'd cast a curse that was then stolen by an owl, he'd be hard on him as well. I sigh and lean back, taking a big breath.

I wish I understood the curse more, wish there were more examples I could look to or texts I could read, but the only thing I can point to is the story my mom told me as a child, and that had a catastrophic ending. I don't know how the curse will impact the region or what it will do if it gets unleashed. The only thing I know for certain is that it will turn Pike into a mage, which is bad enough. That he could burn to death, which is even worse.

But what about all the other things?

My heart begins to race as I imagine myself back on that field, surrounded by wildflowers and lavender, watching a council of witches take seven turns around me. I want to cry, picturing my mother off to the side, watching me with an irrevocable love she could never shake.

But it isn't just about me. It's about Pike and his family. It's about the region this curse could affect.

Pike pulls out his map and compares it to the coordinates on my phone, looking at the trailheads in the area. After a few minutes, he taps on the map and says, "This one."

"How far of a drive is it?"

"Probably only twenty minutes or so. But we need to stop at a store on the way to get a few more supplies. I didn't plan for this long of a trip."

The comment makes me ache for the refuge and my mom and Winter, ache for the relief of having the owl back where I can undo the curse and finally feel at peace.

Pike starts his car, and we drive down the mountain, listening to the same music as when we drove up here two days ago.

It's overcast out, blanketing the world in shades of gray, and I lean my head against the glass and let the cold permeate my skin. It isn't long until we turn into a gravel parking lot and stop in front of a small general store with a steep pitched roof and dark wooden planks, set against the mountains in the distance. That's something I love about living out of the city: once you get far enough out, even the general stores have incredible views.

Pike walks in like a man on a mission, checking a list he's pulled up on his phone, then going up and down each aisle with purpose. Every time he finds something he wants, his routine is the same: he picks it up off the shelf, flips it over to read the back, checks the list on his phone again, then sets the item gently in his basket.

He does this several times, and when he finds the ingredients for s'mores, I take them from him and put them in my basket instead.

"I'll get these," I say.

I pick up a few more snacks, then we both check out and head back to the car.

"Hey, do you mind waiting a few minutes? We actually have pretty good reception here, and I'd love to give my mom a quick call."

"Oh, that's a good idea. I'll call my parents, too," Pike says.

I wander a few feet away from the car and pace back and forth. Mom picks up on the third ring.

"Hello?" She sounds calm and happy, the same as she did the day I left. It makes me miss her.

"Hi, Mom," I say, so relieved to hear her voice.

"Iris! I'm so glad you called. We miss you around here."

"I miss you, too," I say. "How's everything going?"

Sarah says something in the background that I can't make out, then Mom is back on the phone. "Your timing is actually great. Cassandra just called."

Everything inside me turns cold at the sound of her name. My palms begin to sweat, and the hair on the back of my neck stands on end. Nausea flares to life in my stomach, and for a moment I think I'm going to be sick.

"Why?" It takes everything I have to make that one word come out clear. Even.

"She offered to help with the owl. You know the council keeps pretty close tabs on the amplifiers, and since she's working in the area anyway, she called and asked if we needed anything."

I can't think straight. My mind is racing and the parking lot begins to spin. I rub my temples and try to focus, try to think, but all I can see is Cassandra turning off my sense of magic. I'm relieved that help will be available if I need it, but I thought I'd have more time to try to fix this.

The owl is safe right now; there's no immediate risk. But once the council gets involved, that's it. They'll know about the curse, and I'll be put back on trial.

I've been silent for too long, and Mom speaks again. "Honey, are you okay?"

"I'm fine," I say, but my heart is racing and I feel lightheaded.

Even after everything—seeing my best friend kill the person she loves, losing my dad, moving away—I still can't imagine a world without magic.

I don't want to have to change to fit in, to be loved and known and seen. I would rather live a life without love than a life without magic.

"Is everything okay with Pike?" Mom asks, and I realize she's starting to worry.

"Shockingly, yes," I say, forcing the words to sound casual. She laughs at that, but I'm too distracted to revel in the sound.

I was at Amy's trial with my parents, clutching my mother's hand so tightly my fingers ached for days. When Cassandra walked toward Amy, when she held both her hands and removed her ability to sense magic, tears were streaming down both their faces. Mom and I were crying, too. I respected Cassandra then, not letting anyone else do that to Amy. Choosing to be the one who carried out the sentence.

But I always got the sense that she looked at me with resentment, wishing I had done something more on the lake that night. Or wishing it had been me instead. And I don't blame her, but I really wish she wasn't the council member stationed in this area.

"Well, enjoy your last night. Cassandra mentioned a training exercise she's doing, so it sounds like you've got another day before she comes to offer her assistance. I'll give you her number just in case you need it—she has one of those fancy phones that works with the satellites."

I save the number and thank Mom for the heads-up.

"How's the owl?" she asks.

"He seems to be taking an immense amount of pleasure in making me come after him, but he's otherwise fine."

She breathes out in relief, and it makes me happy, how much she loves this bird. How much she values him.

"Good. Tell Pike I said hi, and find that owl so you can come home."

"I will. Love you, Mom."

When I hang up the phone, I listen to the sound of gravel crunching under my boots. I still have time to get to the owl before Cassandra does. This doesn't have to end in darkness, in a vote that will make all the magic of the universe flicker and dim, until it finally goes out.

There are other endings, and I will find one.

fourteen

As we drive up the narrow dirt road to the next trailhead, the clouds above us get darker. It's the middle of the afternoon, but it looks like twilight, everything muted behind a filter of gray. I sit forward and look through the windshield, watching the treetops sway as the wind picks up.

"This should make for an interesting night," Pike says as we pull into the parking lot.

"You're not worried?"

"A little rain never hurt anyone," he says, putting the car in park. "Why don't you check on MacGuffin before we start our hike? I'll unload the back."

He doesn't wait for an answer and instead gets out of the car and opens the hatch.

I pull out my phone and open the app, just in case he's watching, then close my eyes and find my connection to the owl, feel as all our particles snap together in one crisp line leading directly to him.

"Yep, he's still in the same place."

"Great," Pike says through the back. "We've got about an hour hike up this time. I've actually been here with my dad before, and there's a beautiful spot by the river where we can set up camp."

I get out of the car and pull on my North Face shell and a baseball cap. "Do you and your dad go backpacking together a lot?"

"We try to," Pike says. "When my mom travels for work, we typically schedule something and take off for a few days."

I slip my pack over my shoulders and tighten the straps, then check the back of the car to make sure I'm not leaving anything. "Is that how you decided to become an ornithologist?"

Pike closes the back of the Subaru, locks it, and adjusts his pack. "Yeah," he says, "that's part of it. We spent a lot of time outdoors growing up, and my little brother loved birds. He'd always point them out and try to identify them by their songs."

We start up the trailhead, the wind sounding louder now that we're under the cover of the trees. "How old is your brother?" I ask.

Pike falters just slightly as he steps over an exposed root. "He would have been fourteen this year."

Would have been.

"Oh. Pike, I'm sorry, I didn't know."

"Why would you?" he asks, reminding me of what I said when he found out I have asthma. It isn't said in a mean way, just realistic. This trip is the first time we've ever talked about anything of substance, and it's odd, knowing that the intern who competed with me and gave me such a hard time was always this multilayered person with his own history and tragedy and pain.

Of course he was, but I never saw it.

"I don't know," I say quietly.

We fall into silence after that, and a slight rain begins to fall. A storm is rolling in, and I briefly wonder if we should turn back, try to find nearby lodging until it passes. But we're close to the owl, and with Cassandra somewhere nearby, I don't want to risk it.

It sounds like we have another day before she starts to look for the owl herself, but it doesn't feel like enough time, and I'll need every minute I can get.

I keep my eyes on the ground, being especially careful now that the rocks and roots are slick with rain. It will be much easier for Cassandra to track me if I'm using magic, so from now on, I can't use it.

I shouldn't even be checking the location of the owl, but that takes just seconds, and if Cassandra isn't trying to find me in that exact moment, it won't matter. But something that would take more time, like healing an injury or trying to relax a cougar is strictly off-limits.

I don't know if Cassandra pleaded with the council to reconsider Amy's verdict or if she accepted it readily. I don't know if she tried to save Amy from her fate or if she felt bound by her duty as a council member.

Part of me thinks Cassandra would be furious with me if she knew the curse I'd written for Pike, not because of the consequences but because of what I watched my best friend go through. Cassandra was my best friend's older sister and one of my mom's closest friends—she was more family than anything else, but that all changed two years ago.

Now I don't know how to look her in the eye, how to tell her how sorry I am for what she went through with Amy, how to say I shouldn't have gone to sleep when I did. I should have stayed, listened to my gut when it told me Amy was planning something.

But I didn't, and because that isn't a crime, I got off easy and Amy suffered.

Deep down, though, I know Cassandra's feelings on the curse won't matter. What I've done with the owl is so egregious that I deserve whatever punishment the council sees fit to hand out.

It's not too late, I tell myself, and I cling to it and force myself to believe it because it's the only way I can continue to put one foot in front of the other.

The rain is heavier and the earth is darker by the time we reach the river. Pike was right—there's a perfect spot for camping a few yards back from the shoreline, and we start setting up for the night. The trees are providing decent protection from the rain, and I'm able to get my tent up and my things inside in just a few minutes.

Pike pulls rope from his pack, then anchors his tarp around four large pines, pulling it tight. He puts a blanket underneath, and proudly motions at his makeshift shelter.

"How's that for prepared?" he asks.

"Not bad," I admit.

The owl is only a quarter mile from here, not even, but the terrain gets steeper with lots of rocks and boulders, so this is as close as we can get. Still, it's good being this close to him again. Hope fills my chest and spills over into my shoulders and down my arms, a physical reaction that calms my racing heart.

Hope is my lifeline right now.

Pike assembles a bunch of rocks in a circle and is able to get a fire going, even in the rain.

"Okay, I actually am impressed," I say, ducking under the tarp and sitting on the blanket. The fire is just a few feet away, and I reach my hands toward it, gathering its warmth.

"Fire starter kit," Pike says, sitting down next to me. He hands me one of the premade subs we picked up at the store, and we eat our dinner with the slight tapping of rain on the tarp and wind in the trees.

It's...nice. Being here with him.

"I used to go camping with my dad all the time," I say, looking at the fire. "He would love this."

"Are you close? You and your dad?"

"We used to be," I say.

"What happened?"

I set my sub wrapper off to the side and lean back, watching the flames as they reach toward the sky. "There was a bad situation in our old town, and Mom and I decided the best thing for us would be to move. My dad agreed and even helped us plan for it, but when it came down to it, he wanted to stay. So he did. Mom filed for divorce not long after, and I haven't seen him since."

"Really? He sent you off on your own and just stayed behind?" I almost flinch at the disgust in Pike's tone, and my instinct is to stand up for my dad, protect him in some way.

"Yeah, but we'd had to move before. He was just tired. He wanted to put down roots somewhere."

"But you're his family," Pike says, his voice rising. "You *are* his roots."

I look at him, and all the fight drains out of me because he's right. I know that he is. "We used to be."

"I'm sorry, Iris. That's a shit deal."

"Thanks," I say, feeling shy and overexposed. I curl my knees to my chest as if taking up less space will make my feelings smaller, more manageable.

The wind gets stronger, making the flames dance chaotically in front of us. The tarp shudders with the gusts, and I pull my hair into a bun to stop it from flying every which way.

The river rushes through the forest, and another gust sends a branch crashing into the water.

"Do you think we're safe here?" I ask, peering out from the tarp toward the trees. The tops sway left before snapping right, and a constant stream of needles and pine cones showers the campsite.

"These winds are definitely higher than the National Weather Service predicted," he says.

I hope the owl is okay. I hope he's burrowed into the trunk of an old, loving fir, contentedly waiting out the storm.

"That didn't really answer my question."

Then he looks me right in the eye and says, "We're safe."

He holds my gaze for several seconds, and a lump forms in my throat. Did he know that was exactly what I needed to hear? Can he tell that sometimes my worry gets so big it overwhelms me?

I swallow hard and look away.

"My grandmother used to say that to hear the wind is to hear the earth breathe."

Pike smiles at that and leans back on his hands, closing his eyes. "I think I would have liked your grandmother."

I can picture it, Pike and my grandma sitting around a table, him joking around and her not taking any of his ego. It makes my heart ache thinking about how much she would have liked him.

"She would have liked you, too," I say.

She died the year before we moved, and sometimes, in my worst moments, I'm thankful she didn't see the mess that followed, thankful she didn't have to pack up her lifetime of things and move across the country with us. But the truth of it is that I know she'd absolutely love it here. She would have connected with this place in her bones, and I'm devastated she couldn't come with us.

"What was your brother's name?" I ask quietly.

Pike doesn't answer right away, and I think maybe he didn't hear me above the river and wind. Then he says, "Leo."

"I like that name."

Pike nods, looking at the fire. "Me too."

The air between us feels charged, and even though the wind is building to a roar, I'm completely focused on the distance separating us. It suddenly feels too vast, and when I look up from the blanket, Pike is watching me. Our eyes meet, and my mind screams at me to look away, to hide behind the wall I'm supposed to be keeping between us.

He leans toward me just slightly, and I'm mortified when I find myself doing the same, closing the distance instead of expanding it.

Then a loud crack sounds through the air, and I jolt back. I look away just in time to see a huge branch slam into my tent.

I grab the flashlight from the corner of the blanket and rush over to inspect the damage. Wind batters me from all directions, and I pull up my hood and widen my stance to keep steady. It's so loud that I don't hear Pike when he comes up behind me, and I jump when he speaks.

"I should have had you set up your tent in a less vulnerable place," he says. "It was pretty exposed out here."

"We didn't know the storm would be this bad." I look up at the treetops swaying back and forth, bending deeper as the gusts get stronger. "Do you think we should leave?"

"I was wondering the same thing, but hiking down the trail in the dark feels more precarious than sticking it out in one place. I think our best option is to stay put."

"Okay," I say, turning my attention back to my tent. "You're probably right."

Several of my tent poles are broken, and the nylon top is split all the way through, from corner to corner. I pull it back up and try to salvage the poles, but it doesn't work. I can't get the tent to stay upright, and each gust of wind blows it back down before I can make any real progress.

Pike is watching me with an amused expression on his face, which frustrates me even more.

"This isn't funny," I say above the wind. "My tent is completely ruined, and I have no way of fixing it."

"It's a little funny," he counters.

I sigh and keep working on my tent, but it's no use, and if I get it to stand upright just for the wind to knock it over again, I'll probably cry.

"We do have another tent, you know."

I look at Pike, shocked. "Are you really that prepared? You brought a backup?"

"Seriously?"

"What?"

Pike motions to his tent, and heat floods my cheeks as I realize what he's suggesting. "Well, you're not nearly as prepared as you thought, now are you?" I try to keep my voice calm and even, but my mind is screaming. Sharing a tent with Pike Alder is out of the question.

"Yeah, silly me, I can't believe I forgot to bring the *extra tent.*"

I ignore Pike and shove everything into my pack, then pull it from the tent and haul it over to the tarp where it has a better chance of staying dry. I sit back down and lean toward the fire, trying to get warm again. Darkness has claimed the earth, banishing the twilight hours ago, and I can only see Pike by the light of the fire. Once the flames go out, I won't be able to see him at all.

"I can sleep under the tarp," I say.

"You'd really rather sleep out here, where there are wild animals, than have to share a tent with me?"

"Yes?" I say, but it comes out like a question. Pike set his tent up next to a rock face farther up the incline, so it isn't as vulnerable to falling branches. I know I'd feel safer there during the storm, but I still can't make myself move.

Pike laughs and holds out his hand to me. "Come on, Gray. Let's get some sleep."

I watch his hand, unsure of what to do.

I like the woods, and sleeping outside wouldn't bother me if not for the storm. But then I think of Cassandra and the curse and how it feels as if my life is slowly coming unraveled, and I realize I don't want to be alone.

Hesitantly, I reach out and take Pike's hand, his fingers closing around mine.

He helps me up, then we walk to his tent. Together.

fifteen

Pike leads the way with a flashlight and holds open the front of his tent for me to climb in. His pack is tucked in a corner with his sleeping bag stretched out on top of a folded blanket. It's tiny, obviously meant for one person, and I sit off to the side and try to make myself as small as possible.

Pike crawls in after me and switches off his flashlight in favor of a dimmer lantern. He sets it in the middle of the floor and zips the tent closed.

"Since your stuff got wet, we'll have to improvise a little." He pulls a blanket out from under his things and unfolds it to its full size, then unzips his sleeping bag and lays it on top. "It won't be as warm this way, but it's big enough to cover us both. It'll have to do."

When I don't move or say anything, Pike stops and looks at me. "Now that we're in here, I suppose it is a bit tight for two people. I can sleep outside," he says.

But I don't want to be alone to worry about the curse and

Cassandra and what it would mean if the curse was unleashed. I don't want to think about Alex and that night on the lake and the terrifying possibility that I doomed Pike to the same fate.

I can't tell Pike any of the things I want to talk about, but I can sleep in his tent and distract myself with the closeness of another person.

I swallow and finally meet his eyes. "I don't want you to sleep outside."

"You don't?"

I shake my head, then slowly scoot onto the blanket. Pike lifts up the sleeping bag for me, and I lie down on my back. He does the same, and once we're both covered, he turns off the lantern.

The wind continues to roar, and the nylon tent flaps and shakes with the stress of it. Creaks and snaps come from outside as the trees sway back and forth, their branches working to hold on through the storm. I jump when a large splash sounds in the distance, something heavy and big landing in the river.

"Are you okay?" Pike asks.

I nod in the dark, even though he can't see me.

"Iris?"

"I'm okay," I say, keeping my voice even. Something about being this close to him makes it impossible to ignore that his life is hanging in the balance, and he doesn't know.

He doesn't know.

What would he say if I were to tell him I cursed him? If I were to look him directly in the eye and tell him I'm a witch?

I'm terrified to realize I want to find out, I want to say the words I vowed to never say and wait for whatever reaction lies on the other side. I'm sick of hiding.

But behind the Pike who makes me s'mores and comes looking for me in the dark is the Pike who hates witches, and I can't show him that part of me because he wouldn't understand. And I can't even blame him because I wrote an awful curse for him that I never should have written.

I cursed him, yet I want him to understand.

Impossible.

The rain gets harder, pelting the tent so loudly I'll never get to sleep. Not that I would have slept anyway.

"I hope MacGuffin is holding up okay in this storm," Pike says, and my heart starts to race.

"Why wouldn't he?"

"Rain can be risky for owls. If their feathers get soaked, they can't fly, and if they can't fly, they can't hunt. But drenched feathers can also lead to a loss of body heat, so hypothermia becomes a risk."

It's suddenly hard to breathe, and my chest gets tighter and tighter imagining all the things that could happen to the owl before we reach him. I'm unreasonably upset at Pike for telling me this, reciting what he learned in a textbook without thinking through the weight of his words.

"No, we can't let that happen. He has to be okay," I say, sitting up in the dark. I look around the tent for my shoes, but I can't see anything.

"I'm sure he's fine," Pike says. "He's a wild animal—he's used to the rain."

"Which is it? One second you hope the owl is faring okay in the storm, and the next you're sure he's fine." My voice is too frantic, too fast, and I can feel the panic rising in my body. I can't be in here anymore, in this too-small space with this person who will never understand.

"Whoa, whoa, calm down," he says, sitting up next to me. "I was just talking. I'm sure he's fine."

"You don't know that," I say, embarrassed when I almost choke on the words.

I need to see the owl, see him safe in some hollow or nest, riding out the storm just like we are. It isn't enough to track his location and feel that he's in the same place. I need to know he's sheltered and safe and well, protecting that curse until I can get to it myself.

I keep feeling around the tent until I find my shoes.

"Turn on the lantern," I say, trying to get them on so I can leave.

"What? Why?"

"I'm going after him." I don't care how outrageous it seems. Pike doesn't have all the information, and that isn't his fault, but it means I have to make some decisions he won't understand. I have to overreact because he won't. He thinks it's all about the owl, but it's all about him. That's the awful truth of it.

"You can't be serious," Pike says, shuffling around for the lantern. When he finally turns it on, I tie my shoes and grab my phone and jacket.

"I am," I say, reaching for the zipper. Pike takes my hand and pulls it away from the tent, looking at me with confusion.

"I don't understand," he says, not angry or upset, but almost hurt. Sad.

A large gust of wind slams into the tent, the fabric shaking furiously, and I slip into my jacket and reach for the zipper once more.

"You don't have to understand," I say, unzipping the tent. "But I'm going."

"This is totally absurd," Pike says, frustration sharpening the tone of his voice.

"Then don't come."

I step out of the tent and turn on my flashlight, then go to where my stuff is drying out under the tarp. I pull my headlamp out of my backpack, turning it on, and put my phone safely in my pack. I slip the straps over my shoulders and start off in the direction of the owl.

I ignore the way the trees snap and the wind howls, the way rain pelts my hood and the river surges through the woods.

The forest feels infinite, ferns and moss and huckleberry bushes covering the earth, large roots snaking through the dirt, and fallen trees resting on their trunks. It's untouched and wild, exactly as it should be, beautiful in its abandon.

Lightning splits the sky in two, and seconds later thunder rumbles in the distance. I look up, but my light can't reach the treetops, limiting what I see to only a few feet ahead.

I keep walking.

"Iris!" I hear behind me. "Wait!"

I turn and see Pike in the distance, his headlamp moving up and down as he follows after me. I don't know why seeing his light makes my eyes burn and my throat ache, why I want to run toward it until I'm blinded.

I don't move, watching through the rain as he gets closer and closer, until finally I could reach out and touch him. I could, but I don't.

"What are we doing out here, Iris?" he asks, confusion and anger lacing his tone, pulling at his eyes and mouth.

"I have to get to him," I say, my voice shaking. I need to keep moving, and I turn around to walk, unwilling to wait any longer.

"Why? Why right now?" Pike asks, his voice getting louder as he follows behind me. "He's a bird; he knows how to survive in the rain." He says it as if it's the most obvious thing in the world, as if I'm ridiculous for thinking otherwise.

"Don't do that. Don't chase after me just to tell me how ridiculous you think I am. I already know." I walk faster, my pack bouncing up and down as I jump over roots and rush around tree trunks.

"That's not what I'm saying," he says, catching up to me, staying by my side. "I just wish you'd talk to me. You're so in your head that you forget there's someone else here."

"Yeah, well maybe I'm so in my head because you aren't in yours enough," I say, frustrated. "And if I'm not giving you enough attention, you're free to leave."

Pike exhales so loudly I hear it over the wind and rain. "That's so unfair. I'm here, aren't I? I want to be here."

"You definitely don't sound like it," I say, slipping on a rock and righting myself.

He catches my hand, stopping me, making me look him in the eyes. "That's because I'm angry," he says. "I'm allowed to be angry. This doesn't make any sense, and you refuse to talk to me, running off without any explanation. This storm is only getting worse, and we should be back at camp, waiting it out, not walking directly through it in total darkness. But that's what you insisted on doing, so here we are, standing in the middle of the woods at midnight simply because you felt like it."

I breathe heavily, watching him as he speaks, watching the way his hair sticks to his forehead and the way raindrops run down his face. Watching his mouth and his eyes and his jaw as it tenses, the light from my lamp casting harsh shadows on his skin. His glasses are covered in drops of water, and there's a small twig that I want to pull from his hair. My fingers ache with it, with the desire to reach out and touch it, with the restraint of staying still.

I push my curls out of my face, wanting to see him as best I can.

"You're angry, and you still came," I finally say.

Pike sighs, exasperated. "Well...yeah. You didn't really give me a choice."

"You could have stayed back at the tent."

"No, I couldn't have."

I want to ask him why, want to know what made him come after me as I track down an owl in the middle of the night while a storm is raging. I want to know. But maybe it's nothing, and he's here out of some sense of obligation to keep me safe, as if I can't do that myself.

It's probably nothing.

I turn away from him and start walking, the wind pushing back against me. It's so strong that even the brambles are shaking with it, everything hissing in unison. The owl hasn't moved, and I tell myself it's because he's waiting out the storm in a dry hollow, safe from the weather taking place around him.

Another bolt of lightning illuminates the sky, so big I can see it through the canopy of trees. Thunder sounds right after, the storm getting closer, shaking the ground as it marches on.

Then a loud crack pierces the night.

"Iris, look out!" Before I know what's happening, Pike grabs me from behind and throws me to the ground. He lands on top of me just as a huge evergreen falls through the trees and slams into the earth, my body lifting off the ground and dropping back down as the shock moves through me.

Something is poking through my hood, and I slowly lift my hand to touch it. A huge branch is lying over Pike, resting on the part of my head he isn't covering, and my breathing gets quicker as I realize how close the tree is to us. How I would have been crushed by it if Pike hadn't thrown me off to the side.

"Pike?" I ask, my voice shaking. I'm not loud enough, though, and the words get lost in the wind.

"Pike?" I ask again, this time dragging myself out from under him. I scramble on the ground until my headlamp finally points right at him, and I'm horrified to see branches covering the full length of his body.

"Pike!" I rush over to him and he groans, the sound making me want to cry with relief.

He slowly crawls out from under the branches, covered in mud, his movements unsteady and sluggish. His glasses are sitting crookedly on his face, and he adjusts them before finally meeting my eyes.

"I want you to know," he says, taking a jagged breath and wiping his forehead on his hand, "that I blame you entirely for what just happened."

I'm shocked by how easily he can make a joke of this, how his mind isn't running with all the ways this could have ended, images of our bodies buried beneath a tree, the life crushed out of us in an instant.

"I'm sorry," I say, my voice trembling, trying so hard not to lose myself in what could have happened. I take several deep breaths and try to calm down, but the wind is still blowing and the rain is still falling and the world is still dark. "Are you okay?"

"I'm fine," he says. "But can you believe the audacity of that tree? It almost went right through us."

I don't know why but the words make me angry, and I fight to keep myself from screaming. "God, is everything a joke to you?"

I push myself off the ground and wipe the dirt from my clothes, even though it's hopeless. I'm covered in mud, and I can feel it seeping through my pants and caked on my face.

"No," Pike says, standing as well. He shifts his backpack and adjusts his headlamp, and I squint when he points it directly at me. "Most things aren't."

"Then why do you act like they are?"

"Because this world is fucking brutal, and laughing is the only way I know how to deal with it." He sounds more upset than I've ever heard him, and he keeps his eyes on mine, daring me to respond.

I look down, mad at myself for shrinking beneath his gaze.

When I don't say anything, he starts walking back the way we came, and I don't have it in me to fight. I follow him in silence all the way back to our campsite, flinching every time a branch snaps or a pine cone falls to the earth.

Pike drops his pack under the tarp, and I do the same. I grab some dry clothes, then follow Pike to his small tent meant for one person. We climb inside, keeping our backs to each other so we can change.

I pull off my wet clothing and slip into dry pants. Before I put on my sweatshirt, I slowly turn. Pike pulls his shirt over his head, and I watch as his shoulder blades shift with the movement, his muscles stretching across his back in the dim lantern light. But Pike keeps his gaze on the wall of the tent, not once looking my way, not even after he's fully dressed.

"Done," I say quietly, pulling my sweatshirt over my head and turning back to face him.

Without a word, he lifts up the sleeping bag and waits for me to crawl in before he does the same. He rolls onto his side, facing away from me. Then he turns off the lantern.

The storm continues on, and I try to ignore it, try to remind myself that this is part of the owl's natural environment and he's better equipped for it than we are.

I roll onto my side, away from Pike. There are only inches between us, but it feels like so much more, an entire ocean of past hurts and secrets, of experiences and fears that the other knows nothing about.

So many unknowns.

"Good night, Iris." Pike's voice finds me in the dark, and even though he's still upset, the sound of it eases some of the tightness in my chest.

"Good night, Pike," I say, wondering what the sound of my voice does to him, if it has any effect at all.

He scoots just slightly, closing some of the distance between us, and I decide that it does.

sixteen

When I wake up, a soft blue light filters in through the tent. The wind has died down, but the rain is still falling, tapping against the nylon in a way that makes me want to fall back asleep. Soft, rhythmic breathing comes from beside me, and I suddenly remember that I'm in this tent with Pike.

I slowly turn my head to look at him. He's facing me now, a shift he must have made in the middle of the night. His right arm is stretched toward me, his hand resting against my hip, and his left is tucked under his head. It's the first time I've ever seen him without his glasses on, and the image does something weird to my insides. He looks vulnerable in a way, a vast difference from the confident, sarcastic person I'm used to.

A stray piece of hair has fallen down his forehead, and my hand reaches for it, acting entirely of its own volition. I gently tuck the hair behind his ear, lingering longer than I should. His skin is warm, and he stirs when my fingertips brush his face.

His words from last night reenter my mind. *This world is*

fucking brutal. I watch him, wondering what secrets he keeps, what hurts and pains he carries inside him, hidden beneath easy laughs and constant jokes. Maybe our secrets could keep each other company.

But it's a foolish thing to think. Secrets are secrets for a reason, and mine belong deep in my chest, far from the surface.

Pike's eyes blink open, and I'm mortified to realize my hand is still hovering over his ear. I quickly pull it back, but it's too late. Pike looks to the side, to the empty space my hand just occupied, then slowly turns to me.

"My vision is admittedly terrible without my glasses, but it looks an awful lot like you were watching me sleep." His voice is groggy and low, sleep still thick in his throat. Heat flares in my stomach, and I look at the roof of the tent, the zipper on the door, my shoes on the ground. Anywhere but his face.

"That's a gross misrepresentation of what was happening."

"Is it?" he asks, reaching over his head for his glasses. He puts them on and watches me, his vulnerability fading away with the dawn.

"It is. How embarrassing for you."

Pike laughs and rolls onto his back, then stretches his arms up and over his head. He arches into the stretch, and I feel like I'm intruding, seeing him like this. It's a common thing, waking up, but it's something he normally does alone. There probably aren't many people who have seen Pike Alder wake up, and it's odd, knowing that I have.

"I don't get embarrassed often," he says, looking back at me.

"That's one of your personality flaws," I say casually, even though my mind is racing, fully unprepared for this version of Pike.

"You're feisty in the morning." He sits up, and I want to tell him he's wrong, that I'm not feisty. I'm trying to act normal, trying to make sure he doesn't feel the shift that's happening, doesn't notice the way I'm relearning him.

Last night, my panic took over everything, forced me into the woods in the middle of the storm because that's all I could think of to do. And Pike didn't shy away from it or ignore it or try to stop it. Instead, he stood in it with me, trudged through the darkness and high winds and pouring rain so I wouldn't be alone.

Even though he was angry. Even though he didn't understand.

He stayed next to me when that was the toughest place to be, and I want to forget it. I want to forget because it was so heart-breakingly kind, because for a single second, it made me wonder what it might be like to be fully accepted. Fully known.

But I'm not sure there even is such a thing as being fully accepted, and if there is, it certainly wouldn't come from Pike. I embody the magic he hates.

Pike scoots out from under the blanket, but I catch his arm before he leaves.

"Thank you," I say. "For last night."

"You're welcome." His eyes stay on mine for one, two, three breaths, then he unzips the tent and walks out.

As soon as he's gone, I find my magic and reach for the owl. I exhale when I feel the curse strong and steady in his chest, pulsing in time with his heart. Now that it's morning, I realize how irrational it was of me to worry, terrified that the owl couldn't survive a storm. These owls have lived in forests for hundreds of years—they know how to handle the weather.

But that's the thing about anxiety, it doesn't care if something is rational or not. It takes hold of your mind and squeezes tighter and tighter until it can't be ignored, demanding your undivided attention. It turns from insignificant to all-consuming in the span of a breath, a fog so thick it's impossible to see through, and no amount of breathing or counting or visualizing undoes it.

I went after the owl last night, not because I wanted to, but because I had to. And even though it seems senseless in the light of the morning, I don't fault myself for it.

I change into warmer clothes, then grab Sarah's granola and put on my shoes before slipping outside. The cool morning air greets me, and I breathe deep. Everything feels vibrant and fresh after the storm. New. The campsite is littered with branches and pine cones, and the river is surging, swollen with rainwater.

Pike hasn't lit a fire and instead goes through his pack, checking off items on a list.

"Have some breakfast," I say, handing him the bag of Sarah's granola.

He takes it and checks one more thing off his list before pausing to eat. Once we've gotten our fill, I tightly seal the bag and put it back in the tent. I'm about to go over our plan for the day when a high-pitched moan comes from somewhere in the distance.

"Bear?" I ask.

"Sounds like it. A very unhappy one." Pike stands and puts

on his pack. We both listen, but the morning is quiet again. "I have bear spray with me, just in case. Is MacGuffin in the same location as last night?"

"Yep. I checked when I got up."

"Good. Let's go then."

We both start out of the campsite at the same time, neither relinquishing our hold as the leader. Pike sighs, heavy and loud, making sure I hear it. Then he begrudgingly puts his hand out in front of him and says, "After you."

"Thank you." I walk in front of him, feeling some of my tension dissolve the closer we get to the owl.

If I don't get MacGuffin home today, curse-free, Cassandra will come looking for him herself. And if she finds him, she'll sense the curse as clearly as if it's a river in the desert, impossible to ignore.

"Are you still mad about last night?" I ask Pike as we get deeper into the woods, wanting to distract myself.

"Grudges are a lot to carry—I try to be discerning in the ones I hold."

I expect him to make a joke or recount the evening back to me, highlighting all the ways in which I acted poorly, but his response is genuine. It's real.

"And my running through a storm at midnight isn't worth the weight?" I ask.

"No, it's not."

I find myself wanting to ask what is worth the weight, what grudges he carries to bed at night, but I don't.

"Besides, you were doing what you thought needed to be done. I'm not so much of a jerk that I'd give you a hard time for that," he says.

"Aren't you? You've given me a hard time for much less."

I hear him laugh behind me—a light, easy laugh that plays on the wind and carries through the trees.

"That's not entirely fair. Sometimes I do it *for* you," he says.

"Oh, this ought to be good."

"It's true. You're so in your head sometimes that it's almost painful watching you, like you're stuck in some kind of loop you can't get out of. But when I give you a hard time, your brain seems to switch into 'bicker with Pike' mode, and it almost acts as a reset, like you forget whatever it was that was bothering you."

I slow my steps, turning to look at him. I'm not sure if I'm annoyed at his words, at his arrogance over thinking he knows how my mind works, or if I'm moved by the sentiment. I think it's both.

"I'm sorry I'm so painful to watch," I say, because I'm not sure how to respond to the other part. The vulnerable part.

"That's not what I meant."

I watch him for another moment, holding his gaze. "I know." Then I start walking again.

"Now who's giving who a hard time?"

I'm about to respond when I take a breath and a strong, metallic scent fills my nose. The unmistakable scent of magic. But I'm not using any magic, and we're out in the middle of nowhere—it's the last thing I should smell out here. My heart beats faster, and a cold sweat breaks out along my forehead and in my palms.

Too much magic.

Pike won't be able to smell it; it would have to be much stronger for anyone other than a witch to notice. But it crashes into my senses like a tidal wave, and I'm covered in it.

I pick up my pace, rushing to where the owl was this morning, the scent getting stronger with every step. If Cassandra starts looking for the owl early and beats me to him, that's it—she'll already know about the curse, and there will be nothing I can do about it.

She'll take me back with her to the council, where I'll be tried in court for attempting to turn a boy into a witch. Even though that's not what I meant. Even though I was just trying to manage my frustration. Even though I'm starting to not-dislike the boy.

He hates witches, I remind myself, something I haven't been thinking of enough on this trip. He hates witches, and I cursed him to become one. That's what this trip is about, and that's where my focus needs to stay.

I follow the scent of magic, rushing over large roots and through dense brambles, ignoring the incessant rain and my too-fast heart and all the what-ifs running rampant in my mind.

We're in the thick of the trees, and I weave out from behind a large spruce when another moan like the one we heard earlier breaks the silence. Only this time, the sound makes my ears ache and reverberates in my chest, so close.

Too close.

"Pike?" I say, stopping cold, holding out my arm so Pike doesn't go any farther. He jolts to a stop by my side, and we both watch the black bear as it lets out another devastating moan.

"Shit. Shit," Pike says under his breath, slowly bringing his pack to his front.

I survey the bear, too afraid to use my magic until I know what's going on. There's a large burn on his backside, red, raw skin interrupted by patches of singed fur. He has been burned, badly, and on the ground next to him are several brown feathers dappled with white. The colors are distorted by blood, and I take a step back as I realize what happened.

The owl's wing is still healing, and he was likely staying close to the ground to avoid strenuous hunts. The black bear must have found him and thought he was easy prey. My stomach twists into knots, picturing their fight. The only way the bear would sustain burns like that—and the air would smell so sharply of metal—is if the owl was injured. As an amplifier, he carries so much magic inside him that it's leaking out of his body from whatever gashes he sustained. That's what burned the bear, and that's why the air is thick with magic.

It's the only explanation.

Pike isn't a mage, though, so I know the owl is still alive, still carrying the curse. I reach for him, following our connection through the magic-drenched trees, and exhale when I find him about a quarter of a mile out.

"We need to do something," Pike says.

The bear lets out another moan and takes a step toward us.

"Whoa, whoa!" Pike shouts, throwing his hands up over his head, standing tall, looking as aggressive as possible.

It's what he's supposed to do. He's responding exactly as he should, but the bear is injured, and I want to help him. If I can get him to the river, that will soothe the burn. I have to try.

But the only way to do that is to run. Anything else would make Pike suspicious. It can't, under any circumstances, look like magic.

I grab at my hem and start shaking where I'm standing, trying to seem panicked.

"Easy, Iris, we're okay," Pike says, falling for it.

I hurry my breaths, making them fast and shallow, and Pike gently touches my arm.

"It doesn't want to hurt us. It's injured," Pike says, his voice steady.

Work with me, I say to the bear, finally sending my magic toward him, coaxing him to come closer.

He listens and takes another step forward, locking his eyes right on mine. Pike stiffens next to me and grabs the bear spray from his pocket. But he's too late.

I run, and the bear takes off after me.

seventeen

It's risky. I send as much magic as I can back to the bear, reassuring him that I'm helping. But I'm also running away, and every instinct inside him is telling him to attack, screaming at him to run faster and faster.

He could easily overtake me, and I drench him in a steady stream of magic, doing everything I can to show him he's safe. I feel the rhythm of his heart, feel the pounding of his paws as he chases after me. His gait is unsteady, favoring the side that isn't burned, but still he runs.

I weave through trees and jump over roots, rain pelting my face, making it difficult to see. I run toward the sound of the river, my hair flying behind me, my heart lifting as if running through the forest with the animals I love is exactly where I'm meant to be. As if nothing, not even a curse or the council or my own loneliness, can touch me out here.

I try so hard to plan for everything, checking and rechecking my lists, staying up at night practicing conversations in my mind, but maybe I've worked so hard to fit my life into a tidy, well-defined box that I've forgotten the most important thing: I'm as wild as the magic in my veins and the dust of the stars, and so I run.

Pike's voice rises above the sound of my heavy breathing, shouting at the bear. Trying to get his attention, to stop him from pursuing me. I feel the bear's focus shifting, getting aggravated with Pike's yelling, and I send more magic his way, telling him it's not much longer.

Pike keeps shouting, chasing after us, and when I risk a look back at him, he's waving a lit flare above his head, trying to pull the bear away from me. It almost makes me laugh how ridiculous it is, but it's also making my job harder. I run faster, and my chest aches, desperate for the inhaler in my pack.

Finally, I see the river up ahead. I tell the bear that relief is coming, that he's doing great, and that the water will make him feel better. When I'm a few feet from the river's edge, I dive to the side, and the bear launches himself into the water.

He sighs with instant relief, and I stay on the ground, heaving, trying to catch my breath. I shift my pack to my front and dig for my inhaler, taking two puffs before lying my head back on the wet earth, closing my eyes.

Pike rushes over and drops to the ground beside me, the lit flare still burning in his hand.

"Put that thing out," I manage to say between breaths.

Pike buries the flare and comes back to my side, watching the bear warily. But the bear isn't paying attention to us, too fixated on submerging his burned flesh. He'll be okay, though; he'll heal.

"What the hell were you thinking?" Pike looks frantic and angry, his eyebrows knit together and his jaw tense.

"I don't know—I got scared," I say, hoping he believes me.

"You know you're never supposed to run! You know that. You could have been killed." Pike looks over my body as if he's reassuring himself that the bear didn't maul me.

"I just... I wasn't thinking. I'm sorry." I look at him, at his wide, anxious eyes, and I suddenly feel guilty for what I put him through. He truly thought the bear was going to attack me.

"You're sorry? Hell, Iris, I just watched you get chased by a bear. I thought—I thought—"

"I'm okay," I tell him, sitting up, forcing him to look me in the eyes. "I'm okay."

"I don't understand. It could have easily caught you."

"The burn on his backside is huge. I'm guessing that was my saving grace."

"Fuck, Iris," Pike says, running his hand through his hair. "That was so reckless."

"I know," I say, hating the way I feel embarrassed, even though I ran intentionally. Even though this was exactly how I needed Pike to react. Angry and relieved, not suspicious.

I touch his arm, and he looks to where my fingers are resting. He slowly brings his eyes to mine. "I'm sorry," I say again, and I mean it.

He holds my gaze, and I'm overcome with the urge to get closer to him, to trace my fingers along his jaw or curl up in his arms. I could do it, scoot closer, lean in, keep my eyes on his even though every part of me is yelling to look away.

I could.

A cold surge of water rolls over me, and I jump, the moment washing away with the river.

"It's flooding," Pike says, pulling me to my feet. We run a few yards away, and when I turn back, the bear is getting out on the opposite side. He looks at me for a moment, and I know he understands what I did for him. I know he's thankful.

"We need to get back to the campsite. Our stuff will flood if we don't move it." His voice is still tense, angry, and I realize how deeply I upset him, how shaken he is by what happened. He starts walking toward the campsite without another word.

Then I remember why the bear was injured in the first place, and I stop.

"Camp is an hour hike in the wrong direction, and we need to go after the owl. Did you see his feathers on the ground? He's injured."

"We won't have anything to help him with if all our gear floats away."

Pike keeps walking, moving farther away from the riverbank, and I follow after him, helpless. He will never understand if I go after the owl alone, and with all the magic in these woods, after everything that happened with the bear, I can't afford his questions. I can't afford for the magic pulling at his mind to crystallize in any way. Deep down, Pike knows I would never make that mistake, I would never run. He knows that's not how I would react.

But my stomach feels as if it drops to the earth as I replay what happened with the bear, the feathers on the ground, the burn. I slow my steps and fall back, seeking out the owl. With the curse still bound to him and his proximity to me, I can survey his injuries, get a sense for how bad things are. But regardless of the extent, he's at a greater risk of being sought out by predators. He's at a greater risk of dying.

And if the owl is at risk, so is Pike.

I stop walking and steady myself against a tree, trying to catch my breath.

It was one thing when the owl was healthy, when I had plenty of time to find him and bring him back to the refuge. But now he's bleeding, an undeniable invitation to other animals, and I can't risk it. I can't keep doing this on my own.

I'll follow Pike back to the campsite, make sure we have the gear we need, and call for help. And if it's too late, if the owl is too injured, I'll grab the herbs I need for the binding ritual and undo the curse right here, in the middle of the trees, with Pike nearby.

I close my eyes and survey the owl, letting my magic move through him. He's bleeding, but his heartbeat is steady and his breathing is even. As long as he's safely off the ground, in a hollow or cavity, he isn't in any immediate danger.

"Stay put," I whisper, more a plea than a command. "Stay alive. I'm coming."

I rush to catch up with Pike, and he turns around when he hears me.

"How the hell did that bear get burned?" Pike asks, talking

more to himself than to me. "It's been pouring rain for the past twenty-four hours, and we haven't seen a single person since we got here."

"Lightning?" I ask, hoping it sounds plausible. "Maybe the bear was up against a tree that was struck?"

Pike is quiet for several minutes, and I don't think he's going to answer. "Maybe," he finally says, and I can hear in his voice how he's trying to put the pieces together, pieces that don't make any sense. Pieces that only fit if magic is part of the equation.

He doesn't speak again, and the silence is awful. I wish I knew what he was thinking, if he's on to me in some way, if his mind is screaming at him that the world is just a little different when I'm around. Animals are just a little calmer.

He's going to find out. Once I call for help, I'll be put on trial for a second time, and Pike will know the secret I've tried so hard to keep from him. From everyone. And I know it's selfish, but I want this time with him, these last moments when he looks at me with curiosity and wonder, as if I'm the best subject he's ever studied.

I'll tell him once the curse is undone and we're back at the refuge, once his life is his again and there's no more risk. I'll tell him, and he'll no longer look at me with curiosity and wonder.

He'll no longer look at me at all.

"What were you planning on doing with that flare?" I ask, trying to get his mind off whatever it's circling around.

"I was trying to distract the bear. Get it to come after me instead."

"Why would you do that?" I ask, and I genuinely want to know. I was the one who ran—whatever came next was mine to endure.

"I don't know. I didn't stop to think about it, but I assume it had something to do with not wanting you to die."

I catch up to Pike and gently touch his wrist. He stops walking and turns to look at me. Sweat is lining his forehead, his hair sticking to it. His glasses are covered in raindrops and his eyes are tired.

"Thank you for what you did," I say. I cursed him, and he tried to stop a bear from attacking me. I've been so worried about the danger that Pike is to me and my family that I haven't stopped to consider the danger I am to Pike. It's his life hanging in the balance, not mine.

"You didn't look scared," he says, watching me. "When you were running. You didn't look scared."

"How did I look?" I ask, meeting his eyes. I won't shy away, won't give him a single reason to think I'm hiding something.

"You looked...free," he finally says. "Wild." He pauses, and his gaze falls to the ground. "Beautiful."

My breath catches in my throat, and I'm speechless. Pike doesn't know who I am, not really, and yet he says certain things that make it feel as if he knows exactly who I am. It's unnerving and terrifying. It's wonderful.

"I don't think I ever developed the proper fear response to animals," I say, going back to his original comment, even though the words that followed have already lodged in my chest.

Free. Wild. Beautiful.

"No, I don't think you did," he says. We watch each other for several seconds, then we start walking again.

The river continues to rise, and when we get back to the campsite, water has already reached my backpack. I silently curse, wishing I would have put it safely in the tent before leaving this morning. The whole thing is soaked, and I get to it just before it floats away. Pike moves his things out of the tent and pulls the stakes from the ground, then he carries it all deeper into the trees before it, too, is claimed by the river.

I survey the damage, and that's when I notice that I left the top of my pack open and multiple things are gone. They must have fallen out and floated away when it tipped over, and I dig in my bag, frantically looking for my herbs.

"No," I say, pulling things out and tossing them aside, desperate to find my supplies. My eyes burn and my head pounds. Once I've emptied everything out, I drop my pack and rush toward the main part of the river, following the current, hoping to see my herbs floating on the surface. But they're gone. All I see are branches and leaves.

I stare at the river, unable to accept it, willing my herbs to materialize at any moment. I need them to unbind the curse— they were the vessel the curse was originally written for; they're powerful enough to hold it.

And now they're gone.

I shove my hands through my hair and pace back and forth. I tell myself it's okay, that the owl is safe for now, but all I can see is Alex on the lake. A sob breaks free from my chest as I picture Pike the same way, flames and smoke and ash, and for a moment, I can't breathe. I pull the inhaler from my day pack, but it isn't enough to fill my lungs, to ease the tightness that's squeezing my airway.

I have to call for help.

I rush to where Pike is setting up the tent, a stretch of earth between two large oaks, mostly free of roots and brambles. It's at an incline, far enough away to avoid the flooding river. A bunch of ferns sit at the base of the trees, their leaves somehow even richer when covered in rain, and pale lichen crawls along the oaks' bark, climbing and climbing. I wish I could enjoy it.

"I have to get down to the trailhead," I say, too fast. "I need to call my mom, and I don't have reception up here."

"Is everything okay?" Pike asks.

"I just want to update my mom. Let her know we need more time." He studies me for a minute, then kneels down and opens his backpack.

"I have a satellite phone," Pike says. "You can use that."

"You have a sat phone?"

"Of course. I wouldn't be very prepared if I didn't."

"Well, you didn't have an extra tent, so I was starting to question it," I say, and it feels good, joking with him. Pretending that things are normal. That things are okay.

Pike laughs and shakes his head, digging through his pack until he finds the phone. He turns it on and waits for a signal, then hands it over to me.

"Thanks. I'll be right back," I say, moving far enough away so he can't hear me. Then I grab my phone and go to my contacts, pulling up the number Mom gave me for Cassandra.

I take a deep breath, press the numbers, and make the call.

Cassandra answers on the third ring, and even though the connection is weak, her voice distant, distorted by static, it's enough to make my eyes burn. She used to feel like family, like an older sister, but Amy's verdict and my trial changed everything, and I'm not prepared for the rush of memories and emotions that accompany those two words from her mouth: "Cassandra Meadows."

I'm silent for a moment, unable to speak.

"Hello?" she asks.

I clear my throat and finally find my voice. "Cassandra, it's Iris."

"Hello, Iris. Your mother informed me that you're trying to track your lost amplifier."

"That's why I'm calling," I say, holding the phone with one hand and balling up the fabric of my shirt in the other. "It's injured." I tell her about the bear we encountered, but I leave out the curse for now.

"That explains the change in energy we've felt on the mountain," Cassandra says once I'm finished. "There's been a large influx of magic, and I suspect it's coming from the amplifier."

"I need your help," I say. "I think we can save him if we can get him back to the refuge, but I haven't been able to catch him on my own."

Cassandra is quiet for a moment, and I can hear her talking in the background to someone else. "Where are you in relation to the owl?"

It took us about an hour to reach the bear, and with the owl flying even farther away, into dense woods with no trails, we're probably looking at twice that. "At least a two-hour hike."

"If there's a chance of survival, we want to take it. But given the rain and how far out you are, I want to wait until the morning to go after him, and you should do the same. Otherwise, you'll be hiking back in the dark."

"I don't think waiting is a good idea. I'm worried he won't make it through the night." I try to keep my voice from betraying my panic, but it's so hard. My entire body pulses with it.

"We want to heal the amplifier as much as you do, but we won't risk our witches to do it. The terrain here goes from tricky to treacherous once the sun goes down, and the rain only makes it worse. Hold on," she says, talking away from the phone to whomever she's with.

"We'll spell the owl," she finally says. "We can reach him using the magic he's leaking. The spell will slow down his injuries and give him more time, if the situation is truly that dire. It won't last very long, but it will get him through the night. You can resume your search in the morning, and I'll be on my way as well."

I breathe out in relief. Cassandra is more experienced than I am, more powerful. If she says her magic will get the owl through the night, I believe her.

"I'll start back up first thing in the morning," I say, giving her our exact location. She's farther out, so she'll be a few hours behind us, but she's coming. She'll help.

I thought I'd be scared, terrified of what Cassandra might do to me when she arrives and feels the curse that's lodged in the owl. And I am. But more than anything, I'm relieved. Cassandra will help, and Pike will be safe.

"I'll see you tomorrow," she says, then she hangs up before I can reply.

I clutch the phone in my hand for several seconds as raindrops roll down my face, and I take a deep breath. This is my last night before Cassandra arrives and finds the curse—she's too far from the owl to sense it now, even with her spell, but it will be impossible to miss once she's closer.

It's my last night knowing my mom will sleep soundly, mercifully unaware of what I've done.

It's my last night with Pike before he learns more than I ever wanted him to know.

I walk back to where Pike is standing and hand him his phone. He was nice enough to haul my stuff up to the new campsite, and I reach for my pack, knocking it over instead. The pockets are all still open from when I searched for my herbs, and I'm horrified when the condom falls out onto the dirt, directly in front of Pike.

"I'll get that!" I say, dropping to the ground to pick it up. But I'm too late, and Pike holds it out to me, raising his eyebrows.

"That's not what it looks like," I say, grabbing it from him and shoving it back into my pack. I might never forgive my mom for this, for the way Pike watches me with a tight expression, as if he's trying his hardest not to burst out laughing. My skin must be a million shades of red, and I look behind me and down and up, anywhere to avoid his face.

"It isn't?" he asks, amusement dancing on his lips.

"I mean, it is, but it isn't mine," I say, stumbling over my words. I've never really been in a relationship before, save for a few crushes, a few dates here and there, and this moment might ensure I never am, since I'm fairly certain I'm about to die from embarrassment.

"Whose is it?" He barely makes it through the question without laughing.

"Can we not talk about it anymore? That would be great," I say, zipping my pack closed and shoving it aside.

"Whatever you want." He shakes his head and laughs, and I'm tempted to get his sat phone back and call my mom, just so I can express my extreme dissatisfaction over the situation she created for me. But that will have to wait.

"Thank you," I manage to get out.

Pike moved our campsite far enough up the incline to avoid the rising river, and he clears a new spot for a small fire under his makeshift shelter. It's relatively dry, a large boulder leaning against the trunk of a tree that's shielding the ground from much of the rain, and there's a small circle of rocks he found that reminds me of my stone circle back home.

Pike is completely soaked. His hair rests flat against his head, and I watch as raindrops fall from the ends. He looks up at the sky and shakes his head.

"We're not going to have enough light to get the owl back here," he says, and I'm so thankful we're moving on to a new topic.

"I know."

We look at each other, and I wonder why my stomach feels too light when Pike's expression turns serious, why my heart beats faster when his eyes linger on mine for a breath longer than I'm expecting.

"I've got another night in me if you do," he says.

"You're not missing your *National Geographic* special too much?" I ask, getting us back to normal, letting the routine soothe all my worries and what-ifs.

But he doesn't laugh, doesn't come back with a sarcastic comment or a witty retort. Instead, he holds my gaze.

"No," he says. "I'm not missing anything."

And just like that, I no longer want our normal. I no longer want our routine. As his words slide through me, all my frayed edges and empty spaces wake with the sound, coming alive in a way I don't expect.

It isn't magic, per se.

But then again, maybe it is.

eighteen

The rain has stopped, and the wind is dying down, the constant roar of it dulling into a gentle rustling that will be perfect to sleep to. The fire is almost out, and I watch the deep amber flames as they crackle and spit in the night. I've checked on the owl close to a dozen times, and each time he's in the same place. His heartbeat is even. The curse is waiting.

I tell myself over and over that I have no reason to believe he won't survive. Cassandra's magic is powerful—far more than mine—and she cast a spell that will keep him safe through the night. Even still, I reach for him, and like every other time this evening, he's stable, just as Cassandra promised.

I feel a gentle tug in the magic between me and the owl, as if he knows I'm here, as if he believes that I'll come for him as soon as I can. He's waiting for me.

"Iris?" Pike asks, sending my magic scattering into the night, my connection to the owl broken.

"Sorry, what?"

"Where were you just now? You looked like you were in a trance or something."

"I must have been lost in thought," I say, bringing my focus back to the present. To the boy sitting next to me.

I look at him, firelight bouncing off his glasses, casting a warm orange glow over his features. I have an overwhelming desire to tell him about the curse, to lay it all out there and see how he'll pick up the pieces. He has surprised me a lot over the past few days, and it makes me hope that maybe he can surprise me again. Maybe I can tell him exactly who I am, and maybe he'll accept it. Accept me.

Mom could be right. His jokes and comments could be empty, with no real weight to them. But then I think back to that day in the office, to the tone of his voice and the intensity in his eyes, to the cruel words he spoke about Amy, and I know deep down that he's carrying something that has unquestionably shaped his view of witches. And it isn't good.

"One of these days, I'd like to get lost with you," he says, and I laugh.

"Trust me, you really don't."

Pike hands me a small twig, my whole body responding when his fingers brush mine. "Here, this might help."

"What's it for?" I ask.

"A wish. My brother made it up on one of our camping trips, and it kind of stuck. Just as the fire is about to die, you make a wish on the twig and toss it into the flames. The wish will burn, half of it drifting away on the wind, the other half turned into ash for the soil."

It reminds me so much of what my grandma taught me, of my own ritual to give things to the earth, and it makes me want to cry. He makes wishes and I craft spells—are the two really that different?

"I love that," I say quietly.

"Yeah, me too. Maybe it will help with whatever's on your mind."

"Maybe," I say, the word getting caught in my throat, barely audible.

Pike holds his twig out in front of him. "Okay, close your eyes and make a wish."

And I do. I squeeze my eyes shut and clutch the twig in my hand. I wish for a successful morning where I find the owl and unbind the curse before anyone gets hurt, eliminating the risk to Pike and this region that I love so much. I want so badly for it to happen that the twig shakes in my hand.

I open my eyes, and Pike is watching me. "Ready?" He asks.

I nod, and Pike counts to three. Then we throw our twigs into the fire, watching our wishes turn to smoke and ash. It's not as therapeutic as casting a spell, but it's nice. Calming in a similar way.

I lean toward the fire and hold my hands to the weakening flames, gathering the last of their heat. Then the final flame dies out, and all that's left are glowing embers filled with wishes.

"We have an early day tomorrow. Should we get some sleep?" Pike asks.

Smoke rises between us, and I watch as it twists and curves in front of his face until it's gone. Then I stand.

"I can sleep outside tonight if you'd rather," he says, pouring water over the hot embers.

"No, I'm comfortable with it if you are," I say, even though my stomach twists tighter and tighter the closer we get to the tent. Pike leads the way with a flashlight and holds the flap open for me to crawl in. He follows and turns on the lantern to the dimmest setting, and somehow, the tent feels even smaller tonight.

We stick to the same routine, facing away from each other as we change out of our damp clothes, then Pike holds up the corner of the sleeping bag for me and I slip under. When I can finally bring myself to look at him, I'm disappointed to see he's in sweats instead of his pajamas.

"Why aren't you wearing your pajamas?" I ask, partly because it's fun but mainly because I find them devastatingly cute.

"They sadly didn't survive the fall," he laments. "Thin fabric."

"Ah," I say, keeping myself from laughing as I remember him falling face-first out of his tent. "You should get another pair."

"Way ahead of you. I placed an online order while we were at the general store."

"Of course you did," I say.

Pike turns off the lantern, and I burrow into the sleeping bag, thinking of how calming it is to be under the cover of the trees. Or how calming it would be, if Pike Alder wasn't right next to me. Every part of me is aware of how close we are, of how easy it would be to move my hand and brush his fingers with my own. Each of his inhales makes the sleeping bag rise just slightly, and each of his exhales fills the space between us, waiting for me to breathe it in. Breathe *him* in.

And I do.

I breathe him in.

"Do you miss your dad?" Pike asks, catching me off guard.

Something about being in total darkness with him, about the way he can't see my face or read my expression, makes me want to say the things I wouldn't normally say. Maybe that's what this last night is for, to say whatever we want, to wrap our words in darkness and give them to the other person.

"Yes. I wish I didn't though."

"Why?"

"Because I don't think he deserves to be missed after what he put us through."

Pike shifts, the sleeping bag sliding over me as he moves. I remain perfectly still, as if taking too deep a breath could put me on top of him.

"That's fair," he says, his voice quiet and thoughtful. "But the missing part. That isn't really for him. It's for you."

"What do you mean?" I ask.

"Missing someone is just a form of grief. Grieving that they're gone, grieving that they're too far away, grieving that you'll never see them again. Whatever kind of grief it is, the missing is just a symptom of it."

"But I don't want to grieve someone who was never supposed to leave."

"Then don't grieve that he's gone," Pike says. "Grieve that he turned out to be such an asshole."

I almost laugh, the words surprising in such a delicate conversation. "I like that shift."

"It's all about perspective," Pike says. "Or so they say."

There's a pause, and I think he's done talking. Then: "Do you think we could ever get to a place where you'd miss me?"

"Are you planning on going somewhere?" I ask, keeping my voice light, compensating for the way his got heavy.

"I'm being serious."

I stare up at the ceiling, even though I can't see anything. My throat feels tight, aching, and I'm terrified of what I'm about to ask. I take a breath. "Why would you want to be missed by me?"

"Because you're special, Iris. You're strange and surprising, and I'm endlessly curious about the things that take up space in your mind."

"A lot of worst-case scenarios," I say in a casual tone, trying to ignore the way his words enter my bloodstream and rush through my body, the way my heart beats faster and my mind whispers that this is maybe the best thing anyone has ever said to me.

"You do tend to jump to the worst possible outcome," he says, pulling the sleeping bag up to his chin.

"You're very observant."

"I am. And that's not the only thing I've observed."

"Oh yeah? What else have you noticed?" I ask, keeping the conversation light. Light is good. Light is safe.

Pike shifts and rolls onto his side, facing me. All the air in the tent becomes charged at once, and I finally take the breath I need, holding it in my lungs, hoping he can't tell how tense I am, how hard I'm working to keep it together.

"You double-check everything, sometimes triple-check. You pace when you're stressed. You push your palm to your chest when you're worried about something. You add vitamin D to your mom's coffee every morning when she isn't looking. You wear your hair up when we have group tours and down the rest of the time. When Sarah brings in doughnuts, you let everyone else pick theirs before you pick your own, including me. Your favorite color is green. And when I say something that annoys you, you give me an expression I've never seen you give anyone else. So I keep annoying you, just so you'll make the face you only make for me."

My heart pounds and my mind races with everything he just said. "Pike," I say, slowly rolling to my side, so close I can feel his breath on my skin. "We both know you can't help how annoying you are."

"It's only because I'm right all the time, and you hate that." His tone is low and heavy, at odds with the words he just spoke.

"I suppose I would hate it," I say quietly, "if you were ever right."

He laughs, so quiet I feel it more than hear it. "Here's the thing. You spend all this time in your head and carry around all these worries, but it doesn't actually change the fact that there's something about you that seems entirely at home in this world, more so than anyone I've ever met. I don't know how to describe it," he says, trailing off.

I'm afraid to move, afraid to breathe, afraid to speak. Afraid of losing this moment that feels as if I'm seeing myself for the first time, as if Pike is holding up a mirror, allowing me to look past all my fears and see the girl beneath them all.

"Effortless," he says, reflecting someone who can't possibly be me. "You're effortless."

His fingertips find my face, slowly tracing down the bridge of my nose and over my mouth. I inhale sharply, thinking this is probably the worst idea I've ever had, second only to the curse I put on him.

I close my eyes and part my lips, feeling his touch in every part of me, my body coming to life as his fingers move over my chin and down the center of my neck before pulling away. Everything is heightened due to the dark, every sound and touch, my senses wild with how close he is. I reach out and take his hand, wrap it around my waist and push his palm into the small of my back. For several moments we stay that way, unmoving, listening to the wind and the river and each other's breaths. Then he pulls me closer, and his mouth meets mine.

He kisses me slowly, moving his fingers up my spine and into my hair. I know I should pull away, should tell him about the owl and the curse, let him decide if he wants to be kissing a witch. But instead, I push into him more, getting closer.

Either I will unbind the curse and make this right or I won't and I'll ruin everything, but either way, I want this moment that's untouched by tragedy and curses and magic, this moment that's wholly ours, away from whatever is waiting for us in the morning.

Right now, I can be a girl kissing the boy she likes instead of a witch kissing the boy she cursed.

I open my mouth just slightly, and Pike exhales, the sound traveling all the way through me. He rolls me onto my back, and I reach up with both hands to touch his face and jaw and neck. I feel the plastic of his glasses and pause.

"Wait," I say.

Pike pulls back and asks if I'm okay.

"Will you turn on the lantern?"

He turns it to its dimmest setting, illuminating the tent in a soft glow. He sits back on his heels, breathing heavy, searching my eyes. I sit up on my knees so I'm facing him, watching him in the light.

"Are you okay?" he asks again, his voice gentle and concerned.

"Yes," I say. "I want to see you without your glasses. Really see you."

Pike takes my hands and guides them to his face. I slowly take off his glasses and set them aside, never once looking away. He blinks but keeps his eyes on mine, and I'm struck by how vulnerable he looks, how unprotected he is in this moment. No arrogance or ego or witty remarks, no perfectly fitted T-shirt or unfairly cool glasses.

Just Pike, honest and raw and perfect.

He takes my breath away, and I gently trace the corners of his eyes before pressing my mouth to his once more. His hands come to either side of my face, and he kisses me with urgency and need, turning off the lantern and laying me back, his mouth moving from my lips to my jaw to my neck.

Goose bumps rise all over my body when his fingers trace the skin above my pants. I want to pull them off, to get closer to Pike than I've ever been to anyone else, but that foolish hope in the back of my mind tells me to wait, says that maybe Pike will choose me, magic and all. Maybe he'll still want me in the same way once he knows.

I slide his hands up to my ribs and arch into him, deepening the kiss, trying so hard to forget the things that are waiting for me come dawn. Trying so hard to hope that whatever this is can survive in the daylight.

I think I hear the owl in the distance, so close to where we are, but it could just be a trick of the wind. A trick of my mind.

I pull the sleeping bag above our heads, Pike's arm around my waist and lips against my mouth, shrinking our world to the tiniest of points in this impossibly vast universe.

And for just a moment, I do. I forget.

nineteen

When I wake up, Pike is gone. Birds are singing from all directions, and just enough light is pouring into the tent for me to see. The dawn is here, and with it, all the heaviness of the day. The fear. The enormous ramifications if I don't get this right.

But also, hope. So much hope.

I hear Pike out in the campsite, and disappointment stirs in my gut, wishing I could have seen him as he woke up, tired and groggy and without his glasses. The thought makes my breath catch, and I immediately reach for the owl, needing to feel his heartbeat and the curse and know that everything is as it was last night.

And it is. He is in the same place, waiting, just like he promised.

I crawl out of the tent and brighten considerably when I see Pike warming two bagels over the fire, spreading them with butter. He really is good at this.

He looks up and smiles when he sees me, a soft, happy smile that lodges right in my chest. "Morning," he says.

"Morning."

I walk over to the fire, unsure of how to act, but he pulls me toward him and kisses me softly. "How'd you sleep?"

"The best I've slept since we left the refuge," I admit.

"Me too."

He hands me a bagel, and I gratefully take it, eager to get on with the day. I sit down on the blanket and realize how clean the campsite is.

"Did you pack up this morning?"

"A little. I know you wanted to get an early start, so I figured I'd help out. I hope that's okay."

"That's great, thank you."

"Is the owl in the same spot?" Pike asks.

I nod, the hope in my chest getting bigger.

"Good; he's not too far away then, but with the rough terrain, it'll probably take us a couple hours."

Pike finishes his bagel, then sets his napkin aside and pulls up his legs so he's sitting in a V shape. He rests his arms on his knees, and his hair is perfectly disheveled with sleep. He's wearing joggers and a sweatshirt, and I don't know how else to describe how he looks in this moment other than *lived in*.

Lived in, like my favorite pair of jeans or the blanket my grandmother knit for me.

I almost tell him, right now, the words that I've refused to say for over two years.

I'm a witch.

I almost say it as if it's nothing, as if I'm commenting on the weather or the birds singing in the trees. Almost. But I don't know how I'd handle it if his expression slipped into something unrecognizable, and I have to save all my energy for finding the owl and unbinding the curse. Those are the only things that matter right now.

We finish our breakfast and get cleaned up, then ready our day packs for our hike. I run through my list in my head and make sure Pike has the supplies for our makeshift trap. Once we're ready, I slip my pack over my shoulders and put on my cap.

It's overcast and cool, the earth damp with rain, and I inhale slowly, knowing this will all be fixed today, knowing Cassandra is coming. Maybe Pike would be one of the lucky ones who would survive being turned into a mage, and maybe I would be strong enough to get him through it. Maybe the effects on the region wouldn't be as bad as I fear and things would be okay, even if the curse was unleashed.

I'm not willing to find out, though. Amy's magic was strong for her age, a Stellar whose effect on those around her was profound. And she couldn't stop what happened to Alex. I used to think that falling in love was her catastrophic mistake, the failure point that led to that night on the beach.

But it wasn't. Her mistake was her arrogance, believing that death wasn't a risk because she'd be strong enough to stop it.

I won't make that same mistake.

"Ready?" Pike asks.

I take a deep breath. "Ready."

He squeezes my hand. "Let's go get him."

"Did you know that crows can hold grudges against people?" Pike asks as we veer off the main trail and begin our hike up the rugged mountainside. In true Pike fashion, he doesn't wait for me to answer and instead keeps talking. "They're extremely smart birds. If they feel threatened by you, they can remember your face for years. Not only that, they can warn their crow buddies about you, and they'll hold a grudge against you, too."

"That's pretty amazing."

"It is. Leo thought if crows could hold grudges against people, they could also learn to like him, so he started to feed a couple of the crows behind our house. They were hesitant at first, but over time, they started to trust him, and sure enough, they stopped by our house every day around the same time, waiting for Leo."

"I love that he did that," I say, keeping pace with Pike, hope building in my chest with each step forward.

"Me too. One of my biggest regrets is that we forgot about the crows in the days after his death. I wish I would have remembered to feed them, but I didn't, and they stopped coming once they realized he was gone. I still feel awful about it."

"What happened to him?" I ask gently, unsure if I'm allowed to ask or not.

Pike doesn't say anything at first, and I start to tell him he doesn't have to answer when he finally speaks. "He got sick. Really sick, with a rare kind of cancer. By the time the doctors found it, there was only one treatment option available, and it would have made him even sicker with no guarantee of being successful." Pike steps over a large tree trunk, and I hear him take a breath before he keeps going.

"Anyway, we tried it and it was terrible. It made him so sick, and after the course of the treatment, his PET scan was worse than before we started. It didn't do a damn thing. My dad knew a woman in his rowing club who did alternative forms of medicine, and he asked her about it. She urged him and my mom to let her care for Leo, told them she'd had successes with kids in the past, even one who had the same type of cancer as him. My parents fought about it a lot; my mom wanted to keep Leo home and comfortable, and my dad wanted to try the alternative medicine. I'm not sure how he won out, but they went with the woman, and she ended up being a total fraud. They paid her thousands of dollars and completely depleted their savings to do it. As soon as she got the money, she left town, and Leo died not long after."

"Oh, Pike, that's devastating," I say, my entire body hurting with the weight of his story. "I'm so sorry your family went through that."

Pike stops and turns to face me. "Thank you," he says, running his fingers up the straps of my pack. "It was a really difficult time for our family, and obviously something we won't ever fully recover from. Mom and Dad were able to stay together though, after lots of counseling, and I'm thankful for that."

I nod, thinking about what it would take to rebuild a marriage after that kind of tragedy. Pike looks at me, and I can tell there's more he wants to say, debating with himself on if he should or not.

"You asked me once why I hate witches so much," Pike says, my blood turning cold. "That's why. The woman, she was a witch. She convinced my dad that magic was the only thing that could cure cancer as aggressive as Leo's. That was her alternative form of medicine: magic. Nothing we could see or feel. We just had to trust that every time we brought Leo in, every time they wrote her another check, she was doing something for him. And when she got her final payment from them—the biggest one—she left. We found out later we weren't the only family she did that to; she'd pocketed over a million dollars from families like ours."

For a moment, I can't speak. I can't think. My legs start to shake and threaten to buckle beneath me.

All that bravado and joking in the office, rolling his eyes and making harsh comments, it was all to cover up this deep, gaping wound left by an unimaginably cruel witch who took advantage of his family in the most unforgivable way.

I should tell him. He has a right to know, but how can I tell him that the reason we're out here is because I too am a witch, and I cursed him?

I cursed him.

My eyes sting and a lump forms in my throat, so big I can't swallow around it. It's suddenly hard to breathe, and I pull my inhaler from my side pocket, taking two long puffs.

"Are you okay?" Pike asks, searching my eyes, so much concern and care. So much honesty.

"I'm sorry," I say, trying to steady my breaths. "I just... That's horrible, what happened to you and your family. I can't even imagine." I wrap my arms around him and hold him close, not wanting to let go. He rests his head in the crook of my neck, then pulls back and kisses me on the forehead.

"Thank you for listening," he says. "I haven't talked about it in a long time. I think maybe I needed that."

"Thank you for trusting me with it," I say, hating myself with each word.

Pike kisses me once more, then begins hiking again. He tells me more facts about birds and the ones that were Leo's favorites, and I listen to it all as a slow dread builds inside me, devouring all my hope and telling me over and over that this will never be okay. Even if we find the owl and Pike never knows I cursed him, we can't be together.

Because being together can lead to love, and you can't be loved without being known. If I show Pike who I am after everything he told me, he will never accept me, let alone love me. And I refuse to keep up this lie so that we can be together, because he can't choose me if he doesn't know who he's choosing. And I want to be chosen.

After everything that has already happened to his family at the hands of a witch, he met another one who went and cursed him.

My lungs strain with the effort to take a full breath, and I push my palm to my sternum, pleading with my body and mind to get me through this. I can't have an anxiety attack right now, can't lose myself to it and make it about me when Pike just shared so much of who he is. This is his story, his past, his life, and I have to absorb it all until every cell in my body understands what an awful thing I did.

I remember that situation with the witch who defrauded Pike's family. It was a huge deal in the witching community because it was one of the only recent cases where a witch was both rid of her ability to use magic and sent to jail. Or it was, until Amy. I remember sitting around the dinner table, talking about it with my parents and grandmother, remember how disgusted they were to learn of it.

I want to reach out and tell Pike that we aren't all that way, that damning every witch for the actions of one isn't fair. That we could be together and he could trust me and we could be happy.

But it isn't true.

If the curse is unleashed, it will spread for miles and miles, affecting Pike and everyone he has ever loved. If what I know about curses and amplifiers is correct, some of them won't survive, and it will be my fault.

That's unforgivable.

The best thing I can do now is lay to rest any hope of what Pike and I could have been in another life and instead focus on this life and this curse and making sure it never touches Pike. Making sure he can live the way he wants to, not with magic he was cursed to carry by the girl he fell for.

My thoughts are interrupted by a faint, metallic smell that tinges the air. I catch it just briefly before it's gone, but I'm sure of it. I stop and look around, trying to find the source, but it's long gone by now, carried away by the wind.

Then I smell it again, and I know the owl has gotten worse. Magic leaks into the air like a poison, and I search the ground for any signs of him. But there's nothing here. Cassandra's spell has faded, and the magic inside the owl is draining into this mountainside, too much and too fast.

I rush around Pike and start running, faster and faster, my legs burning. If there's enough magic that I can smell it, then it won't be long before Cassandra senses it, too. If she hasn't already.

"Iris, are you okay?" Pike yells behind me, running to keep up. "Iris, stop!" he says, reaching out for my hand, pulling me back. It takes everything in me not to yank my arm away and keep running, desperately trying to reach the owl.

"We're close," I say, my voice frantic, looking everywhere except his eyes. "We have to find him."

"That's what we're doing," Pike says, confusion lining his face.

He pulls out his map and compass, and I put my hands on top of my head and pace back and forth, needing to move.

"If he's still where he was earlier, we're about twenty minutes away," Pike says. He tucks his things back into his pocket and cuts through the trees, deeper into the woods where a northern spotted owl can hide.

The metallic scent gets stronger the farther into the forest we go. He must be in bad shape, perhaps from his wing or the bear or both. Magic is everywhere, coating everything, and all I can hope is that the trees absorb most of it, keep it from the humans and other animals in the area.

It's so much worse than I thought, and I can't stay still. Even when I tell myself to walk at Pike's pace, to not make a scene, I can't listen. I run ahead, willing the owl to come into view, searching the trees and the stumps and the hollows. My boot catches on an exposed root, and I fall to the ground, hard. My knee crashes into a sharp rock on the way down, and I cry out.

"Shit," I say, pulling my leg to my chest. Pain radiates from my knee, and I rock back and forth, angry at myself for being so careless.

Pike comes up from behind me and drops to the ground, gently placing a hand on my back. "What did you hurt?"

"My knee," I say, taking a shaky breath.

"Let's have a look."

I can already see the blood seeping through my pant leg. Pike carefully lifts the fabric so he can get to the cut, and I close my eyes, cursing when I see how bad it is.

"It's pretty deep," Pike says, inspecting the gash. "I can bandage it up, but it's going to need stitches." He sighs and gives me an apologetic look. "I think it's probably time to go home."

"What? No," I say, too aware of the panic that's entered my voice. "We're so close." I try to ignore the pain in my leg and the blood running down my shin.

"I know, but this needs medical attention. I don't want it to get infected."

"Just bandage me up, okay? We can clean it, wrap it up, and look for the owl, then I can go to urgent care as soon as we're done."

Pike looks at me, obviously conflicted by what I'm saying.

"Please," I say. "We're so close."

He sighs, heavy and loud, then digs through his pack for his first aid kit. He starts cleaning the cut, and I hold my leg steady and look up at the trees. My knee is throbbing, and the gash stings every time Pike goes near it. I suck in a sharp breath and hold it, trying to stay calm.

"I don't understand," Pike says as he cleans up the blood. "This clearly hurts like hell, you need stitches, but you keep going on about the owl. I don't get it."

"That owl, he's important, okay? He's important." My tone is pleading, begging him to understand, but how could he? How could he possibly know the weight of the situation we're in?

"Why is it so important? Explain it to me, please."

"I've told you before, it's a threatened species, and this one is ours. He's my responsibility." I hear how weak it sounds, how ridiculous it is given our current situation. But it's all I can think of to say.

It starts to rain, small drops at first that turn big and cold in the span of a breath. I look up and blink, water pouring over us and washing away the blood on my leg.

"There's something you're not telling me," Pike says, not looking at me. He pulls a bandage from his kit and tears it open. "You always know exactly where the owl is, and sometimes it looks as if you're in a trance," he says quietly, almost like he's thinking out loud.

He's gentle as he cleans the cut on my leg, even as he's questioning me. Even as he's realizing I'm not telling him the truth. It breaks something open inside me.

"Please tell me what I'm missing." He's so close to me, and I have the incredible urge to reach out and touch him, to feel the raindrops on his skin.

"There's nothing. It's been a long few days and we're both exhausted. Let's just find the owl and get down the mountain so I can deal with my leg." The words sound hollow coming out of my mouth.

"Don't patronize me," Pike says, and it kills me, the way he sounds more upset than angry. He trusted me with his deepest hurt, and I can't even give him the truth.

A million different words form in my mouth, but I can't make myself say any of them.

Pike finishes wrapping my leg, then he packs up his things and his eyes meet mine. His gaze is intense, willing me to speak, but I don't say a word.

He shakes his head and walks away.

twenty

I want to go after him, but I'm frozen in place. My vision fades, replaced with total darkness, and tiny pinpricks of light appear, bright and sparkling, like the stars away from the city. Relief rushes through me as I realize Cassandra is on her way, using magic on me to find my location.

Almost as soon as it comes, though, it's gone. She got what she needed. I know it's a good thing, I know I'm in over my head, but I can't help the way my stomach rolls with unease and dread crawls up my throat. I want her help. I *need* her help. And yet all I can see is the look on Amy's face in that field when Cassandra removed her ability to sense magic, as if the entire world had vanished to nothing. Total emptiness.

I'm relieved Cassandra's coming, relieved for Pike and anyone else who could get in the way of this curse. And I'm terrified for me.

I push myself off the ground and try to get reoriented, unsteady from Cassandra's magic. Pike is in the distance, and I tell myself to ignore him, to let him go and finish this on my own. But seeing him walk away, his back to me and his head down, it's unbearable. It physically hurts, my body aching with the sight of it. I replay our conversation from earlier, the way he shared his pain and grief, and I can't let him walk away. I can't.

"Pike, wait!" I call after him, running away from the owl and toward the person who has become so much to me in so little time. My knee screams with the pain of it, and I can already feel fresh blood moving down my leg. But still, I run.

Pike keeps walking, and I hurry after him, slowing when the decline gets steeper. The rain falls steadily, and the moss-covered rocks and fallen trees are slick as ice.

I want to yell at Pike that we don't have time for this, that he's being childish by walking away. But more than that, I want to beg him not to be mad at me, to hear me out when the time comes, still holding onto a foolish hope that I won't have to give him up.

"Pike, please!" I finally catch up to him, but he doesn't stop. I grab his wrist and turn him, forcing him to meet my eyes. "Pike, I'm sorry, okay? I'm exhausted and my leg is killing me, I'm afraid the owl is hurt and I miss my mom, and watching you walk away from me did something weird to my insides and I don't like it." I take an unsteady breath. "Please don't give up on me now. Please." I'm out of breath by the time I'm done talking. The patter of rain-drops echo around us, and my clothes are soaked through, but I don't care.

Pike exhales, and I watch the way his shoulders lower with the motion. His jaw is tense, and I can't read his face. "So you aren't keeping anything from me?"

I don't want to lie to him, but there isn't enough time for the conversation we need to have. I will tell him, one day, when there isn't an owl carrying a deadly curse. And when I do, I'll tell him everything, leaving nothing out. Then I'll ask for his forgiveness.

But for now, I look Pike directly in the eye and say, "No, I'm not keeping anything from you." The words taste awful on the way out, and guilt burns hot in my throat.

"Okay," he says, watching me. "I believe you. I'm sorry I walked off like that." He takes a deep breath. "Are we okay?"

"Yeah, of course." His apology makes this so much worse. I try to give him a reassuring smile, but I can't form one under the weight of my lies.

"Good," he says, not seeming to notice. He cocks his head to the side and looks at me. "What did you mean when you said your insides did something weird when I walked away?"

I almost laugh because it's so Pike Alder to make me say it. And after what he just asked me, all I want is to tell him something true. "You seriously can't help yourself, can you?"

"I just want to make sure I understand what you're saying," he says, and I'm so thankful for the playful tone entering his voice. So thankful that he isn't completely done with me.

"I like you, okay? That's what I'm saying."

He takes a step closer to me and looks down, a smile tugging at the corner of his mouth. "I like you, too."

He leans down and kisses me, and I feel so much relief that I could collapse right here on the soaking wet earth. His mouth is warm against the cold spring rain, and I breathe him in as if he is the solution to all my problems, the only thing that matters.

I reluctantly pull away, memorizing the way his hair is slicked down his forehead, the way his glasses are dotted with raindrops. There are so many things to do, but kissing in the rain is not one of them.

"Please don't go," I say, looking at him. "MacGuffin is just as much your owl as he is mine at this point. And we're close to him."

Pike frowns, looking down at my pant leg soaked through with blood. "Are you sure? That looks really bad."

"I can barely feel it," I say casually, even though my knee is throbbing in pain.

"I'm pretty sure that's a bad thing," he says.

"You know what I mean. I'm fine for a while longer."

"Okay, but if you pass out and die from infection, I can't be held responsible."

"Deal," I say, marveling at how quickly he's joking with me again. He believed me when I said I wasn't keeping anything from him, took the words at face value and moved on.

Grudges are a lot to carry—I try to be discerning in the ones I hold.

The words rush into my mind, and I want to cry, knowing the ones he's holding. Wondering if he will ever be able to get over my deceit when I am the thing he hates most in the world.

I clear my throat and turn around, making my way through

the thick of the forest. Pike walks next to me, and we go slowly to account for my leg. It hurts to put weight on it, and each step seems to open it up a little bit more. But we're getting closer to the owl, and that's all that matters.

The rain is starting to let up, and I'm thankful for the weather, relieved that no one else is here. Pike and I climb steadily, not stopping for conversation or water or rest breaks. My lungs are heaving with the effort, and I take a puff from my inhaler as I climb.

I can sense how this is shifting, and I know in my gut these are our final hours. Cassandra is on her way, close enough to use her magic on me, and the owl doesn't have another night left in the absence of care, either medical or magical. It's almost over, and I will have fixed this or not. There's no in-between, not with something like this. Not with a curse.

As quickly as I can, I reach for the owl. I know we're close, but the connection is weak, so much dimmer than it was earlier. I can feel him, but barely. He's losing a lot of blood and a lot of magic, and his time is running out.

I force myself to concentrate on the steps in front of me, refusing to spiral into all the consequences of what happens if the owl dies.

We're deep in the forest now. Ferns cover the ground, their leaves heavy with the recent rain, and moss clings to stones and hangs from branches. Shades of green color the woods and remind me of how much life is here. The rain makes everything more lush, more vital, and I wonder at all the magic held in these trees, all the magic that has been absorbed over hundreds of years.

I don't know who I'll be if I lose my connection to this. My dad didn't get it and Pike doesn't trust it, but magic is the one constant that has made sense to me my entire life. I don't want to lose it.

"We're here," Pike says, looking at his maps. He slips his compass back into his pocket and reaches for his binoculars. I take off my cap and push back my hair, pacing around while Pike begins to search. There isn't time for me to pretend to look, though, and I'm about to follow the magic when four loud hoots catch on the wind, the middle two closest together. He sounds farther away than expected, and I wish he'd stop moving, stop asking things of his already frail body.

But that's him. That's our owl.

"Did you hear that?" I ask.

Pike is looking in the same direction I am, up the mountain. He nods, and we take off toward the sound, my knee begging me to slow down. The scent of metal is so strong it's hard to breathe, sharp and stinging, magic coating everything, including me. Including Pike.

I jump back when an old spruce tree begins to crackle and spark. Then the whole thing goes up in flames, rain-soaked and vibrant in one moment, engulfed in fire in the next. Trees can absorb an incredible amount of magic, but it's spread out over time and throughout the entire forest. The owl must have been in this tree, the magic living inside him seeping out onto the bark and branches, creating too much energy in one place. Too much heat. Amplified magic so intense that a single spark could ignite the whole thing.

Pike is staring at the tree as if it's a monster from a children's book, something he knows can't be real yet stands directly in front of him. The rest of the landscape is still, save for the slight breeze that is ever-present on the peninsula, coaxing the branches to shake and sway in the salty sea air. He squeezes his eyes shut, then opens them slowly, looking around as if the problem is him, a figment of his imagination.

I want to tell him that what he's seeing is real, that he isn't imagining it, but I'm supposed to be just as confused as he is. "What is happening?" I whisper under my breath, loud enough for Pike to hear, angry at myself for holding onto my secret when I know it's about to reveal itself no matter how tightly I cling to it.

"I don't know," Pike says, shifting his pack to his front and digging inside. "I have to call it in before it gets worse. Before it spreads." His voice is uneven as he speaks, unsure, because he knows it doesn't make any sense for a single tree to go up in flames in the middle of a damp spring.

Thick gray smoke drifts toward me, and my eyes burn. Sweat rolls down my neck in large beads that soak into the fabric of my shirt, and heat distorts the air around me as if I'm looking through imperfect glass.

I'm horrified when an image of Pike bursts into my mind, burning just like the tree in front of us. Burning just like Alex.

No, I tell myself, backing away from the tree, away from the image. Backing away from a possibility that seems far too close.

I no longer care what Pike thinks. I'm going to find the owl, right now, before things get any worse.

Pike is holding his sat phone up to the tree line, waiting for a signal, eyeing the burning tree as if it might uproot itself and walk toward him at any moment.

"I'm going after the owl," I say, pulling Pike's attention away from the flames.

"No," Pike says, shaking his head back and forth. "Something isn't right; I think we should stick together."

"The owl isn't far from here. If you can't find me once you make your call, just shout for me. I'll be close by."

Pike is about to argue when his call goes through and someone answers. I catch his eye and signal that I'm going, then walk away before he can say anything. Once I'm safely around the fire, too far away for Pike to see, I run.

Without Pike here, I don't have to pretend that I'm unsure of where the owl is. I can feel that I'm close, and I keep running, deeper into the trees. My knee is stinging, and my pant leg is soaked with blood. I ignore it as best I can and follow the trail of magic. The owl is giving off so much I'm surprised this entire mountain doesn't go up in flames, and I suspect he's avoiding the trees after seeing what happened to the last one. He loves these ancient forests as much as I do; he doesn't want them to burn.

I trip over an exposed root and force myself to slow down. The earth is damp and slippery, and without a clear path to stick to, I'm trudging through plants and over roots, loose stones and fallen trees. The farther in I get, the denser the trees and underbrush—the perfect place for a runaway owl to hide.

The air is getting heavier with the metallic scent, and it stings when I breathe through my nose. I know I'm close when my skin starts tingling with the sensation of magic, even though I'm not using mine.

Then I see him, not in a tree or on a branch but on the soggy ground, unable to fly. I rush over to him, and he doesn't flinch or try to get away. Instead, he looks directly at me, his large black eyes piercing mine.

"Hi, MacGuffin," I say, kneeling next to him.

I can feel the pain he's in before I even summon my magic, and any animosity I felt toward him vanishes in an instant. All I want is for him to survive.

"I'm going to help you," I say, looking over him.

Then I see the injury, a large, gaping wound on his left side, spanning from his wing to his abdomen. Even though I know he was attacked by the bear and this is how it works in the wild, my eyes sting with the threat of tears.

I wish I could have been there to protect him.

"I'm here now," I say out loud, steady and clear, taking off my pack and getting ready to work. "I'm here now."

twenty-one

I unclasp the top of my daypack and pull the drawstring open. The gray day is making it hard to see, especially this deep in the forest, and I pull off my cap and set it aside, giving myself more light. The ground is wet, branches and ferns hanging heavy with rain, and I inhale deeply, filling my lungs with the cool, salty air.

The owl watches me with patient eyes, reinforcing what I've always known deep down: he has been orchestrating this from the very beginning, and for whatever reason, he wanted me to have to trek through the woods to find him.

"Why did you do this?" I ask, not out of anger or frustration but out of genuine curiosity. I want to know.

He looks at me and tilts his head to the side, blinking once.

I sigh and pull the towel from my pack, gently placing it around MacGuffin to keep him warm. Pike has the boxes with him, so I'll have to wait until he gets here to safely transport the owl. But at least I can keep him warm and survey the damage. The wind picks up again, the sound of the swaying treetops almost tricking me into believing it's a peaceful day, that everything is as it should be.

But this single curse is pulling on all the threads of my life, and at any moment, the entire thing will unravel.

I look through my pack and grab the first aid kit, rifling through the pockets, Band-Aids and disinfectant wipes spilling onto the ground as I do. I don't even know what I'm looking for—MacGuffin needs to be on the steel table back at the refuge, with sanitized instruments and Mom's steady hands. He needs magic *and* medicine, and there is only one of those things here.

Wind moves through the branches, picking up pine needles and tossing them into my hair. My pants are soaked through from sitting on the wet ground, and my chest is aching with the familiar pain of dread. There is no way the owl will survive the trek off the mountain; I have to act now, in the middle of the forest, and hope that I can heal him enough to get us more time.

I shove my hands through my hair and try to calm my racing heart. MacGuffin looks up at me, catching my gaze. His wound is still bleeding, leaving bright red streaks along the dirty white towel, and even though his eyes are steady, his breathing is not.

I need to know what I'm dealing with. Maybe his injury isn't as bad as it looks, and if I can use just enough magic to make him stable, maybe we can get him back to the refuge. I think of my binding herbs, floating somewhere down the river, completely out of reach. I don't have the tools I need to undo the curse, and if he dies before I can figure it out, that's it. All of this will have been for nothing. My only choice is to try to heal him now so he's alive later.

Fog rolls in through the forest, and I can no longer see the treetops moving back and forth or the gray sky peeking through the canopy. It brings with it a welcome chill, cooling my skin and making it easier to breathe. I turn around and look behind my shoulder, the tower of smoke still rising up, a single tree completely overwhelmed by magic.

That's what happens when there's a rush of it, too much all at once. It's what happened to Alex, and it's what could happen—I force myself to end the thought before it shines too bright a light on what's at stake.

I close my eyes and connect to my sense, all the magic in the area making itself known to me. I force myself to ignore that Pike is close by and Cassandra is somewhere on this mountain, and how this could be one of the last times I ever use my sense.

I force it all out until all that's left is me and my magic.

I marvel at the way it feels to have this kind of connection to the world around me, what it's like being one of the few people who can experience the universe in all its splendor. Magic has been here from the beginning of time, and I get to call it and direct it and feel the energy of the stars from which it came.

I am infinite because of it.

Magic assembles all around me, heating my skin and crackling against me, my own perfect security blanket. I reach for the owl and send magic rushing into him, feeling his unsteady heartbeat and too-shallow breaths. I inhale sharply when I feel the pain he's in, this deep ache that reaches to his very core.

My eyes snap open and I look at him. He's watching me, and

yet he looks as calm as he has this whole time, refusing to let me see his pain.

But there's so much of it.

And that's when I realize he's been doing his very best to skirt death, staying alive solely so I could find him. Maybe he regrets stealing my curse as much as I regret casting it, forcing himself to survive just long enough for me to make this right, like we're in it together.

I close my eyes again and send a stream of magic to his system, wrapping his nerves in thousands of particles that absorb his pain. He breathes out, and a small whistle follows his breath, as if he's sighing in relief.

"That's it," I say, giving him as much magic as I can. "You're okay."

He's still bleeding, though, and I have to find the source if I want to get him back to the refuge alive. Magic scours his system, but there's so much blood I can't tell where it's coming from.

"We have to clean you up a bit," I say, grabbing my water bottle from a side pocket. I remove the towel from around MacGuffin so I don't drench it, then I pour water over his wound. Red liquid runs from his feathers and into the earth.

He looks so fragile, and my eyes burn. I swallow hard and my throat aches with the effort, but the owl stays calm, letting me clean him up as best I can. Once I've rinsed him off, I replace the towel and grab some gauze from my first aid kit. I gently press it into the wound, soaking up as much blood as possible, then set it aside and try again.

Magic rushes back to the owl, and I close my eyes and send it searching for the source of his bleeding. Soon, hundreds of particles cluster around a nick in an artery, and I breathe out in relief. I found it. I cover the cut in thousands of flecks, magic reinforcing the artery and stopping the bleeding until we can get him to the refuge.

I lean on my heels and push back my hair, exhaling heavy and slow. Maybe I can get him off this mountain after all.

Then all at once, the gauze in his wound turns from white to red, and I know it wasn't enough. I bend over him and send more magic into the area, but the cut is too severe. Magic can only do so much, and MacGuffin needs more than what I can give him.

He needs more.

"Iris!" Pike calls, and I feel like my heart will beat right out of my chest. It's going so fast.

"Over here!"

I stand up and pace around the owl, waiting for Pike. Trying to figure out what to say to him, but none of the words are right. The curse I wrote is meant for a human, and since I'm not a Stellar, I don't know how powerful it will be. If I can get Pike off this mountain and far away before the curse is unleashed, maybe it won't be powerful enough to reach him. Maybe it will die out in these hundred-year-old trees and never find him.

I have to stay with the owl, keep him alive as long as possible in order to give Pike the best shot at getting far away from here. But I don't know how to convince him to leave. I don't know how to make it make sense without telling him who I am. And I can't do that. I can't.

"Okay, it's been reported," Pike says as he comes around a corner. "Firefighters will be out here as soon as they can." His eyes go to my pant leg, soaked through with blood, and he frowns. "That doesn't look good."

"Pike," I say, ignoring his words, "I need you to listen to me."

"What's wrong?" he asks, coming closer, searching my eyes.

"You have to leave. Right now."

"What? What are you talking about?"

"I just need you to trust me," I say as panic seeps into my voice, making it louder and faster. "It's not safe for you to be here. Please go."

"You're starting to scare me. What's going on? Did you find the owl?"

I point to the ground behind me where MacGuffin is cradled in a white towel, watching us both as if our conversation matters in some way. As if he cares.

Pike drops to his knees beside the owl and looks at the injury on his side. "Oh, buddy, I'm so sorry," he says, but we don't have time for this.

"Pike, please. I need you to go, right now. Run down the trail and get in your car, then drive back to the refuge and stay with my mom; she can explain everything." Mom doesn't know about the curse, but Pike has to be with another witch in case the curse finds him, in case he can't get far enough away. Mom will know if that happens, and if it does, she can help him. She'll know what to do.

Pike stands up and looks at me, but I can't read his expression.

I can't focus. "I'm not going anywhere until you tell me what's going on."

"Stop being so stubborn, and just listen! I will tell you everything one day, I promise I will, but for now I need to see you running down that trail and not looking back." I'm pretty sure I'm crying at this point, but it's hard to tell between the raindrops that fall from the branches above us and the sweat that's covering my face. My voice is shrill and unsteady, and I can only imagine what Pike must think.

But I can't care about that.

"Who's the stubborn one? You don't tell me shit and expect me to just follow your orders with no explanation. You aren't making any sense."

"We don't have time for this. I don't care if you think I'm stubborn or unfair or not making sense. All I care about is that you get off this mountain."

"Sorry, Iris, not good enough."

Pike drops to the ground and crosses his legs, resting his forearms on his knees as if he's about to chat with the owl. His eyes scan the length of MacGuffin, up and down and back again. Then he slowly turns to me. "He's not wearing a tag," he says.

"What?"

"A tag. We've been tracking him in the app, but he isn't wearing a tag." He says the words slowly as if he's trying to solve the puzzle as he speaks. It doesn't make sense. None of this does.

"Maybe it fell off," I say, exasperated, angry that he's not listening.

"They don't just fall off."

"The tag doesn't matter," I say, pacing around, frustrated and mad and scared. "You need to leave. You can't possibly begin to understand the magnitude of the mistake you're making."

The words hurt to say because I don't think Pike being turned to a witch is a bad thing. Not really. The risks are too high—the chance of him burning up and the council punishing me and the curse being amplified. The fact that Pike would be turned into the thing he hates. That's all bad, and I'd undo it if I could. But the magic part? It's brilliant, and I would never begrudge anyone their own sense.

But I can't just give him magic, even if he wanted it the way Alex did. It doesn't work that way; the risk is too great. It always has been, and I should have recognized that before crafting the curse in the first place.

"Then explain it to me," Pike says, his tone sharp.

I ignore him and keep walking, trying desperately to figure out what to say, what to do to get him to leave. And that's when it hits me, all at once, barreling down on me like an avalanche. My heart aches with understanding and my insides feel as if they are hollowed out. Nausea coats my stomach, and I wonder if I can even get the words out, wonder if my body will let me say what I need to say.

Once I speak the words, I can never take them back. He will have all of me, see all of me, know all of me. And I'll have no other option but to stand here and wait to find out if he'll accept me.

That's my only choice.

I slowly sink to the ground in front of Pike, with MacGuffin next to me. I take Pike's face in both my hands, leaning into him and pressing my lips against his. I kiss him gently, the salt from my tears coating his mouth. He's hesitant at first, but he kisses me back, going from slow to urgent in the span of a breath. He opens his mouth, deep and desperate, and maybe he knows that this is the last time we'll ever kiss, the last time we'll ever breathe each other in and run our fingers through the other's hair.

I pull away and force the tears from my eyes. The wind picks up, blowing my curls across my face. I reach out and tuck them behind my ear, then look at Pike.

"Fine," I say. "You win."

His expression is confused and intense, and he watches me with a pain in his eyes, as if he knows I'm about to break not only his heart, but all of him.

Then I take a deep breath, close my eyes, and reach for the magic Pike hates.

twenty-two

Magic rushes to me in an instant, flying through the forest and assembling all around me. My skin gets hot as I gather enough to answer Pike's questions, enough for him to never doubt exactly what I am. Enough to shatter whatever bond we forged beneath the cover of the trees.

Pike's vision will fade, and the images of this forest, these ferns and the owl and me will all give way to a total darkness, with little pinpricks of light the only disruption in the infinite black. Starlight, in the middle of the day, with his eyes open.

Magic. Undeniable, unquestionable, indisputable magic.

I'm not gentle with it. I send it toward him in a surge, wrapping around his heart and mind as if I'm trying to track him, just as I did with the bird. Just as Cassandra did with me. I feel his heart rate increase and his stomach contract, a physical reaction to the knowledge of who I am. I have a sudden urge to pull it back, try to explain it away somehow, but I don't. I open my eyes and watch as the magic rushes through him, as it turns his world dark.

His eyes widen, and he blinks several times. He shakes his head back and forth and blinks some more, as if that will get rid of the starlight, get rid of the magic. He rubs his eyes and puts his face in his palms, and it breaks my heart, watching him fight against what he knows is happening. Watching him fight against me. My eyes sting and my throat aches, and I know the way he looks right now will haunt me for the rest of my life.

"Stop!" he yells.

I halt my magic, and Pike's vision returns, his eyes focusing on me. He scrambles back, pulling himself through the dirt, then pushes himself up off the ground. I stand, too, but he takes a step away from me, and I stop moving.

"What was that?" he asks, his voice low and strained, tight enough to break in half.

I want to speak, but the words are stuck in my throat. I can't make them come out.

"Answer me!" he shouts.

I flinch at his words, my heart racing and my palms sweating. Everything narrows around us until all I can hear is the blood rushing through me, all I can see are Pike's hazel eyes.

"You already know what it was," I say, my voice trembling with the exposure of it. The vulnerability.

"No, no, I don't," Pike says, shaking his head some more, shoving his hands through his hair. "Because if it is what I think, then it's—it's—"

"Magic," I say, finishing the sentence for him. I'm so mad at him for making me do this, so hopeful that it might turn out okay. So foolish for wanting it to.

I watch him and brace myself as the walls I've worked so hard to build collapse all around me. Then I take a deep breath and speak.

"I'm a witch." The words echo in the trees, loud and harsh, and I bring my hand to my chest, shocked that I've said them. Shocked that I spoke the words I vowed to never speak again.

Something shifts inside me, as if my secret was the scaffolding holding me together and without it I might crumble.

For a moment, we stare at each other, breathing hard and waiting for the other to say something. Do something. React in some way.

But he's still here, standing in front of me. Maybe it will be okay.

Then Pike takes several steps back as if the words have finally reached his brain and he understands what I just confessed. He holds his arm out to me, telling me not to move, not to take a single step toward him.

"I'm not going to hurt you," I say gently, realizing he might actually be scared.

"How nice of you."

A gust of wind blows through the woods, and I wrap my arms around my chest. I turn in the direction of the burning tree, the smoke dying down now. I haven't heard a single person on this mountain, though, and it must have finally burned through itself, nothing left to give to the fire. It makes me indescribably sad.

I turn back to Pike, ready to talk, to answer whatever questions he has or accusations he wants to throw my way. I open my mouth, but he holds up his hand, shaking his head, and I stop, the words dying in my throat.

He takes several steps away from me, turns around, and runs.

Tears flow freely down my face as I watch him recede into the distance, getting farther away from me and farther away from the owl. That's what I've been trying to get him to do, run, get as far away from here as possible, and I'm relieved that he's leaving. I am. But it also hurts, a physical pain that throbs in my chest.

Pike is running away from me, an image that I'm sure will live with me the rest of my life, right along with Amy losing her sense and Alex on the lake, with my dad choosing to stay when Mom and I left. All these things telling me that my magic should have always been kept a secret, something I delighted in on my own.

And now the secret's out.

I walk back to the owl and sink to the ground. MacGuffin looks at me, and if I didn't know better, I'd think his eyes were filled with compassion. Maybe they are. Animals understand a lot about humans, a lot more than we give them credit for. Sometimes I wonder if they understand more about us than we do about them.

Now that Pike's gone, I can work on unbinding the curse. Even through all the pain, I feel hope sprout somewhere deep inside me—after everything, maybe all I will have lost is Pike's affection.

Still, it feels insurmountable, and I force myself to breathe, to focus on the curse. Without my binding herbs, I'll need to improvise, and I scour the forest for something to use.

Then a scream cuts through the silence.

Pike.

"I'm so sorry," I say to the owl. "Please, hold on just a little longer."

As quickly as possible, I send more particles to his nicked artery, hoping to give him more time. I wrap his nerves in magic to take away some of the pain, and I gently stroke his feathers before promising to be right back.

Then I jump up and run in the direction of Pike's scream.

"Pike!" I yell, moving through the trees as fast as my knee will let me. "I'm coming!"

I hear a groan and follow the sound, but it's so faint, far quieter than his scream. "Pike, where are you?" I shout, standing still to hear his reply.

It comes in the form of a moan, and I rush toward it, then stop abruptly when the earth beneath me starts to fall away. I scramble back from the crumbling dirt, and that's when I notice the ravine, gaping and deep, covered with sideways trees and boulders the size of truck tires. The ground is uneven and steep, full of dense vegetation and jagged stumps left by fallen trees, and I peer over the edge in search of Pike.

"Pike, I'm here!" I call, straining to see through the snarl of branches and underbrush.

"Iris?" He says it like a question, and I squint into the distance and finally find him, spread out halfway down the ravine, covered in mud.

"Just hold on—I'm coming," I say, lowering myself to the ground and sliding down the ravine. I wince when my hands go over sharp rocks and sticker bushes grab at my skin. I see his glasses halfway down, and I grab them and stick them in the collar of my shirt. I keep moving, lower and lower, until I'm finally close enough to hear Pike's breathing. It's shallow and quick, and I scramble over to where he's sprawled out on the dirt, clutching his right leg to his chest.

"I'm here," I say, stopping beside him and trying to assess the damage. I hand him his glasses, and his fingers linger on mine for a beat longer than I expect, images from our night in the tent flooding my mind. Then he takes them from me and the memory recedes.

"Let me look at your leg," I say.

He doesn't reply but lets go of his knee with shaky hands. I slowly extend his leg and pull up his hiking pants, inhaling sharply.

"What is it?"

I look at him. "Your leg is broken."

"How can you tell?" he asks through clenched teeth.

"Because your bone is sticking out through your skin."

His breathing gets faster, and he tries to sit up, straining to see what I'm looking at. "Shit shit shit shit shit," he says over and over, his voice getting more panicked.

I gently push his chest back and take his hand in mine. "You're okay," I tell him. "You're going to be fine."

He lays his head back and looks up at the sky, wincing in pain. "Grab my sat phone," he says, trying to roll onto his side. "It's in the first pocket."

I unzip the pocket and pull out the phone, but there's a huge crack down the center. "It's broken," I say. "You must have gone over a rock when you fell."

"Shit," he says, leaning back, his breaths shaky. "You need to go for help. There's no way you can get me up the ravine by yourself."

I follow his eyes, watching the layer of fog drift over us like a blanket, hiding us from the rest of the world. The wind doesn't reach us here, and I haven't seen a single soul on this mountain.

"Who am I going to find? It's just us up here."

"We can wait"—he pauses, sucks in a breath—"for the fire-fighters. They said they were coming."

"I don't think they're coming," I say. "The fire is out."

Pike leans back in the dirt, inhaling sharply. Then I remember Cassandra. She said she was coming, and I felt her magic tracking me. She must be somewhere on this mountain. I wish I could call, tell her that things have deteriorated with the owl, but I have no way of reaching her, no way of making her come any faster.

I exhale and push my hands through my hair, thinking. I can get him out of here; if I can stabilize his leg enough so he can help me, I can get him up the ravine. I'll have to use magic to dull the pain, otherwise he won't be able to tolerate it. But if he'll let me, I can do it.

"I can get you out," I say.

He looks at me then, and his eyes widen when he realizes what I'm saying. "No, absolutely not."

"Why?" I ask, impatience lacing my tone. "We're not all bad, you know."

"The fact that you've been lying to me since the day we met suggests otherwise," he says through a grimace. He brings his leg to his chest and rocks back and forth.

"I don't owe you my secrets," I say, lifting my eyes to his. "The idea that I would share myself with you just because we work together is as ridiculous as me thinking you owed me your brother's history. We don't have a right to those things—they're earned."

"Yeah, well I wish I could take mine back, because you definitely didn't earn it."

"And you're doing such a good job of earning mine?" The words sound more aggressive than I mean, and when Pike doesn't answer, I let out a long breath. Rainwater rushes over the edge of the ravine, carving its own stream through the brambles and tree trunks. I wish I could lie back and listen, let the sound calm me, but there's no time. "I didn't come all the way down here just to fight," I finally say. "Let me help you."

He doesn't respond, and I take that as an invitation to continue. "First, can you feel your foot? Can you move it?"

He flexes it and lets out a sound between a bark and a cough. "Yes."

"Good. I'm going to rinse off your injury and make you a splint, then we'll get you out of here."

I scour the area for two large sticks, then pull my fleece out of my pack. I wrap it around his leg, avoiding the bone, then set the two sticks on either side. I grab my pocket knife and cut the hem of my shirt off, using the fabric strips to tie the splint in place.

"Your leg is going to swell, so let me know if this starts to feel too tight at any point."

Pike nods. His breathing gets faster and his eyelids start to close.

"Hey, hey, stay with me," I say, scooting up to his face, touching his cheek with my hand. He opens his eyes and looks at me. The right lens of his glasses is cracked and caked with dirt, and I take them off his face. I wipe them clean and gently put them back, Pike watching me with angry eyes and a tense jaw.

"Let's get you out of here."

"What are you going to do?" Even when he's delirious with pain, he manages to sound disgusted at the prospect of magic.

"I'm going to send enough magic to your nerves to ease the pain. Your leg will feel a little warm, and you'll notice the pain lessen right away. I'll move behind you and hook my arms under yours, and I'll drag you up as you use your good leg to help."

"You can't make us fly or some shit?" Pike asks, and I roll my eyes.

"No, I can't make us fly or 'some shit.' Magic works with the universe, it doesn't defy it." I look at him. "Are you okay with that plan?"

"I guess I don't have a choice."

"Fine," I say. I close my eyes and concentrate on the magic

around me, so many millions of particles living in this old forest, witnessing this place before the trees were ever even here.

I draw enough magic to direct into Pike's leg, wrapping his nerves in tiny flecks that will feel better than any medicine he could take. There are areas of human magic that I'm unskilled at, but this isn't one of them; humans are built remarkably similar to animals. We break the same bones and feel the same pain. I can help him with those things.

Pike sighs next to me and his eyelids get heavy. "That feels better."

"Good," I say, moving behind him, "because we're going to get you up the ravine now." I try to ignore the way he flinches at my touch, telling myself he's just in pain. But I know better.

When he meets my eyes, it isn't relief or exhaustion or even fear that I see.

It's fury. Intense, searing fury.

twenty-three

I position myself behind Pike, looping my arms under his. He tenses, his back rigid and straight, and I move closer to him to get a better hold. I can see the sweat on the back of his neck and the way goose bumps appear when my breath meets his skin.

"Relax into me," I say, ignoring the way the cut on my knee feels as if it's ripping open, wider and wider. It's nothing compared to Pike's leg, and it'll feel better once I can straighten it out again.

He doesn't move at first, then I feel him take a deep breath. On his exhale, he relaxes into me, his back getting heavy against my chest, his head leaning into the crook of my neck. His skin feels warm against mine, and I close my eyes for a single moment, committing the way he feels to memory.

I'm about to start pulling him up when he speaks. "Wait," he says, his voice quiet and strained. "Tell me something real."

"Something real?"

He nods, his head moving up and down against my neck.

Something real. I think for several seconds, with Pike's full weight resting against me, and something about the way I can't see his face makes me feel brave. "I want to be known by you," I finally say. "And I'd rather you know all of me and hate me than only know parts of me and like me."

He's quiet for several moments, his breathing labored and unsteady. "Let's go," he says.

I nod and grip him tighter, letting my words drift away on the cool mountain air. The rain is light now, drops falling on nearby leaves and stones, the gentle tapping the only sound. "On my count, I'm going to pull you back. Hold your right leg up and plant your left foot firmly on the ground and push. Are you ready?"

"Yes."

"One, two, three," I say, pulling him up as he pushes off the ground. I swallow a cry of pain, the gash on my knee splitting open, warm blood crawling down my leg. But we moved; we made progress. It will be slow, but we can get up the ravine this way.

Pike's weight gets heavier on me the longer we go, and I grip him tighter, making sure he doesn't fall back or slip. He's so close to me that I feel his labored breaths and tensing muscles, and after several more rounds, he asks for a break. I welcome it and sit behind him, extending my leg to ease the strain in my knee. Even when I sit, he doesn't move his weight from me. I tell myself it's because his leg is broken, because he's weak and doesn't have the energy to sit up straight. But whatever the reason, I like the feeling of him against me.

"Why can't you just fix my leg? Why all this go-around?" Pike asks, not turning his head to look at me.

"You want me to use more magic?"

"No. I want to know why you aren't."

I sigh, and Pike sinks deeper into me, as if the question took all his energy. "It isn't like that. Magic is an innate part of the world, an extension of it. It works in tandem with things like medicine and expertise and experience. It honors the natural world by working *with* it; it can't create something out of nothing or destroy something that already exists. It works within the parameters of our world."

At first Pike doesn't respond, and I wonder if what I said made sense or if he thinks it's ridiculous. His head tips down. "It can't destroy something. So cancer, for example. It can't destroy cancer cells."

My stomach drops as I realize what he's asking, a physical pain I feel in my center. I slowly shake my head. "No. It could make someone more comfortable. It could bolster their healthy cells to put up a stronger fight. It could keep them nourished and help protect against the effects of the harsher treatments. But it couldn't eradicate the disease, no."

"So Leo never had a chance?" Pike asks through gritted teeth, his voice rough and unsteady. "We were lied to from the start? No amount of magic could have saved him, even if it hadn't been about the money?"

Tears build up in my eyes and spill over my lashes, and I quickly wipe them away with my free hand. "No," I say. "Not on its own. It would have to work in tandem with some kind of treatment."

Pike inhales sharply, and it sounds like a gasp. His shoulders start to shake and he lets out one choking sob. I want to hold him tighter, to take all his weight and let him rest for as long as he needs, but I don't dare move, scared that even a breath will make him realize who he's touching, scared that he'll recoil from me.

And as much as I want to comfort him through this, I know that I can't. I cursed him. I wrote a curse far crueler than what he deserved and let it get away. Now we're sitting in a ravine, Pike with a broken leg and the owl with a broken artery, and I'm no closer to fixing this than I was three days ago.

He's right to lean away from me, to flinch when I get too close and look the other direction when I tell him I care.

We sit in the ravine for a long time, and I watch the fog move overhead and the raindrops sitting on leaves, reflecting the world above them.

"We need to go," I finally say when I can no longer stand being away from the owl. He's the same as he was when I ran after Pike, but that could change in an instant, and if I'm halfway down the ravine when it does, I won't be able to do anything.

Pike grabs his right leg and I loop my arms under his once more, starting our slow climb up the ravine. I count out loud the first few times, but we eventually find a rhythm, and we don't speak for the rest of the way. By the time we get to the top, we're both out of breath and drenched in sweat. Pike scoots up against a nearby tree, and my front is flooded with cold air, used to the warmth of his back against my chest. He takes a sip of water, and I pace around with my hands in my hair, trying to figure out what's next.

The owl. I need to get to the owl.

My magic is buying him minutes, nothing near long enough to get him to our campsite, let alone the refuge. And any extra time I did get him was spent going after Pike. Every single thing that could go wrong in the past several days has, and I want to scream and cry and yell and blame Pike for falling down a ravine, but I can't.

This is my fault, and I will have to live with that knowledge for the rest of my life.

"I'm going back for the owl," I say, walking over to Pike. "Once I get him back here, we can try to head to camp."

"Here, take the boxes out of my pack," he says, leaning forward. "The makeshift nest will be more comfortable for him."

"Thank you," I say, grabbing what I need. "Let me check your leg before I go."

Pike braces himself against the tree, avoiding my eyes the whole time. I pull up his pant leg and check on the splint. The bleeding has stopped, and the splint is holding up well.

"How's your pain level?" I ask, gently sticking my hand between his leg and the sticks, making sure the splint hasn't gotten too tight with the swelling.

"Fine," he says, looking up at the fog.

"You don't have to say that, you know. I can help with the pain if you need it."

"I said it's fine." He rubs the top of his thigh with his free hand,

and when he finally looks at me, I wish he wouldn't have. Even in the absence of the curse and the owl, Pike never would have accepted me for who I am. It's written all over his face and in the depths of his eyes, a hatred so strong not even love could overcome it.

The line between the two is paper thin and razor sharp, and we ended up on the wrong side of it. Maybe it was always inevitable, but if that were true, it wouldn't feel like losing something.

"You should eat while I'm gone," I say, digging into my bag and pulling out a KIND bar. At first I don't think anything of it, the joke so far away by now. But the way he looks at it brings it all back, and it makes the ache in my chest get stronger. I roll my eyes so he can't see the way it hurts.

"Just eat it," I say, handing it to him. "I shouldn't be gone too long."

I take off toward the owl without another glance at Pike, going as fast as my leg will let me. It's hazy and gray through the dense woods, and the earth moves easily under my feet, soft and damp. Goose bumps rise on my skin, my stomach exposed to the cold air after using my hem for Pike's splint.

I follow my trail of magic to the bird, impatient to get back to him. I feel awful for leaving him alone as long as I did and force myself to move faster. I step through a particularly thick patch of brambles, then I see my baseball cap on the ground, right where I left it.

One more step, and the owl comes into view. As well as a coyote standing aggressively over him.

My heart jumps in my throat, and I stop moving, not wanting to spook the coyote. I'm so angry at myself for not leaving the owl somewhere safe, in a hollow or branch, high enough off the ground to avoid predators. But the coyote isn't burned or injured, which means he hasn't touched the owl yet.

"I'm sorry for leaving," I whisper to MacGuffin, and I hope he knows how much I mean it.

Then I turn to the coyote. "No," I say firmly, locking eyes with him. "Get out of here."

The coyote doesn't move from his place over the owl, and he lets out one low growl. Something inside me snaps, and I don't use magic or gently try to coax him away from the injured bird. Instead, I scream as loudly as I can, waving my arms over my head and making a mad dash toward the animal.

At first I think he's going to lunge at me, tearing me to shreds, but at the last minute, he runs in the opposite direction, through the trees and behind a large boulder until he's out of sight.

I drop to the ground, and MacGuffin looks up at me. He's tired. His eyes are heavy and glassy, but he still looks happy to see me. I can't believe how attached I am to this stupid bird after everything he's put me through, but I am, and I'd give anything to get him through this alive.

"I'm happy to see you, too," I say, removing the towel to assess the damage. His bleeding has started again, but there are no new wounds to address.

I take the same steps as before, rinsing the gash and soaking up some of the blood with gauze. Then I send more magic to the nicked artery, but I've done all that I can do.

I want to work on the curse, try to undo it right here, but with my binding herbs gone, I'll need time to come up with a replacement, and I can't leave Pike alone for that long. If he starts to show any signs of infection, I have to be there.

"I'm sorry, MacGuffin," I say, assembling his makeshift nest. "I have to move you, but it's not far." I line the boxes with the towel, then gently pick him up and lay him down on top. "Pike will be happy to see you," I say, grabbing my cap and carefully lifting MacGuffin's nest.

The owl watches me at first, looking up at me as I carry him through the trees, making my way back toward Pike. But his eyes get heavy, and soon he's struggling to keep them open.

I'm going to have to unbind the curse out here in the wild, with Pike and his broken leg, with no hope of getting help from my mom or Sarah or anyone else. Cassandra should be here by now, but she isn't, and she hasn't used magic on me again, which means something must have come up.

I'm on my own.

Pike's eyes are closed and his head is tipped back against the tree when I reach him. The empty KIND bar wrapper is sitting on his chest, and I'm embarrassed when my eyes fill with tears.

Pike's head snaps up, and he looks at me. I blink the tears away and clear my throat.

"He's dying," I say. "I have to work on him right now."

"Here?" Pike asks.

"Yes."

He looks at MacGuffin, and a sad expression settles on his face. "What if it's just his time?" he asks, and I remember that

Pike still doesn't know about the curse. He knows I'm a witch, but I haven't shared the worst part with him.

I swallow hard. "I want to try," I say, hoping Pike doesn't hear the way my voice cracks at the end.

I think he'll question me, tell me to let it go. But he doesn't.

"Okay," he says, sitting up straight. "Tell me how I can help."

I wish I knew, I think to myself, more and more magic pouring into the air as I try to figure out where to begin. My grandmother used to say that curses are the most unpredictable of spells because they tend to have minds of their own, and without my herbs I'm terrified of trying the wrong thing and releasing the curse to the wild. To Pike. I've never had to unbind a curse before, and I'm stuck in this forest without the supplies that I need.

But magic is fluid, and there has to be something among these ancient trees that I can use to carry the curse, something strong enough to hold the weight of it. There has to be, and I will try every single plant and root until I find what works.

All I need is for MacGuffin to give me the time to try; I need time. But for an owl so full of magic, so full of wonder, time is something he doesn't have.

twenty-four

The fog is lifting higher, and I realize how long we've been at this—Cassandra used her magic on me hours ago. A cool breeze moves through the woods, and it feels good against my sweat-soaked body. Wet leaves and thick branches rustle in the wind, and songbirds sing in the distance.

"What's the plan?" Pike asks, and I look at him, suddenly too aware of what I'm about to do. I have to remove the curse right in front of him, so close together. He's stuck here with me, and if I don't do it right or I can't unbind it in time, Pike will suffer for it.

My chest is tight, and I can't get a big enough breath. There isn't enough air in the world to get me through this, and I stand up and pace around the owl, so scared of what the next few minutes will bring.

I wish my mom was here. I wish Pike's sat phone wasn't broken and I could call for help. I wish I could talk to my grandmother and let her raspy voice soothe me. She had a way of making even the worst situations feel manageable, of lining even the most horrible days in strands of gold. I miss her so much.

I grab my inhaler and take two long puffs before sitting back down and bending over the owl. I unwrap his towel and look at his injury again. There's too much blood.

I rock back on my heels, unable to stop the tears from running down my cheeks. Focus. I have to focus.

"What's going on?" Pike asks, his voice more apprehensive than mean, and when I meet his eyes, he looks scared. "Please, tell me."

I look around as if there's something in the woods that can change this somehow, but there's nothing. I take a shaky breath and move closer to Pike, sitting right in front of him.

He deserves to know.

I lick my lips and taste salt, but I don't care. He's seen so much of me now that crying in front of him doesn't matter the way it used to. "It's bad," I say, my voice shaking. "It's really bad."

"For the love of God, Iris, just tell me."

I wipe the tears from my face and nod. "I cursed you," I finally say, the words so quiet I'm not sure if I even said them.

Pike stares at me. "You what?"

"I cursed you," I say again, louder. "I didn't mean to. Or—I did, but I didn't mean for it to get out."

Pike is looking at me as if the words I've spoken don't fit, as if they can't possibly go together. He rubs his thigh with his hand and exhales. "Explain it to me."

So I do. "My grandmother taught me this ritual as a way of

dealing with the things I couldn't quite let go of. Stressors and anxieties and frustrations. She taught me to craft spells or curses that would carry those things, then bind them to something inanimate like a bundle of herbs before burning it all away. Kind of like writing letters you're never going to send—I came up with curses I never meant to cast as a way of working through my feelings." I pause and look at Pike. "It reminds me a lot of Leo's tradition of throwing wishes in the fire."

Pike flinches when I speak his brother's name, so angry at himself for sharing that with me—a witch.

"Okay," Pike says, nodding his head. "Keep going."

"Well, I know you'll be shocked to hear this, but I didn't really like you before this trip. And when you started making those comments about witches, I got scared. It made me nervous having to see you every day, knowing how much you hate magic. Then you made that comment about how Amy should have been the one to burn." I take a deep breath and look at him, his features blurring with my vision.

"Amy was my friend. My best friend. I was there that night, when her boyfriend burned on the lake. And when you said that about her, I was scared that you'd find out about me and my family and do something to jeopardize our life here. So I wrote a curse for you to make myself feel better, to try to work through my fear, but before I could burn it away, the owl swooped down from the trees and the curse got bound to him instead. Then he flew away with it."

I wipe my face again and take a shaky breath, my chest aching with the effort.

Pike looks at the owl. "So MacGuffin is carrying a curse," he says slowly, working through the words I just said.

"Yes, and the curse is bound to his life. If he dies, the curse will be unleashed."

"Unleashed," Pike repeats, grimacing. Then his eyes narrow and he looks at me. "What did you curse me with?"

I shake my head back and forth and back and forth, not wanting to answer. I don't think I can. I choke back a sob and look at the ground, my whole body shaking with fear. I cursed him with something that could end his life in the exact way as Alex, but the risk didn't feel real. I've written dozens of spells over the years, and not once has one gotten out. I didn't think it through enough, and now I have to look Pike in the eye and tell him what he's cursed with, tell him it was deliberate. It was intentional. That I wanted to do it, and I did.

"Iris, tell me," Pike says. He doesn't yell and his tone isn't harsh; he sounds tired, exhausted, as if he's given up—and that somehow makes this so much worse.

"I cursed you to become a witch," I say. "A mage." My eyes widen and my heart races as I replay the words, as I watch them hit Pike in slow motion. He visibly recoils and his eyes fill with tears.

"You did what?"

"I'm so sorry," I say too quickly, the words rolling together into one. "It was this stupid curse meant to ease my frustrations— that's it. You were never supposed to know about it; it was never supposed to even exist. It should have burned away like all the curses before it, but the owl changed everything." I wish I could be stoic and emotionless so Pike can react however he needs, but I can't find my breath, can't calm myself down. "I'm so sorry," I say again.

"You're sorry?" Pike says, his words loud and angry. "You're sorry? Jesus, Iris, you cursed me to turn into a witch!"

"I know!" I shout back, getting to my feet and moving. I have to move. "I know."

I wonder what it must be like for Pike, so angry and scared, stuck where he is because of his leg. He keeps rubbing his thigh, and I see him shift against the tree, his whole body tense with what he just learned.

"How's your leg?" I ask, knowing he needs to get to a hospital, get out of these woods, away from the witch who cursed him and the owl who can amplify it.

"It fucking hurts," Pike says.

"Then let me help you."

He looks up at me, his eyes red and wet. "Haven't you done enough?"

The words cut right into my chest, and I push my hand to my sternum but it doesn't stop the pain. I turn toward the owl and kneel, running my fingers over the feathers on his head. He looks up at me, hissing as he breathes, his lungs so tired from the work.

"I have to try to unbind the curse before we lose him," I say.

Pike closes his eyes and leans his head against the tree. "Even if he dies, there's got to be someone who can undo it, right? One of those witches on your council who can fix it?"

I slowly shake my head, my gaze falling to the dirt. It's so hard to look at him. I wish I could say something that would give him reason to hope, something for him to hold on to, but there's nothing.

"I don't think so," I say, being as honest as I can be. "If a curse finds the person it was meant for, that's it. It lives and dies with you."

A tear runs down Pike's cheek, and he quickly lifts his hand and wipes it away, the image searing itself into my memory. I try to blink it away, erase it somehow, but it's still there.

He looks up at me then. "You really hated me so much that you did this to me?"

For a moment, I can't speak. I've lost my voice in the hollow of my throat, completely unreachable. I try to remember what it was like working with Pike before this trip, so many days I was sure I disliked him. But I think about what he said about giving me a hard time so that I'd bicker with him, so that my mind could reset from whatever it was spiraling around, and maybe it worked. Maybe I didn't dislike him at all.

"I was scared of you," I finally say, settling on the one thing I know is true. "My life imploded after Amy's trial, and the people around me latched on to the fact that I was a witch in a way they'd never done before. Even my dad couldn't handle it anymore. Mom and I decided to start over, and we came here. When you started talking about witches, all I could see was having to move again. Having to start over again. Having to give up this place I love more than anything." I pause and look at him. "You terrified me."

He watches me as I speak, flinching when I say the last three words. "I'm sorry. I hate that I made you feel that way." His voice is rough and quiet, and he rubs his thigh, taking a sharp breath.

"But I'm not some asshole out on a mission to destroy witches. I just don't trust magic, and if I had found out about you, I would have left. That's all. I wouldn't have tried to ruin your life."

I would have left.

I don't expect the words to hurt the way they do, sliding in through my ribs and going straight for my heart. I look away, not wanting him to see. Then I give myself one deep breath, one silent moment to react, before pressing on.

"That doesn't matter now," I say, keeping my voice steady. "Once we deal with the curse, you'll be free to leave. But I need you to listen. As soon as the owl dies, a switch will flip in your brain and you'll be able to sense all the magic around you. It will be thrilling and exciting, and you will have no control. Your instinct will be to pull an astronomical amount of magic to you solely because you can, but your body isn't used to it, and it will burn you." I pause and swallow hard. "If you aren't careful, it will burn you to death."

I try to stop the images of Alex on the lake from flooding my mind, but it's no use. There he is, burning while my best friend watches in horror. While I sprint down the lawn, trying to help in some way.

I blink several times and lock my gaze on Pike. I will not let that happen to him. I won't.

"That's what happened to your friend's boyfriend?" he asks, his voice shaking.

"Yes."

Pike swallows hard, then clears his throat. "Okay, what do we do?" My heart breaks, hearing the fear in his voice.

"I'm going to help you through it," I say, holding his eyes with mine. "I swear I will not let that happen to you."

Pike nods, but it's impossible to know if he believes me. I want to tell him that I mean it, that I've never meant anything more in my life, but that won't change anything. He doesn't trust me anymore.

I look over at the owl, and he's calm. He seems to be listening to our conversation with interest, moving his eyes from me to Pike and back again. I stroke his feathers gently, then keep going.

"That's not the worst part," I finally say.

Pike stares at me but doesn't respond. I've never been looked at like this before, like I'm everything that's wrong in the world, a total letdown of a person. It's too much to bear, and I look away.

"It's almost impossible for me to describe the power of this owl," I say, forcing myself to keep going. "He's an amplifier—he can literally magnify the intensity of the magic inside him, including the curse. If I can't unbind the curse in time, you will be turned into a mage. But the curse won't stop with you. It will stretch on for miles; I don't know exactly how it will manifest, but the worst case is that it turns many more people, not just you."

"And those people," Pike says, working through something as he speaks. "Are they at risk of burning to death?"

"Yes, it's always a risk." I try to keep my voice even, but it makes me sound callous instead. I soften my tone and keep going. "It's not a guarantee. People have turned before and been just fine. But I don't want to lie to you anymore, and the truth is that it's a risk. A considerable one."

"Fuck," Pike says, scrambling on the ground, trying to stand. "Fuck." He manages to get to his feet, but his leg buckles and he collapses, crying out in pain.

I rush over to him, but he pushes me away. "Don't touch me," he says, clutching his leg and bringing it to his chest.

"Let me make this better for you," I say, trying to reach his leg.

"No. Don't come near me. Don't touch me. Don't say my name. Do whatever you need to do to save the owl or the curse or whatever, but don't you dare touch me."

"Okay," I say, holding up my hands. "But sitting there in pain isn't making this any better."

"Don't talk to me like I chose this, Iris. I didn't. I'm here because of you, and from where I'm sitting, you haven't made a damn thing better." His breathing is too shallow and too fast, and he winces and rubs his thigh.

"You're right," I say, moving away from him. "But I'm still going to try, and you need to rest."

He closes his eyes and keeps rubbing his leg, and I turn my attention back to the owl. The air is so heavy with the metallic scent I'm surprised Pike can't smell it yet. I breathe through my nose and it stings, sharp and crackling with magic.

I quickly get up and walk around the area, gathering enough pine branches and roots to bind the curse to. Old growth forests hold more magic than any other place on Earth, and while I didn't write the curse specifically for them, I'm hoping they'll be strong enough to hold it.

Once I have more than I think I'll need, I dump them next to the owl and get started. I tune out Pike and his words and the way his voice sounds when he's scared and instead close my eyes and concentrate on the curse, drawing from all the intent and frustration and fear I felt when I first created it. I put myself back in that place, imagining myself standing in the backyard next to the cottage, upset with my mom for not caring about Pike and angry at Pike for his callousness.

All I wanted was to give it to the earth, like my grandmother taught me. I never meant for any of this to happen.

I feel the curse materialize in the owl, coming together in a dense, tangible form I can hold, a living thing I can take from the owl and give to something else.

I keep my breathing even and my focus sharp, narrowing my world to this one task.

I can solve this.

Here we go.

The owl takes a heaving breath, and as he does, I grab hold of the curse. When he exhales, I pull it from his chest and cast it to the bundle of pine, but something isn't right. The curse fights against me, unwilling to go where I'm directing it.

I push it to the pine and roots, imagine it clutching their needles and being absorbed by their bark, waiting to be burned away just as it should have always been.

But it doesn't work.

I release the curse, and faster than it takes a heart to beat, it snaps back to the owl, binding itself to him once more.

twenty-five

I open my eyes and stare at the owl, terrified of what just happened. I search the ground as if it can tell me exactly what went wrong, but there's nothing. I must have rushed the spell or not prepared the pines enough, and I close my eyes and begin again, forcing myself to be patient. But the result is the same, and the curse snaps back to the owl. I frantically try again, over and over, but it doesn't work.

"What's happening?" Pike asks, his voice panicked. "Did you fix it?"

"No." I shake my head, watching the owl. "It isn't working. I don't know what I'm doing wrong."

"What do you mean it isn't working?" Pike raises his voice and shifts where he's sitting as if he's going to come over here and do it himself. Now that I've started working on the owl, I can see how the smallest seed of hope has sprouted inside of Pike, and he clings to it with both hands. Hope is a powerful thing, impossible to turn away from, a lighthouse on the rocky coast of the Pacific, and everything within him is reaching toward it.

"I don't know," I say, dread crawling through my body, threatening to take over everything. "It should have worked."

"Well, try it again." Pike looks at the owl and back to me, his eyes wild.

"I am," I say, wiping my palms on my pants. "It isn't working."

"Try harder," Pike shouts.

"Shut up," I yell, glaring at him from my perch over the owl. "You aren't helping. Just sit there and be quiet and let me think." I stand and rest my hands on my head, walking through the woods.

I go through everything I know about the curse and the owl, about amplified magic and bound curses, and that's when I realize why it isn't working.

Binding the curse to the owl made it stronger, more powerful. The owl's magic amplified that of the curse, nurturing it with the blood in his veins and the beating of his heart. The curse grew while wrapped in life, and now I can't bind it to anything without a life of its own.

It needs a heartbeat to attach to.

A kindred home, just like the book said.

I breathe out, a cross between a choke and a cry, and my legs feel weak. This is so much bigger than me, and I don't know if I can handle it on my own. I don't know if I'm strong enough.

The fog is starting to burn off for the day, revealing golden streaks of light that reach through the trees, unafraid of the curse that lives here. Unafraid of the unimaginable consequences if I can't figure this out. Sunlight touches my face, and I close my eyes and, for just a moment, let myself bask in the feeling of warmth.

Then it comes to me as suddenly as the sun broke through the clouds. I can bind the curse to myself. It's not common, but back before the Witches' Council was established and there wasn't any formal process for governance, witches who committed crimes were often cursed as punishment. The curses were written to fit the crimes, and they were handed out by the most powerful witches in their communities.

It's been generations since that kind of punishment was seen as acceptable, but I remember reading about it in our old family texts. Cursing a witch is possible, and that's what matters right now.

It isn't a permanent fix—I don't want Pike living his life terrified of what happens to me—but it's a fix for now. If I can bind the curse to myself, I can get back to the refuge and find help.

I rush back to the owl and drop to my knees. I choke back a cry as pain shoots up my leg, grinding my teeth and forcing myself to ignore it. MacGuffin slowly opens his eyes and looks at me, and I want more than anything to heal his injuries and get him back to the refuge, to give him a long and comfortable life where he can watch whomever he wants and hoot into the night and follow me around to his heart's content.

But right now, the best I can hope to give him is a peaceful death, slipping into whatever comes after without a curse attached to him.

I wrap more magic around his nerves, making him as comfortable as I can, then I get to work.

The curse is tightly clinging to the owl's center, burrowing in, contentedly living in an amplifier that could turn it into a disaster, a curse that could be written about in books and whispered about at night. A curse that could inspire eerie children's songs and lilting rhymes meant to warn others of the power of magic.

A curse so terrible it wouldn't even need a name.

I unwind the curse from the owl's insides, gently pulling it out until it finally lets go and hovers in the air in front of me, a heavy, dreadful thing. I breathe through my mouth to avoid the biting metallic scent and open the magic inside me, ready to take on the curse.

More particles rush toward me, the old trees in this ancient forest giving up some of their magic to help, and my skin heats up with the feeling of it. Even with the curse hovering in the air before me, even with the boy that I like absolutely terrified next to me, this is home. This is me.

My body hollows out, magic pushing things out of the way, making room for the curse to live alongside organs and muscles and bones. A kindred home. It feels as if the wind has been knocked out of me, as if I've left parts of myself behind to give room to this thing I never wanted.

I inhale and let the air of the forest settle deep in my lungs. Then I breathe out, shoving the curse into all my empty spaces. I gasp as it enters my body and tries to grab hold of me, fighting for purchase in a new home. It rushes through me, grasping at my insides as if it's falling off a cliffside, but it can't hold on.

It falls and falls and falls, and when it has made it through my whole body without something secure to grab hold of, it rushes out of me entirely and settles back in the owl.

"No!" I yell, hitting the ground with my fists, screaming into the silence.

I don't understand.

"What's happening?" Pike demands, his eyes moving frantically between me and the bird.

"It still isn't working. It needs a living thing to bind to, and I'm trying to bind it to me, but it won't take."

Something seems to shift in Pike, and I watch as all the hope leaves him, as the lighthouse crumbles into the ocean and he's left in total darkness. He looks defeated, but more than anything, he looks sad. Not angry or afraid or even hurt. Sad. "So that's it, then?"

I look up at him, his shape blurry through my tears. "No," I say, determined to figure this out. "No, I'm going to keep trying."

I wipe my face and sit up straight. Then I try again. The curse is agitated, fighting to stay in the owl, upset that it keeps being disturbed. I yank it out and shove it hard, using all the magic inside me to grip the curse and keep it here.

It stays for one second, tumbling through me, then flies back out. I keep trying, again and again, forcing the curse into my body, then feeling it rush back out.

I'm shaking and heaving on the ground as I repeatedly beat

the curse into me, losing strength as I do. There's so much magic in the air. My skin is on fire, hissing from all the particles I've called over, but I keep at it because I don't know what else to do.

"Iris, stop," Pike says, his voice close to me now.

My eyes snap open, and he's just inches from my face. He must have dragged himself over while I was working on the curse, and I look at him with huge, sorry eyes, wanting so badly to make this right and having no idea how.

He gently takes my hand and pulls up my sleeve, revealing burns all along my skin. I stare at the red welts that have formed up and down my arm, inhaling sharply. I won't be able to do this for much longer without risk of ending up like Alex. No one is meant to have infinite access to things, not magic or land or sea, and that includes witches.

I have to think.

A whistling sound comes from the owl, a high-pitched wheeze that sits on top of every breath.

"I'm trying," I whisper, looking into his big, dark eyes. "I just need a little more time. Please."

I sit back and rock on my heels, hanging my head and closing my eyes. The curse won't bind to the pine because it doesn't have a heartbeat, and it won't bind to me because...

I sink farther into the ground and cover my head. My heart feels as if it falls completely out of my body and lodges into the earth.

It won't bind to me because I'm a witch. And it can't turn someone into a witch who already is one.

I grab Pike's pack and start rifling through it, looking for anything that can help me catch another animal.

"It won't bind to me because I'm a witch," I say, throwing Pike's things all over the ground. "I need to find another animal, a healthy one I can bind the curse to."

"It's awfully quiet," Pike says, looking around. "It's just us out here."

I look at the trees and the golden light slipping through their branches, touching the earth. There is so much life here, the forest is humming with it, but I don't have what I need to track an animal and capture it. Pike is right: we're on our own.

And even if I could find another animal to take the curse, the owl won't make it long enough for me to try.

"Where's the sat phone?" I ask, scrambling toward Pike's pack, digging through his things. I pull it out and jump up, holding the phone to the sky, begging it to turn on and find a signal.

"It's broken," he says.

"Maybe not. Maybe it's just cracked. Plenty of phones still work with a crack." I hold it high above my head, staring at the screen, desperate for it turn on. I need to call Cassandra, find out where she is, get her help. I'm completely out of options, and I need her.

I need her.

But the phone stays dark.

"It won't work," Pike says, watching me.

I look down at him, tossing the phone aside and rushing to where he's sitting. "You have to get out of here," I say, kneeling beside him, trying to pull him up. He probably can't outrun a curse; it's probably impossible. But it's all I have left. "I'll keep the owl alive as long as I can, and you need to get to your car and drive. Drive as fast as you can, straight to the refuge where Mom can help in case the curse still reaches you. Just keep going, and—"

"You know I can't," he says, his voice quiet.

"I'll give you more magic, make the pain go away. You can do this, just don't think about it and go," I say, pulling up his pant leg.

Pike puts his hand over mine and stops me. "Iris," he says, looking at me with gentleness for the first time in hours. "You know I won't make it in time. MacGuffin won't live that long."

I choke on another sob when Pike says the owl's name, this wild animal that stole my curse and my heart. I want to hate him and stop myself from caring, but the truth is that I'm devastated. I want him to live.

"I'm so sorry," I say to Pike and the owl and everyone about to be affected by this curse. I think about my mom and hope she's with Sarah, hope they're laughing and smiling and happy, no idea that things are about to change forever. No idea that what we went through is nothing compared to what is to come.

I will lose my magic and be subject to the council as well as the courts. People will most likely die, and magic will be used by those who can't yet control it. There will be chaos and devastation, all because I wrote a curse for a boy who said he didn't like witches. What an unimaginable tragedy.

"I'm going to turn into a witch, regardless of what happens,"

Pike says, interrupting my thoughts. It doesn't sound like a question.

Still, I nod.

"I'm so sorry," I say again because I don't know what else to say.

"If this is it, if there's nothing else you can do, bind the curse to me."

I look up at him. "What?"

"Bind the curse to me," he says again, this time stronger, making up his mind. "That way, no one else will be put at risk. Just me."

We look at each other in the peaceful afternoon light, and I realize he's right. I've been so desperate to save Pike that I haven't been willing to confront the obvious solution. I can't save him, but I can stop the curse from being unleashed on everyone else. It won't make it better for Pike, it won't save me from my actions or give me another chance with this boy, but it's the right thing to do.

It's the only thing to do.

"Are you sure?" I ask, even though we both know it has to be done.

For a single excruciating moment, I think he might cry. Then he swallows, straightens his back, and nods.

"I'm sure."

"Okay," I say, wiping my tears and sitting up. "I'll do it."

twenty-six

The world around us seems to still. The wind stops blowing and the distant birds stop singing. There are no coyotes howling or critters scurrying across the dirt. It's as if the entire forest has taken a collective breath, waiting for what comes next.

My skin burns as I pull more magic to me, gearing up for the finale of this awful week. My breath shakes when I inhale.

"Pike, I need you to listen to me," I say, pausing what I'm doing, making sure he looks at me. "Once this happens, you will want to pull magic to you as if you're breathing air for the very first time. It will be overwhelming and awe-inspiring, and you will want more, pulling and pulling until you burn yourself to death. You have to fight against that instinct, okay? You have to stop when I tell you to stop and trust that there will be more for you later. The first few minutes are the worst—if you can get through those, you'll be okay."

Pike watches me, his eyes wide and his hands shaking. I reach out and touch him, and to my surprise, he doesn't pull away.

"I will get you through this. I promise you I will. But I'll need your help. Do you understand?"

He swallows hard, his eyes wet and red. "I understand," he says, the words rough, barely audible. He clears his throat and tries again. "I understand."

I squeeze his hand. "Good." I want more than anything to help him relax, to calm him down in some way. "Tell me something real," I say, echoing his words from earlier.

"What?" he asks, looking at me.

"While I unbind the curse, tell me something real."

He nods, and I think he understands. He takes a shaky breath, then closes his eyes and leans his head back against the tree. I turn to the owl and get to work.

"I remember the first time I learned about witches," Pike says, almost as if he's talking to himself. "I was probably six or seven, and I was playing with one of the neighbor's kids. He told me there were people called witches who could use real magic like what we saw on TV."

I keep working as Pike speaks, letting his voice calm my racing heart as I reach for the curse one last time.

"I told him I didn't believe him, and I ran home to ask my parents about it. They said that it was true, and from then on, I was fascinated by them. By magic." His voice is losing strength, getting quieter. Shaking. He's scared and he's injured. He needs to get to a hospital.

I catch the movement of his arm in the corner of my eye, going back and forth as he rubs the top of his leg. I silently pause my work on the curse and send more magic to him, letting the particles absorb the pain. He exhales, and I know he feels it, know he's seeing stars.

"I had books about magic and played witches with my friends, running around zapping things as if we could alter the world around us."

I smile to myself, thinking about young Pike pretending to be a witch. It reminds me of the way Amy and I used to practice our magic, the way we'd run into the Nebraska plains and work on simple tasks long after the sun went down—me on animals and her on me.

I reach for the curse again and start pulling it from the owl.

"When Leo was old enough to understand, I told him about magic, and I remember the way his face lit up. He thought it was so cool. We both did," he says, taking a breath. His whole body is starting to shake now, with either cold or fear or both.

I send more magic his way, just enough to surround him in heat.

"Thank you," he says quietly, and the tone of his voice is enough to crack my chest wide open. I keep working.

"Maybe that's why my dad wanted to treat him with magic so badly." Pike's voice cracks at the end, as if it's the first time he's made the connection. "Because Leo loved it so much. Because what better way to heal his son than with the thing he thought was cooler than anything else in the world."

Pike takes a long, shaky breath, and I realize he's crying. "When Leo died, all the love I had for magic turned into the strongest hate imaginable. Bone deep. I couldn't see past my rage, and for a long time, I thought I'd never recover. I thought it would eat me alive."

The last of the curse releases its hold on the owl and floods into the air in front of me. My skin is burning, and it takes all of my strength to ignore it and press on.

"It's still there. I try to cover it with sarcasm and jokes, but it's still there," he says.

I create a stream of magic from the curse to Pike's chest, a direct line for it to travel through. My hands shake, and I have to stop myself from crying out in pain as my burns spread. It's almost done.

"I thought it was cool once," he whispers, so quiet I barely hear it. "I thought it was maybe the greatest thing in the world."

The wind starts up, blowing my hair across my face. Pike is watching me now, the weight of his eyes heavy on me, and I finally raise my head, looking in his direction. The curse pulses in the air, and I can no longer hold it. It feels as if my whole body could go up in flames at any moment.

"Maybe I can get back there again," he says.

And with that, I heave the curse at Pike, forcing it through the stream of magic and directly into his chest. Pike's whole body convulses, trying to reject the curse, but I hold it firmly in place. He screams, and it takes everything within me not to let go and rush to his side, not to let the curse fly back to the owl, forgotten.

My arms are shaking and tears are streaming down my face, but I keep my hold on the curse. Steady.

The curse writhes inside him, and I feel as it takes hold of his body, as its tendrils wrap around his heart and lungs, as it enters his bloodstream and makes its way to his brain.

Then in one sudden motion, it lunges for his mind and flips the switch.

On.

Pike gasps as he's flooded with the sense, his entire world expanding in the span of a single breath, a single heartbeat. His body stops convulsing and he falls eerily silent.

There is not a single sound, not from Pike or me or the owl. Not from the trees or the wind or the animals that live in these woods.

Nothing.

Then Pike takes a ragged breath, and the magic around him flits to life.

It's over.

I drop my hands and scramble to his side, crawling through the dirt, feeling my way to him. I whimper from the pain, from the way my clothing rubs up against the burns on my skin, from the gash on my knee getting bigger.

"Pike," I say, reaching his side, putting my hand on his arm, "I need you to talk to me. How do you feel?"

At first he says nothing, but he doesn't flinch at my touch or push me away. He stays perfectly still, breathing in the silence.

"It's...everywhere," he finally says, his voice a mix of wonder and despair.

As soon as he speaks, the forest wakes back up. The wind begins to blow, rushing through branches and colliding with my skin. Animals flit across the ground and up the trunks of trees, and birds sing in the distance.

The space around Pike pulses with energy, getting hotter and hotter by the second. That's when I realize how much magic he's pulling, drenching himself in it. It's too much.

"Pike, stop pulling," I say quickly, trying to get his attention. He doesn't hear me, though. His eyes are closed, and he's drawing in magic as if it's water and he hasn't drank in days.

I shake his shoulders and get in his face. "Pike, listen to me. If you don't stop, you will incinerate yourself, just like I told you. Stop pulling."

Pike begins to tremble, and his skin heats up, so quickly I feel the change in temperature through his shirt. But he doesn't stop.

"Pike!" I scream.

His eyes snap open and he looks at me, wild and scared, tears brimming over his lashes. "I can't stop," he says, his voice rough and fast, as if it took everything he has to speak.

I try to form the words to help, tell him what to do to make him stop. But I've had magic my whole life, and everything about it is intuitive to me. It would be like trying to explain how to make my heart beat—I don't know how to do it, it just happens.

"Okay," I say, moving closer to him. "Tell me where your magic wants to go. Do you feel the strongest pull to the owl, to the trees, or to me?"

"What? I don't know," he says through his teeth. His eyes are squeezed shut and his whole body is shaking.

"Focus, Pike! Tell me what you feel the strongest pull to."

His eyes open and lock on mine. "You," he says in a rush. "You."

I try to ignore the way I feel that single word in my core, the way it awakens something in me that I can't want, can't even hope for.

"Concentrate on me. Direct all your energy to me, all your intention. If I'm what you're focused on, the magic will follow."

"I can't do it," he says, panting, his voice tense with pain. "I can't turn it off."

"You don't have to," I say quickly. "Just redirect it."

His skin is turning red, and I know we're out of time. With all my energy, I take in a heaving breath and pull his magic away from him. My skin lights up as new burns appear, and silent tears stream down my face as I try my best to help him.

"Let your magic flow toward me. Just let it happen. Open your eyes and look at me," I say, gritting my teeth and pulling as hard as I can. "Right here."

Pike's eyes meet mine, and I beg him to understand, beg him to stop fighting me. We watch each other, breathless and hurting and panicked. With every ounce of strength I have left, I pull his magic away, claw at it and demand its attention, pulling it toward me with a strength I didn't know I had. Then something in him snaps and his eyes widen as his magic rushes toward me in an onslaught of fire and heat.

I cry out in pain and fall back on the ground, the cool, damp earth catching me. Then all at once, it's gone. Pike stops pulling, and so do I. I try to force myself up, but I can't move. My breaths come in quick, shallow gasps and my heart slams into my ribs. My eyes roll back, catching the light of the sun as they do.

"Iris?" Pike says, dragging himself closer to me. "It worked." His voice threatens to break.

I try to speak, but I can't force the words from my mouth. It feels like the whole world is on fire, but when I look around, I see the shadow of the trees and Pike hovering over me. I see infinite shades of green and sunlight catching on raindrops.

I force myself to breathe and finally get a word out. "Inhaler."

"Yes, okay," Pike says, grabbing my pack. He drags himself back over to me and holds the inhaler to my mouth. I reach up with a shaking hand and press down on the top as I take a long, deep breath.

I wait a few seconds, then take one more. "Thank you," I finally manage to say. Once I feel stable enough, I push myself to a seated position and look at Pike.

"Are you okay?" I ask him, searching his body for signs of burns or trauma, then going over him again once I finish. Other than his broken leg, he's healthy. He survived.

He's a mage, but he survived.

"I think so." He looks down at himself as if to double-check, then exhales, loud and heavy.

"Don't use magic again," I say. "I've used too much today, and I won't be able to help you if you get stuck in it again. You can acknowledge it and feel it and marvel at it, but you can't pull it toward you. Not yet."

He nods, and his gaze falls to the ground. "Did I hurt you?" he asks, and it makes me want to cry, that he's worried about me when I don't deserve his worry.

"I'll be fine," I say, even though my skin is on fire. Even though it's taking all my strength not to dissolve into sobs or pass out. I gather myself enough to speak.

"I don't really know what to say to you right now. 'I'm sorry' will never be enough, but I need you to know that I mean it. I *am* sorry, more than you'll ever know. I don't expect you to forgive me, but I have to say it anyway." I pause and take a shallow breath. "I'll be here for you through this as much or as little as you want me to be. I promise. And I really do believe that one day, you'll love magic. You didn't choose this, and I can't change that, but I think I can help you learn to love it." The words shake, and the world fades in and out as shots of pain move over me in waves.

Pike nods, but he doesn't respond. The muscles in his jaw tense, and his mouth is set in a hard line. He needs time to process it all, and I will give him the time he needs. But he heard the words I said, and that's what matters.

The owl makes a shuddering noise then, almost a cough, and I force myself to concentrate. Force myself to ignore the pain and be in this moment with him, however he needs. My vision is blurry, and I rub my eyes, begging my body not to shut down. Not yet.

I scoot over to the owl, my whole body trembling with the effort, and his big black eyes meet mine.

"I'm here," I say. "I'm not going anywhere."

And I mean it. I will stay with him in this magic-drenched forest for as long as I can, until death separates us.

twenty-seven

I think I hear a twig snap in the distance, but I can't be sure. My mind is clouded with pain, making me uncertain of the things I hear and feel and see. Pike has moved closer to the owl, to me, and he seems stable for now.

It's getting hard for me to move. The pain from my burns is excruciating, my whole body fighting against me as I slide closer to the owl. But I want MacGuffin to feel my presence, to know that he isn't alone. Even if he could hold on for long enough to get to the refuge, I wouldn't be able to get him down the mountain.

I'm not sure how I'll get myself or Pike down, either.

I'm rendered useless, unable to direct my magic. I've already expended too much energy, and even if I hadn't, it hurts too much. I have to heal before I can use it again. Mom knows where we are, though, and Cassandra said she'd be coming to meet us. Help will find us one way or another.

I gently pick up MacGuffin and move him to my lap. He struggles to keep his eyes open, his lids rising halfway, then closing again. I run my fingers through his feathers and pull the towel around him to keep him warm. Pike sits next to me, and we're quiet as the owl moves his gaze from me to Pike and back again.

As he looks between us, I know with absolute certainty that he did this on purpose, that he flew into the wild with an injured wing so I'd have to come after him. I just wish I knew why.

I stroke one of his feathers, and a sharp vision enters my mind, one of me and Pike on a beach, practicing magic. The way Amy and I used to do as kids. Pike is smiling and pulls me into a kiss, my hair blowing in the wind and a flock of gulls circling above us, and the image is so stark, so vivid, I feel as if I'm watching it play out right in front of me.

I pull my hand away from the owl, and the vision recedes, gone as quickly as it began.

I blink several times, bringing myself back to the present, but my chest aches with the images, with how badly I want them to be real. I don't believe the owl would have orchestrated this just to bring me and Pike together, but when I think about him leaving the refuge, when I remember the way he flew from our first campsite only once Pike and I started arguing, when I watch him now, so clearly waiting for us, it's hard for me to come up with a different conclusion.

When my dad could no longer look me in the eye, when he stayed behind in Nebraska and watched me climb into a yellow taxi, I decided I could never trust another person again. It would be me and Mom, and that was it. That was enough. But

I spoke the words to Pike that I vowed I'd never say. I told him I'm a witch, let him see the thing I guard closest to my heart, and the world is still spinning. My life didn't collapse the way I was sure it would.

A tremor runs through MacGuffin, as if he's cold, and I wrap the towel tighter around him. He stills in my lap, and I feel the way his body relaxes.

"You don't have to fight anymore," I whisper.

Pike is watching MacGuffin, his jaw still tense, his eyes rimmed in red. I remember the story he told me when I bound the curse to him, about him and Leo thinking magic was the greatest thing in the world. I'm not foolish enough to think his sense can solve his hurt, his grief, or his anger, but maybe it can help. Pike is a Stellar—that's why his magic was drawn to me. One of the most common jobs of Stellars is pain management, helping sick children and adults get through their treatments more comfortably than with medicine alone.

Leo didn't get the help he needed, and that's unforgivable. It's tragic and gut-wrenching. But Pike could give to others what Leo should have gotten. Maybe that will help, in some way.

Or maybe I'm trying to justify an outcome that never should have happened, and Pike will hate magic and me for the rest of his life.

But I can't shake the feeling that both of us needed this journey, for vastly different reasons, and that the owl recognized that need in each of us.

Owls are sacred to witches, after all. It isn't so outrageous to think he'd help me along. It could all be meaningless, of course, wild coincidences that happened one after the other, but after living with my grandmother for seventeen years, I'm inclined to believe otherwise.

What is coincidence if not a subtle form of magic?

Dad would roll his eyes when my grandmother would say it, but that never bothered her. She was confident in herself and confident in her beliefs, and eventually my dad cut the word *coincidence* from his vocabulary so he wouldn't have to hear her ask the question. But Mom and I knew, and we'd nod along every time she spoke the words.

MacGuffin shifts in my lap, and I pull him closer, cradling him in my arms. His breaths are spaced too far apart, and his heartbeat is getting harder to feel.

"I'm here," I say, and for the first time in too long, he looks at me with wide, alert eyes, watching me the way he has since he first got to the refuge. He burrows into my lap and turns his attention to Pike before coming back to me. He holds my gaze for several moments, then slowly lets his eyelids fall.

I hold him close as he takes his last breath, feel his magic as it leaves his body and enters the forest, scattering among the windswept trees that will take it up and hold it for centuries to come.

Nothing is ever truly lost.

Tears run down my cheeks and drop into his feathers, and I rock back and forth, holding him in my lap, not wanting to let go. And when I can't hold him anymore, when the pain is too great, I do the only thing I can do: I bury him among the old-growth trees that he loved so much, surrounding him in fern leaves and moss and centuries-old magic.

I whisper a prayer for him, thank him for watching over me, and give him to the earth.

I stay over his grave for a long time, then find my way back to Pike. But as I do, the pain in my skin gets worse and the world around me spins. I reach out for something, anything, to catch my fall, but there's only air.

My eyes roll back and I collapse to the ground.

The last thing I hear is Pike calling my name, and the last thing I see is a witch rushing toward me who looks a lot like Amy.

"Iris? Iris, can you hear me?"

I struggle to open my eyes, and when I finally do, the world is still spinning. Cassandra is leaning over me, brushing the hair out of my face, but her features are blurry. I'm vaguely aware of Pike asking her who she is, but I can't see him. I try to look past her, find Pike, but I can't lift my head.

"Cassandra," she says without taking her eyes off me. "From the Witches' Council."

I close my eyes again, my head slipping to the side, but Cassandra keeps talking. I feel her tug at my shirt, lift up my sleeves before moving to my pant legs. I want to push her away, beg her to stop moving the fabric up and down over my skin, but I can't make the words come out.

I wish my mom was here.

"My God," Cassandra says as she looks over me, lifting up the torn hem of my shirt. "How is she even alive?"

Then I hear Pike from somewhere behind her, his voice shaking and upset. I open my eyes, try to see his face, but I can't. "I didn't know it was this bad," he says, looking over my burns. "I didn't know."

"We have to get her to a hospital," Cassandra says, her voice even and cool, just like I remember. "You too."

Then my vision goes dark and bright-white dots appear, twinkling in the vast emptiness. I sigh as the pain in my body eases, as the stinging of my skin lessens and the burning recedes.

"Thank you," I say, trying to focus on Cassandra's face. I take a breath and let her magic move through me, let the muscles in my body relax with relief. Then I meet her eyes. "Him too."

She nods and moves away from me. I hear her make a call, reporting our injuries to whoever is on the other end of the line. I exhale as I realize we'll be off this mountain soon. Someone will tend to my burns and to Pike's broken leg, and I'll see my mom and Sarah.

"I'm sorry I wasn't here sooner," Cassandra says when she gets back to my side. "I was held up by an animal attack."

"I couldn't save him." My voice breaks, and I'm unsure of if I'm referring to Pike or the owl.

"You tried," she says. "That's all any of us can do."

Cassandra has seen amplifiers die. Part of her work is caring for them in the wild, tracking their behaviors, and that means seeing them as they leave this life. Her voice is heavy with the experience of it.

"Help will be here soon," she says, and I nod, finding anything else too difficult.

She sits with me in silence, every so often checking my burns and turning around to make sure Pike is stable. I want to talk to him, to explain about Cassandra and her work with amplifiers, but I don't have the energy. I don't have the words. I want to reach out and touch him, to hold his hand so he knows I'm here, but he's too far away.

"He's okay," Cassandra says, pushing her palm over my hand, forcing me to rest. I didn't realize I'd been reaching for him. "There's no infection and the bleeding is minimal. He'll be fine once the bone is set."

"That's good," I say, keeping my eyes closed. I want to sleep, but I can't get comfortable. There are burns everywhere, and even Cassandra's magic isn't enough to take the pain away. But she's made it bearable, and for that I'm grateful.

"I'm glad you're here," I say, my voice weak.

"Me too." She's being gentle in a way I haven't seen since before Amy's trial, and it breaks something loose inside me, thinking how that trial became a demarcation in so many lives. In Amy's and Cassandra's and mine.

If she can sense that Pike is a mage, she doesn't let on to it, doesn't say anything that would indicate she knows. I want to ask her why she isn't bringing it up, why she isn't berating me over putting Pike in the same position as Alex, myself in the same position as Amy.

But everything hurts, and I don't have the energy to ask.

I don't say anything else, letting the quiet of the afternoon wrap around me and keep me calm until search and rescue arrives.

Pike asks how I'm doing several times, and even though his voice is strained, even though he sounds angry and helpless and defeated, he still asks. And that means something.

"I'm okay," I say, my voice hoarse and soft. I'm not sure if Pike hears me, if I said the words loud enough to reach him, but then I feel a pressure on my foot and open my eyes. I lift my head just enough to see Pike's arm stretching out to me, resting on my shoe. Then as quickly as it happens, he pulls his hand away.

I lean back, drifting in and out. The pressure was so slight, my vision so cloudy. Maybe it didn't happen at all.

I'm not sure how much time has passed when I finally hear footsteps in the distance. Cassandra stands and walks toward the sound. There's lots of hushed discussion, but I can't make out the words. The sun goes down, blanketing the woods in a blue-gray sky, and I think I see a bat flit overhead.

Rescuers come over with a long metal basket and tell me their names before easing me into it. They do the same for Pike, then walk us out of the thick of the forest and down the trail single file. I hate that I can't see him, can't see the expression on his face or if he's in pain. Can't see if he's okay. Pike's entire world changed in an instant, and he's lying in a cold metal basket surrounded by strangers.

I wince with each step, the burns on my back digging into the metal, but Cassandra's magic helps. She follows us for a while but then breaks away, and I suspect she goes to pack up our campsite.

I open my eyes and watch as the sky turns from twilight to night, as the stars appear overhead. I marvel at all the magic in empty spaces that so few people can sense, and I know I'll do everything I can to help Pike love his magic. I hope he'll be awed by it the same way I am, think it's the coolest thing in the world the way he did as a child. I hope that one day, he won't look back on this trip with unimaginable regret.

"Almost there," the woman at my feet says, then I feel my basket level off as they step off the trail.

There are two ambulances waiting, and my chest aches as Pike is put into his, wishing I could go with him. The thought of him in there, by himself, makes my whole body hurt, and I fight back the tears stinging my eyes. I strain to see him as I'm carried past the back door, lifting my head and craning my neck, but I can't catch a glimpse of him. I say his name but he doesn't hear, and I force myself to stay put, to resist jumping out of this basket and rushing toward him.

I did this to him, though. He wouldn't want me in the back of that ambulance any more than he'd want the witch who scammed his family in attendance at his brother's funeral. The thought knocks the wind out of me.

I close my eyes as I'm hoisted into the second ambulance, and when the doors are just about to shut, I hear my mom's voice.

"Wait!" she says, climbing into the back at the last second.

"Mom?" I ask, no longer able to stop my tears. I try not to shake with the relief of seeing her, the burns hurting worse and worse as Cassandra's magic wears off, but I can't help it.

"Sarah's here too, honey. She's riding with Pike." I nod because my throat is aching, because it feels impossible to speak. There are so many things I need to say.

She sits down and grabs my hand, looking me over. "Oh, baby girl, what happened?" Her eyes are wet and gentle, and I grip her hand, so thankful she's here.

"I couldn't save the owl," I say, choking on the words.

"It's okay," she says, smoothing down my hair and kissing me on my forehead. "It's okay. Rest now. You can tell me all about it later."

The ambulance pulls away from the trail, its red-and-orange lights streaking through the dark night. I think of MacGuffin, buried in the woods, resting peacefully beneath the trees, and say a silent goodbye that I hope he can feel.

Maybe it's the pain or lack of sleep, but I swear a single stream of magic flows down the mountain and into the ambulance as we drive away, one final connection between the owl and me.

Never truly lost.

twenty-eight

Cassandra comes to visit on my third day in the hospital. I've tried to prepare myself for whatever comes next, for whatever punishment the council sees fit, but I can't help the way my body trembles when she enters the room. I hope she doesn't notice.

Mom sits on the couch by the window, chewing on the inside of her mouth. I've spent the past three days filling her in on everything that happened, from the curse to the injured bear to turning Pike into a mage. She knows the consequences, understands that the council would be well justified in putting me on trial and removing my sense, and her legs bounce up and down from where she sits. She smooths her palms down the tops of her thighs, trying to steady herself, and it's the way she looks right now, all anguish and fear, that I've been trying to avoid.

I meet her eyes and mouth that I love her.

"It's good to see you, Isobel," Cassandra says. They used to be close, and even though the gentleness I heard in the woods is gone from Cassandra's tone, she looks at my mom with an affection that only comes from years of friendship.

"You too, Cass," Mom says. I'm surprised she'd use a nickname in this situation, but that's Mom. I know that, and Cassandra does, too.

The back of my hospital bed is tilted up, so I'm able to be eye level with Cassandra when she pulls a chair over and sits down next to me. She looks so much like Amy, long dark hair and big brown eyes, and were it not for her wire-rimmed glasses and strands of gray, I might think it was Amy sitting beside me.

Cassandra opens her folio and rests her hand on the paper, reminding me that she is not Amy and this is not a social call.

"How are you feeling?" she asks me.

"Better," I say. "Thank you for everything you did on the mountain."

"I wish I would have gotten there sooner."

I wonder if it would have made a difference, if she would have been able to help. The questions, the what-ifs and if-onlys pile up in my mind, higher and higher, and I wonder if she can see them all.

Cassandra tucks a strand of hair behind her ear and watches me with careful eyes, as if she's trying to navigate how to question me as a council member and not an old family friend. I will never understand how she did it with her sister, the strength and selflessness it took to not let her case go to another member, even knowing with almost certainty what the outcome would be.

"I just have a few questions for you," she says, picking up

her pen. "The work we do with amplifiers isn't only monitoring their behaviors while they're alive—we also keep records of how they die. It's procedural, and I'll be filing the owl's death report this week. But since you were there, I'd like to hear from you how it happened."

My palms are sweating, and I wipe them on my blanket, looking at Mom. I expected Cassandra to open with Pike, with the knowledge of what I did, and I can't figure out if it's because she doesn't know or because she's waiting to see if I'll confess the information freely.

Mom nods at me, and I take a deep breath. I don't want to live my life terrified of a secret getting out anymore. I've done that for the past two years, and it's exhausting. But more than that, I don't want to lie in order to protect myself from what I did to Pike. He didn't have any protection from me; I shouldn't get any, either.

"The owl died in my lap," I say. "I was holding him, and it was peaceful. He had a nicked artery from a bear attack, with lots of internal bleeding. I couldn't stop it all, and that's what killed him. After he died, I buried him in the woods." I'm embarrassed when my voice breaks, and I clear my throat, trying to compose myself.

Cassandra takes notes as I speak.

"That's the simple version," I say. "There is a much more complicated one."

Her pen stills and she looks up at me. "Let's hear it, then."

"The owl was cursed," I say, "with a curse that I wrote, that would turn Pike into a mage. Pike had said some things at work that bothered me, and I never meant for it to get out. It was a tradition my grandmother taught me—"

"Giving it to the earth. I remember," she says, and I nod. Of course she does. She knew my grandmother, too. Her tone gives nothing away, and I keep going.

"The owl dove down from the trees right when I tried to bind the curse to the herbs. I never meant for it to get out, and I've spent this whole week trying to undo it. But after the owl was attacked, I ran out of time. I told Pike what I had done, and he told me to bind the curse to him before the owl died, so that it wouldn't be amplified throughout the region. And that's what I did."

Cassandra listens, watching me the whole time, but doesn't write down a single thing.

"You should have called us immediately, as soon as the owl flew away," she finally says.

"I know. But I didn't think the owl was in any immediate danger. I thought I could bring him back to the refuge, unbind the curse, and fix it without..." My words trail off and my eyes fill with tears. "Without the council finding out. Without losing my sense."

"The way Amy lost hers," Cassandra says, and I nod.

"Yes." The word is just a whisper.

Cassandra closes her folio and checks her watch. Then she turns to my mom. "Isobel, Pike should be waiting outside. Would you please send him in and give the three of us some privacy?"

"Pike is here?" I ask, my heart racing.

I haven't talked with him since we were on the mountain.

Mom gave me updates when he was in surgery, and he was released from the hospital two days ago, but he hasn't responded to any of my texts. I swallow hard.

"I'll be right outside, honey," Mom says. She squeezes my leg as she passes by the foot of the bed, then opens the door. I hear her exchange a few words with someone, and my heart pounds as I stare at her back. After several seconds, she steps fully outside the room, and Pike comes in a moment later.

He pauses as soon as our eyes meet. He's on crutches and his leg is in a splint that goes all the way to his thigh, but the color has returned to his face and he looks healthy. I want to reach out to him, touch him, tell him how sorry I am. How worried I've been. How much I miss him. But I don't move.

Cassandra slips out of the room, and I try to think of what to say, try to find the right words when there aren't any. We watch each other, and I begin to speak but then Cassandra returns carrying a folding chair, and the moment is gone.

"Have a seat," she says to Pike, and he does as he's told.

"I'll get right to the point. It's against the law to turn someone into a mage when it results in bodily harm or death, or when a person is turned against their will. We simply don't have many cases like this because the risk of death is so great, which is why the law is written the way that it is." Cassandra pauses, and I'm sure we're both thinking about Amy. She swallows, then continues. "In the absence of those three things, the charge is downgraded to reckless use of magic, which carries much lighter consequences. Under normal circumstances, I would have this conversation with Pike separately, but when I met with him yesterday, he felt it was important to wait until he could communicate his decision to you in person."

"His decision?" I look at Cassandra, then over to Pike, but he avoids my eyes. His gaze falls to his lap, and his glasses slip down his nose. He pushes them back up and I notice that the lens is still cracked, and for some reason, it makes the pain in my chest worse.

"Pike is alive, and his broken leg cannot be attributed to being turned into a mage. If we are to proceed with criminal charges, Pike must be willing to testify that he was turned against his will."

It feels as if all the air has left the room. I try to steady my breathing and remain calm, but panic rises inside me. This shouldn't be put on Pike, and I hate that after everything he's been through, there's still more for him to carry.

He finally looks up at me, and his expression is sad. Angry. Conflicted.

"It's okay," I tell him, keeping my voice even so he believes me. This is my fault, not his, and I will accept the consequences just as he's been forced to do. "I promise you. It's okay."

Cassandra says his name. "Have you made your decision?"

"Yes." He holds my gaze for one more breath, then turns to Cassandra. My stomach squeezes and I feel like I might throw up. "I will not testify that I was turned against my will."

"Pike," I say, sitting up in bed, forcing him to look at me. "You don't have to lie for me."

"I'm not lying for you," he says, his voice adamant. "There was a time I would have thought this was the coolest thing in the world." He pauses, and it looks as if he might cry. Then he takes a deep breath and regains himself. "I'd rather spend my time trying to find that wonder again than convincing myself that I don't care about what happens to you, because only one of those scenarios seems even remotely possible."

"I don't want you to regret this," I say, my voice barely audible.

"Neither do I, which is why I made the decision I did." Pike turns to Cassandra. "My mind is made up."

"Very well," she says.

"Is that all you need from me?" Pike asks.

"For now, yes."

He nods and stands, grabbing his crutches and looking at me before he leaves. I try not to blink out of fear of breaking the connection, so relieved he's here, in front of me, safe.

"You cursed me, but you also risked your life trying to undo it. That means something," he says.

Then he leaves.

I exhale, loud and heavy, and lean back in my bed, suddenly exhausted. Mom walks back in and sits down on the couch without saying a word.

"He's right, you know," Cassandra says. She takes off her glasses and rubs her face, a break in demeanor I'm not sure how to interpret. "I'm not going to go into the details of what Amy's life has been like since that night. You were there—I'm sure it's not hard for you to imagine. I've spent the last two years wishing I would have tried to find a loophole, wishing I could have saved my sister from losing her magic after losing the person she loved. That is my biggest regret, and I will carry it always."

I'm shocked at her openness, and my eyes burn as she speaks. I'm not sure where she's going with this, but I want to hear it. I need to hear it.

"I don't want to carry the burden of putting another young witch on trial. Certainly not one who once felt like family. So here's how this is going to work: if you plead guilty to the reckless use of magic charge, my recommendation to the council will be to forgo a trial and sentence you to sixty hours of service in the witching community."

I open my mouth to reply, but I don't know what to say. It's far lighter than what I deserve.

"That's extremely lenient of you," Mom says when I still haven't managed to speak. "Thank you."

"Like I said, I don't want the burden. But Iris, you are forbidden from ever engaging in your grandmother's ritual again. No more spells, and no more curses. I don't care how minor it seems. You are absolutely forbidden. Do you understand?"

"Yes," I say, twisting the sheets in my hands. I know it's reasonable, and it's a small price to pay for Cassandra's leniency, but it hurts to give up. Then I remember Leo's tradition of throwing wishes into the fire, and it makes me want to cry, this incredible gift I've been given. I have a replacement for my grandmother's ritual, and suddenly it doesn't hurt as much.

"The level of control and strength you displayed when Pike turned is nothing short of impressive. The truth is that many witches would not have been able to withstand the amount of magic you did, and I know it was in service of trying to protect another person. You should be proud of yourself."

"Thank you," I say, keeping my voice steady. It makes me wish for the millionth time that I could go back to that night on the lake and change it somehow.

"Finally, we feel that Pike is your responsibility, and thus, that you will serve out your sixty hours by being the one who helps him learn his magic."

"What does that mean, exactly?"

"It means that you will have to teach Pike how to be a mage. You will teach him how to use magic and how to be responsible with it. You will teach him the laws and rules, what is acceptable and what isn't, and help him into this next chapter of his life. And until we feel he is ready to practice on his own and no longer needs supervision, we will hold you responsible for him."

Teaching someone how to use their magic when they've acquired it later in life is a huge undertaking, especially at first. The council employs witches whose job it is to do this full-time, and Pike would have to agree to it. The council has no legal authority over him because he hasn't done anything wrong.

"Don't you think it would be better to have someone help him who's done this before? I don't know the first thing about teaching a mage how to use magic."

Cassandra shifts in her seat and rests her hands on her folio. "The Alder family has a complicated past with witches, and Pike has made it clear that if he is going to put his schooling on hold to learn to use his magic appropriately, he wants to learn from someone he trusts. And he trusts you."

I look up at her. "He said that?"

"Yes, he did."

The words settle my stomach and fill me with warmth. After everything, Pike trusts me.

"Okay," I say, meeting Cassandra's eyes. "I'll do it."

"Good." She stands. "We'll get you set up with someone from the council who can help you get started." She walks to the door but pauses before leaving. "I'm sorry for what you went through. Please know that I speak on behalf of the entire council when I say we are all inspired and impressed by the level of pain you endured to try to stop this from happening. You saved his life, Iris. Don't be too hard on yourself."

"Thank you," I say. Cassandra reaches for the door, then turns to my mom. "It really was good to see you."

Mom nods. "It was," she says. Then she stands and pulls Cassandra into a hug. She whispers something I can't hear, but Cassandra closes her eyes and squeezes them tight as my mom speaks.

When she pulls away, Cassandra straightens her jacket and clears her throat.

"Hey, Cassandra?" I ask.

She looks at me.

"Do you think Amy would be open to hearing from me?"

A small smile tugs at her lips, so faint I question if it's even real. "There's only one way to find out." She opens the door and looks at me one last time. "Heal well, Iris."

Then she's gone.

twenty-nine

I'm released from the hospital a week later, and Mom drives me straight to the refuge so I can see Winter. I've only been away for a couple weeks, but spring has brightened everything. The greens are greener, and the soil is richer. Wildflowers push through the earth and songbirds sing for hours on end. I look up to the trees, then remember the owl I'm searching for isn't there. Still, I scan the branches for a moment longer before letting myself into the forest where the wolves roam.

Winter hears me right away and comes barreling toward me, jumping around my legs and nudging my hands when she reaches me. She gives me my distance, careful not to knock me over or dig into my skin, and I kneel down and pet her chest, resting my head into hers.

"I missed you," I say, and she licks my face.

I sit down on the ground and lean into Winter, and she sits beside me, steady and strong. I notice the wolf that Mom and I healed in the distance, no longer separated from the other wolves, and I smile to myself. He'll be released soon, back to the wild where he belongs. Not every animal we take in is able to be released again, and there's always an incredible joy with the ones who are.

After sitting with Winter for over an hour, I go to the office before heading home. Sarah insisted on making me a feast of all my favorite foods tonight, and I can't wait to sit around the table with my family. But the office is empty right now, and that means I can go in and feel him without anyone knowing.

Pike.

He has slowly started reaching out, and it's been hard not seeing him. Not checking in with him every hour to make sure he's doing okay. I want to give him the space and time he needs, but I'm missing him a lot today, so I unlock the office door and walk into the back where he keeps his Foggy Mountain sweatshirt, along with a coffee mug that says *I'm duckin' awesome* above a picture of a duck wearing sunglasses.

I run my fingers along the handle of the mug and touch his sweatshirt. I'm tempted to smell it, but if Pike ever found out, I'd never live it down. He's going to finish up his semester, then start at the refuge full-time, where I can teach him to use his magic. He'll need a Stellar to train him if he thinks he might want to change majors into a human-focused field, but I can teach him all the basics, the laws and rules and expectations of living with magic in this world.

I reach for my phone in my pocket, wanting to text him, but I stop myself, the way I do every time I get the urge to contact him. He'll call me when he's ready. We'll talk when he's ready.

I slip my phone back into my pocket and am about to walk

home when I notice a sticky note on my locker. I pull the note from the door and my heart jumps into my throat. There's only one person who would leave a note like that.

Open with care: the contents inside just might save your life.

I stare at the note, wondering when he wrote it, if he was feeling okay when he did, if it made him smile to himself. Then I carefully tuck the note in my pocket and open my locker door.

I jump back as dozens of KIND bars cascade out, one after the other, so many I could refloor the entire back room with them. I'm stunned for a moment, then burst out laughing, my stomach aching and my eyes watering, the very best kind of laughter.

"Just imagine how long you could survive off of those."

I turn around, and there he is, standing in the doorway, leaning on his crutches for support. He almost looks like himself again, easy smirk and messy hair, glasses that don't have a crack through the lens. I want to rush toward him, but I'm too scared of what he'll do, so I stay where I am.

"A few months, at least," I say.

He puts his crutches out in front of him and swings, slowly moving toward me. He bends over and picks up a single bar from the ground, then hands it to me. "I hope you appreciate how difficult this is for me," he says, any hint of joking gone from his voice.

I look down, my heart slamming into my ribs. "I'm so sorry, Pike. I wish I could—"

"You *know* how I feel about KIND bars," he says, cutting me off.

I look up at him, and there's that smirk again. Relief washes over me, and I roll my eyes. "You're a piece of work."

"I know," he says, looking pleased with himself. "If you think I'm obnoxious as an intern, just wait until I'm your student."

I groan and can't help the laugh that follows. "I can only imagine."

He moves one step closer to me, and I lean into my locker, worried I won't be able to stand on my own otherwise. "I really am sorry," I say. "So, so sorry."

"I know you are." Pike looks at me, his expression turning serious. He searches my face and slowly raises his hand, tucking a stray curl behind my ear. "I've spent the past week thinking. That's all I've done. I've tried to figure out what I want my life to look like, how I want to move on from here, what I want to say to my parents, but I can't focus. Every time I try to think of those things, my thoughts turn to you."

"They do?" I ask, swallowing hard.

"Yes. It's annoying, if I'm being honest."

"I'm sorry," I say, feeling the way my mouth pulls up at the corner.

"You know, I don't think you are." He matches my smile, then turns serious again. He gently pulls up the sleeve of my shirt, wincing as he takes in my red, raised skin, scars that will never go away. I have the urge to pull my sleeve down, to hide from him, but I don't want to hide anymore. He does the same on the other side, his eyes trailing up and down my arm, his expression pained as if he can feel the burns on his own skin. Then he pulls my sleeve back down and looks at me.

"You almost set yourself on fire to save me from this curse, and you endured an unimaginable amount of pain in order to stop mine." He exhales, shaking his head. "It's work, resenting you, Iris. And I don't want to put in the work anymore. I'd rather forgive you instead."

"Do you think you can?" I ask, hope rising inside me. I don't expect to get back to where we were that night in the tent, when he kissed me and touched me and watched me as if I was the only thing in the world that he needed. But if we could be friends, if we could laugh with each other and joke around again, that would be enough.

"The curse is only a curse because of the way *I* feel about witches, right?"

I nod. "Yes. I love being a witch, and I love magic. I would never consider it a curse."

He inhales and moves one step closer, so close I could rest my head against his shoulder or brush his lips with mine. So close I can feel his breath on my skin when he speaks.

"Then teach me how to love it."

We watch each other for several moments, neither of us moving. I don't know how to accept the forgiveness he's offering, but I do know that I can teach him how to love magic, love the way the universe comes alive with a single thought. There is so much for him to discover, an entire world, and I can't wait to show it to him.

Slowly, hesitantly, Pike tips his head down. I'm still at first, making sure I'm not misunderstanding, not seeing what I hope for instead of what is. His eyes meet mine, then trail down to my lips, and it's the reassurance I need to close the space between us. When my mouth touches his, it feels like I can breathe again. His kiss is gentle and patient, soft and delicate, easing something I've been carrying inside myself for too long.

Pike Alder knows I'm a witch.

He knows that I cursed him and that he's a witch, too.

And he's kissing me in a way that lets me know it's all he wants to be doing. I steady myself against my locker and wrap my arms around his neck, his hair weaving through my fingers and his breath entering my lungs. I bring my hand to his face and trace the line of his jaw, feeling his stubble and the way he moves as his lips press into mine.

I want to stay here forever, in the certainty of the moment, but I know there will be other moments and other kisses, an entire life drenched in magic.

When he pulls away, he leans his forehead against my own, closing his eyes as if he can't bear the distance he created.

"I missed you," he says.

"I missed you, too."

I reluctantly pull away, looking at the clock. Mom and Sarah are expecting me, and after being gone for so many days, I'm craving the comfort of home.

"Would you like to come for dinner?" I ask, not quite ready to say goodbye.

"I'd love to."

He brushes my fingers with his, and we make our way through a sea of KIND bars, out into the beautiful twilight.

thirty

It's a cool spring day. A layer of morning fog hangs low over the refuge, and it feels good against my skin. Mom has been doing all the group tours since I just started working full days again and Pike is still on crutches, and it's been nice easing back into my world here. I smile and nod at the group of people as they follow my mom to the birds of prey, and I go in the opposite direction, toward the wolves.

Winter has been following me around as if I might vanish at any moment, whining when I walk away and taking an aggressive stance when we introduce new animals. At times I swear she resents that I didn't bring her with me, as if she could have prevented everything that went wrong.

It takes me a long time to do my chores. Even with Mom's magic, my skin is tight and sensitive, and the smallest motions can bring tears to my eyes. I'm constantly surprised by how quickly my pain level can change, going from manageable to unbearable in the span of an instant, and sometimes I don't even know what causes it.

But I feel myself getting better with each day, and I'm thankful to be back at work.

Cassandra has been true to her word, and the council took all her recommendations. I've been set up with a witch who will help me train Pike, and after sixty hours my sentence will be satisfied. But I'm hoping for many more hours, days and weeks and months and years.

It isn't a punishment. So far from it.

I walk through the woods and to the shed where Mom does most of our medical procedures. Dan is bringing in an injured fox later today, and while Mom works on it, I'll try to teach Pike how to calm it down using magic. Even though his magic gravitates toward people, he loves our lessons with the animals, his scientific brain learning to let go of everything he thought he knew so he can relearn it all with magic in the equation.

It's a gift, being able to connect with animals like we do, and Pike never takes it for granted, not even when he's frustrated or feeling guilty for enjoying the thing he still strongly associates with his brother's death.

I sanitize the large metal table first, then work my way through Mom's instruments, setting them out once they're ready. The shed door opens, and I turn to see Pike, swinging in on his crutches.

"Hey," he says, coming up to the table and looking over the tools I've set out. "What's all this for?"

"Injured fox. Dan's bringing it by in a few hours. I thought it would be good to practice calming it down with magic."

"I love foxes; hopefully the injury isn't too bad."

"It doesn't sound like it, from what Dan was saying." I walk around the table and grab gloves, gauze, and syringes from the cabinets on the wall, then set them out as well. We never really know what we'll need until we have the animal on the table, but there are basic things we use with almost every animal we see.

I wince when my stomach brushes up against the corner of the table, protectively bringing my hand to my abdomen.

"Are you okay?" Pike asks, and it never fails to surprise me how concerned he looks. How even six weeks later, he still asks me as if it's the first time he's noticed something wrong.

"I'm good," I say, reaching out and touching his arm. "Just a little pain."

"I wish you would teach me how to ease it," he says, not for the first time.

"I know you do, and we'll get there. It's just a bit more complicated. Besides," I say, putting my hand against his chest, "magic isn't the only way to make me feel better."

"Oh yeah?" he says, setting his crutches aside and leaning against the table. "Please tell me."

I move in front of him and put my arms around his neck, playing with the back of his hair. "It's honestly better if I show you."

His mouth pulls up to the side, and he tugs on a stray curl, his eyes never leaving mine. "Then show me."

I stand on the tips of my toes and close my eyes, pressing my mouth to his. I'm careful to leave enough space between us to protect my burns, but the way he kisses me makes me ache for a time we can be closer, when I can press my whole body to his and feel him in every part of me.

He puts his hands on either side of my face, holding me tight, touching me in one of the only places that doesn't hurt. It makes me feel as if I'm precious, this treasured thing he found in the damp mountains of Washington and brought back with him.

I open my mouth and press my tongue to his, relishing the way his breath catches in his throat and his hands move through my hair, the way his fingers brush the back of my neck and the rest of his body stays perfectly still, always so careful not to touch my burns.

My fingers move down his neck and over his shoulders, down his chest to the waist of his jeans, his whole body tensing under my touch. I rest my hands on his hips and slow our kiss before reluctantly pulling away.

"I can't wait to be closer," I say, and I feel him smile at my words.

"Closer will be nice," he agrees. "But I'm also a fan of not-as-close-as-we-want."

"It will have to do for now." I squeeze his hand before stepping away, making sure that I've put everything Mom will need out on the table.

Pike catches my fingers and turns me back toward him. "It is more than enough," he says, his tone heavy and serious. "You are more than enough."

I clear my throat and look toward the floor, embarrassed by the way my eyes sting at his words. Embarrassed by the way they settle into my core as if I've needed to hear them my whole life.

"You're only saying that because I've had to clean the sloth enclosure since we got back," I say, giving him a skeptical look.

"And just so we're clear, I don't buy for a second that your leg is preventing you from doing it."

"What a harsh and completely unfounded accusation," he says. "Even if I had to clean it every day for the rest of my life, I'd still feel that way."

"You can't possibly mean that."

"I do," he says solemnly. He pauses, and a slight smirk settles on his face. "It's hard to believe that you cursed me, given how incredibly charming I am."

"Okay, that was *one time*," I say, rolling my eyes, and even though I'm thankful that Pike can joke about it, that he's enjoying magic and accepting its place in his life, I still feel a heavy, tense guilt that stirs in my chest.

He didn't have a choice in this, and I will always feel guilty about it. But his easy laugh and casual comments help me relax a little, help me lessen the amount of space I'd otherwise give it.

And every time his eyes widen when he uses magic, every time his voice is tinged with wonder and awe, it makes me think that one day I'll be able to forgive myself. That one day I'll be able to enjoy sharing the thing I love most in the world with the person who has so quickly become important to me.

"I have a few more things to take care of before Dan gets here. If your leg needs a break, though, feel free to hang out here until I get back." I grab a folding chair from the wall and set it out for Pike, and he gives me a grateful look.

I leave the shed and walk toward the office, but when I pass the trail that meanders through the woods, something tells me to take it. The morning fog has burned off, and I can see the tops of the trees now, perfectly still against the overcast sky.

The air is crisp and fresh, somehow always managing to smell as if it just rained, even when it hasn't. I didn't know there could be soul connections with places, that my entire being could feel rooted to one part of the earth, but that's what I have here.

Amy is flying out in a few weeks. She's going to spend the summer here, helping out at the refuge and getting away from Nebraska for a bit. The salty air has a way of slowing everything down, of making everything feel just a little bit better. I hope she finds that here. I hope it helps her heal. I take mental notes of all the places I want to show her, all the walks we'll go on and beaches we'll visit, but I think she'll love the refuge the most.

I keep walking, far enough into the trees that I can no longer hear the tour group or the animals in their enclosures, the wolves as they run or tires on gravel. I carefully ease myself to the ground, and for several moments, I sit, listening to nothing. A squirrel dashes across the trail several yards in front of me, and I shiver when a breeze picks up, bringing the salty air of the Pacific with it.

Then I hear a horn honking in the distance and force myself to stand. Dan is early.

I walk back toward the shed, shoving my hands into my pockets and keeping my head down, making sure I don't trip over any roots or stray rocks. Just as I'm about to leave the cover of the trees, something sounds behind me. At first I don't think much of it; these woods are home to countless animals, always talking to each other in their own ways.

But something about it feels familiar, and I slowly turn.

I step back onto the trail, then stop and listen, waiting for several seconds. Nothing new happens, though, no more sounds or disturbances, and I shake my head and walk away from the woods. Then it happens again.

One long hoot.

A pause.

Two short hoots, closer together.

Another pause.

Then one final hoot.

It sounds exactly like my northern spotted owl, and I rush back into the trees, scanning the branches and cavities for any sign of him. But he isn't there, he couldn't be. An impossible hope.

Then I remember the story my mom told me, about the witch who used the sacred owl to curse the home of the man who killed her husband. Legend says the bird still circles over the land, hundreds of years later, forever bound to the place it was cursed.

"MacGuffin?" I ask.

A whoosh of air crosses directly in front of my face, my hair blowing back with the force of it. I laugh, big and loud, and my eyes fill with tears.

He must be here to haunt Pike, just like the owl in the legend haunts the land he was cursed to, and I realize with absolute joy that we will never be rid of him, this obnoxious, loud owl that sent us traipsing through the Pacific Northwest just because he felt like it.

"Welcome back," I say. "I know someone who will be *very* happy you're here."

Then I rush from the trail and back to the shed, and while I can't see him, I have the distinct feeling that there is a northern spotted owl, flying at my shoulder the whole way there.

acknowledgments

If you've read this book, thank you, from the bottom of my heart.

My initial pitch for *Wild* went something like "cursed bird in the Pacific Northwest," and instead of being told no, I was somehow met with a very enthusiastic yes. I'm extremely thankful to be surrounded by people who believe in my vision, get excited about the things I love, and help me find my way back to the trail when I wander too far off.

First, to Elana Roth Parker, my amazing agent who helped get me through many of my book two woes. Thank you for all that you do. And to the entire Laura Dail Literary Agency team, thank you for taking such good care of my books.

To my editor, Annie Berger, I'm so lucky to work with you. Thank you for your enthusiasm, incredible insight, and unfailing support—your belief in me and this book got me through my worst days of doubt.

To the entire Sourcebooks Fire team, including everyone who

works behind the scenes to get my stories into the world: What a joy it is to make books with you. To Beth Oleniczak, you are an absolute rockstar. Thank you for tirelessly making sure my books find their readers. To Madison Nankervis, thank you for your incredible ideas and for sending this book out with such a bang. To Jenny Lopez, Cassie Gutman, and Kelsey Fenske, thank you for readying this book for readers. Thank you to Liz Dresner and Nicole Hower for designing a cover I love so much, and to Michelle Mayhall for making the interior so very beautiful. To Margaret Coffee and Caitlin Lawler, thank you for introducing me to so many amazing librarians, educators, and booksellers, and to Ashlyn Keil for connecting me with readers. And finally, to my publisher, Dominique Raccah, thank you for creating such a wonderful home for me and my stories.

Carolyn Schweitz, thank you for all the hours you've given back to me.

To my Pacific Northwest crew, I love you so much. Rachel Lynn Solomon, even with an ocean between us, you remain one of my constants. To Heather Ezell, thank you for being a voice I trust in the moments I'm not sure I trust my own. Tara Tsai, thank you for always lifting me up. Julia Ember, thank you for moving to Seattle and so quickly becoming one of my people. Rosiee Thor, thank you for brainstorming this book with me and helping me find an ending I love.

Adrienne Young, Kristin Dwyer, Adalyn Grace, and Diya Mishra, you make me absolutely love what I do, even on the days when it's awful. Thank you for being my lifeline. Isabel Ibañez,

Shelby Mahurin, and Jordan Gray, thank you for the incredible love and support you show me. I feel so lucky to have you all.

I'd be remiss not to thank Predators of the Heart Animal Sanctuary for inspiring the wildlife refuge in this book, and the board game Wingspan, which was my first pandemic hobby and is singlehandedly responsible for the conception of this idea.

To my dog Doppler, who sits by my side day after day, my constant companion as I write, rewrite, and write some more.

Chip, thank you for being such a steady, calming presence in my life.

Mom and Dad, thank you for showing me the magic of where we live, from Sunriver to Cannon Beach, Ocean Shores to Leavenworth, to our own backyard. I love you so much.

Mir, this book is dedicated to you, but it doesn't feel like enough. I'm only able to do this because of your endless support and unconditional love, and I continue to be amazed that anyone is able to publish a book without you. Thank you for making my life so incredibly full.

Ty, I fell in love with you hiking the mountains of the PNW (even though you always said "the summit is just ahead" when it was *never* "just ahead"), and it's the best thing that ever happened to me. Thank you for loving me so perfectly, for being my true north and very best friend. I love you with everything.

And finally, to Jesus, for the wonder, awe, and perfect love.

about the author

Photo © Dawndra Budd

Rachel Griffin is the *New York Times* bestselling author of *The Nature of Witches*. Born and raised in the Pacific Northwest, she has a deep love of nature, from the mountains to the ocean and all the towering evergreens in between. She adores moody skies and thunderstorms and hopes more vampires settle down in her beloved state of Washington. When she isn't writing, you can find her wandering in the woods, reading by the fire, or drinking copious amounts of coffee and tea. She lives with her husband, small dog, and growing collection of houseplants. Visit her on Instagram at @TimesNewRachel or online at rachelgriffinbooks.com.

FIREreads

⬤ #getbooklit

Your hub for the hottest young adult books!

Visit us online and sign up for our
newsletter at FIREreads.com

 @sourcebooksfire

 sourcebooksfire

t firereads.tumblr.com